DENIZENS OF DARKNESS

THE MERMAID CHRONICLES

BOOK SIX

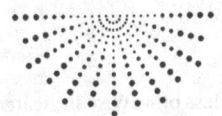

MARISA NOELLE

FIRST EDITION

OTHER BOOKS BY MARISA NOELLE

The Shadow Keepers

The Unraveling of Luna Forester

The Unadjusteds Universe

The Unadjusteds Trilogy

The Unadjusteds

The Rise of The Altereds

The Reckoning

Origin Story Novellas

Silver Melody

Matt Lawson

Joe Rucker

Erica Swiftfield

Paige Starling

Hal Small

Kyle Lewis

Jacob Shea

Sawyer Watson

Addison Shields

President Bear

THE MERMAID CHRONICLES SERIES

REVIEWS FOR DENIZENS OF DARKNESS

"If I could give this 10 stars, I would!" — Goodreads Reader

"Romeo & Juliet for today." — Amazon reader

"Romance, mermaids vs sharks - what more do you need? This is a thrilling read with great characters that you won't want to put down!" – **SJ Willis, best-selling author of *Bite Risk***

"Packed with twists, could not stop reading!" — **Louie Stowell, best-selling author of *Loki: A Bad God's Guide to Doing Good***

"Marisa Noelle does it again with her charming and gripping story of Gal and Una as they navigate the tricky waters of love in a time of change and challenge." — **Lynn Lipinski, author of *God of Internet* & *Bloodlines***

"A refreshing take on an emerging genre. I found this book so hard to put down. Lots of drama mixed with a dollop of romance and just a touch of the supernatural." — **Melissa Welliver, author of *My Love Life and the Apocalypse***

"The premise is laced with conflict, and you'll cheer for Gal all the way through as he battles to overcome inherent differences and conflicts." — **Author Stuart White, CEO of WriteMentor**

"This is a brilliant series! I love it! It's like a mixture of Sirens the TV series and *Aquaman* and a *Romeo & Juliet* forbidden love story." — ARC reader

"*Denizens of Darkness* weaves a spellbinding tapestry of revenge, love, and magical realms—an unputdownable fantasy romance that will linger in your heart long after the final page." — Amazon Reader

"Marisa Noelle's *Denizens of Darkness* is a fantasy romance masterpiece—a breathtaking blend of revenge, friendship, and the intoxicating magic of a love that defies the tides. An absolute gem for fans of the genre!" — Goodreads reviewer

"Enchanting! Mesmerizing! Captivating! Heart-breaking!" — Book Blogger

"Deliciously romantic!" — Goodreads reader

"This series is so good, it got me out of my slump!" — ARC reader

"Gripping, emotional, and utterly enchanting!" — ARC reader

CONTENT WARNINGS

This book contains themes and references that some readers may find distressing, including, but not limited to:

- Violence
- Minor sexual content
- Death or dying
- Blood, gore, graphic injuries
- Mental illness, anxiety
- Swears or curses
- Monsters

DENIZENS OF DARKNESS PLAYLIST

Mermaid - Train
Way Down We Go - Kaleo
Fight Song - Rachel Platten
Head Over Feet - Alanis Morisette
I'd Die Without You - P.M. Dawn.
Why Am I the One - Fun
You Make Me Wanna - Usher
In the Shadows - Amy Stroup
In the Stars - Benson Boone
Paradise - MEDUZA, Dermot Kennedy
Bones - Imagine Dragons
Ghost Town - Benson Boone
Ain't No Sunshine - Bill Withers
The Devil Within - Digital Daggers
Beautiful Things - Benson Boone
Play That Song - Train
Demons – Imagine Dragons
I will Walk 500 Miles - The Proclaimers
Radioactive - Kings of Leon
Glory and Gore - Lorde
I'm Still Standing - Elton John
It's All About You - McFly

For the ones who stay awake dreaming of worlds that don't yet exist. This world is yours now.

RECAP OF BOOK 1 – SECRETS OF THE DEEP

On the approach of Cordelia Blue's eighteenth birthday, she decided it was time to break free from the shadows of her tragic past. The loss of her mother and twin brother in a devastating shark attack had haunted her for five long years, forcing her to abandon her once-promising swimming career. She even shied away from taking a simple bath.

With unwavering support from her best friends, Maya and Trent, Cordelia embarked on a journey to conquer her deepest fears head-on. Little did she know, this leap of faith would reveal a world of enchanting secrets lurking beneath the surface. As she dipped her toes into water for the first time since the attack, Cordelia unearthed her astonishing destiny—she was a mermaid, and her long-lost twin, Dylan, was alive too. Trapped in an aquatic realm, he was unable to shift into human form. Dylan entrusted Cordelia with a mystical pearl, a key to locating the elusive High Council— the sole authority capable of granting mermaids their precious legs once more. However, the mermaids weren't the only ones hunting for this gem. The selachii, shark shapeshifters cursed to the depths, yearned to regain their legs too. And would stop at nothing to find it.

Old flame, Wade Waters, swam back into Cordelia's life. Sparks flew, but lurking in the shadows were Wade's shady cousins, and Cordelia couldn't shake the feeling that he was harboring a deep, dark secret. And keeping her own secret concerning her mermaid lineage under wraps took a toll on their relationship.

When the pearl mysteriously vanished from Cordelia's grasp, she discovered Wade's secret—he was one of the selachii and had betrayed her. Worse yet, Trent, her loyal friend, fell victim to a brutal shark attack and was transformed into one of them.

With trust shattered and alliances uncertain, Cordelia turned to Maya and the ancient tome, *The Mermaid Chronicles*, which held the key to unraveling their intertwined destinies. Maya insisted that merfolk and selachii must unite to reclaim their lost glory. Cordelia delved into the book's secrets, uncovering a forgotten era of harmony between merfolk and selachii on the fabled island of Atlantis.

As Cordelia unmasked Zale, the leader of the selachii, as the thief behind the pearl's theft, she and Wade joined forces to retrieve the precious jewel, but almost cost them Wade's life. When Cordelia and Wade reunited, the pearl's secrets unraveled, whisking them away to another dimension to confront the enigmatic High Council.

The High Council, comprised of representatives from merfolk, selachii, dragon kings, and eelusionists, agreed to grant them legs once more. Yet, it came at a price—Cordelia and Wade were tasked with the monumental quest to unearth their lost homeland, the mythical Atlantis. The epic adventure had only just begun, and the fate of two worlds hung in the balance.

RECAP OF BOOK 2 – QUEST FOR ATLANTIS

When mermaids began mysteriously disappearing, stolen away by humans for display or sinister experiments, the hidden realm of mermaids and selachii was unveiled. Cordelia, Wade, and their friends fought valiantly, rescuing one of their own from a science lab. Yet, the global onslaught continued, casting an ever-growing shadow over their existence.

Their mission was clear: unveil the enigma of the lost island of Atlantis—an aquatic sanctuary where all ocean shifters could find refuge. To unlock its secrets, the team embarked on a quest for the fabled, scattered jewels that held the key to Atlantis' portal. But their journey was fraught with peril.

Beneath the icy depths of Mount Rainier and the treacherous Puget Sound, Cordelia and Wade faced near-death encounters with ice demons. Gal, a formidable dragon king and council member, defied convention to save them. The

Power of the Sea surged through them, healing their wounds and bestowing incredible gifts—a Herculean strength for Wade and the untamed power of fire for Cordelia.

Tensions flared as Wade's ex, Stephanie, intruded on the mission, determined to win him back, fueled by his mother's approval. Cordelia grappled with doubt, their bond tested by misunderstandings and painful infidelities, fracturing their once-unbreakable unity.

Maya's life hung by a thread after a harrowing accident, compelling Dylan to transform her into a mermaid. But the toll of their perilous journey didn't end there—Cordelia's father faced certain death in the unfathomable Mariana Trench, only to be transformed into a selachii through a desperate ritual led by Wade.

Amidst near-tragedies and heartaches, Cordelia and Wade rekindled their love, poised to confront those who sought to tear them apart. Armed with the keys to Atlantis, they crossed dimensions into a magical realm. But a harrowing sight awaited them—an island in ruins, guarded by legions of dragon kings. A savage battle ensued, with Cordelia mastering her fiery abilities to vanquish the malevolent force, at the cost of her dear mentor, Gal.

As the Power of the Sea was plunged into the Fountain of Youth, the island blossomed anew. Amidst the rejuvenation, Cordelia made an astonishing discovery—a long-lost captive, her mother, believed dead for over five years, was alive and well.

In a joyous reunion, Cordelia found her family and a newfound sanctuary where all could walk on land, hidden from prying human eyes. Amidst the serenity, Wade proposed to Cordelia, promising a blissful future, until the pages of *The Mermaid Chronicles* started turning once again.

RECAP OF BOOK 3 – FIGHT FOR FREEDOM

A year after the discovery of the long-lost Atlantis and their showdown with the fierce dragon kings, Cordelia and Wade tied the knot, ascending to their rightful thrones as the rulers of the mystical island. Hidden away from the prying eyes and judgmental gazes of ordinary humans, Atlantis basked in tranquility, shielded by an enchanting veil that isolated it from the rest of the world.

As the brave folks of Atlantis cautiously reconnected with their mainland families, a shockwave of devastating news rocked their world. A cataclysmic nuclear war had erupted, and fingers were pointed squarely at none other than the merfolk and selachii.

This apocalyptic nightmare was set in motion when a wealthy baron's wife met a watery demise. With no ocean shifters around to perform the life-saving resuscitation ritual, the baron pointed the finger of blame at the mysterious Atlantis, threatening to unleash nuclear annihilation unless the world revealed the whereabouts of the elusive merfolk. But nobody had a clue where the merfolk had vanished to, and humanity paid the price with widespread devastation.

Venturing back to the mainland, Cordelia, Wade, and their loyal friends stumbled upon two distinct groups of surviving humans. There were those desperate for survival after the nuclear apocalypse and a faction hell-bent on extracting vengeance from the ocean shifters.

Wade and Trent fell into the clutches of a former mercenary turned captor, the enigmatic Sean Wilson. Meanwhile, Cordelia found herself face-to-face with her high-school rival, the determined Babette, who pledged to aid her in freeing Atlanteans from the clutches of hostile humans, and giving them hope surrounding the latest prophecy in *The Mermaid Chronicles*. While distracted, Wade's ex-girlfriend, the ever-jealous Stephanie, resurfaced as a formidable sea witch, swearing vengeance on Wade and Atlantis.

While Cordelia and her fearless squad embarked on a daring rescue mission to free Wade from the clutches of mercenaries, they crossed paths with Blaze, the last surviving dragon king and Gal's only son, Cordelia's late mentor. With Blaze's remarkable abilities and Cordelia's fiery powers, they launched a mission to free the ocean shifters from captivity. Their journey back to Atlantis, however, took a treacherous turn when Stephanie and Aquaria unleashed the dreaded Hound of the Ocean, a venomous sea monster with a lethal breath.

Simultaneously, Sean Wilson invaded Atlantis, leaving a trail of death and destruction in his wake, including the loss of crucial High Council members. As the situation spiraled out of control and their people faced annihilation, Cordelia's powers went haywire, forcing an uneasy alliance with Babette, her father, and their human army, and fulfilling the prophecy.

Just when all hope seemed lost, Cordelia's wedding ring revealed astonishing powers, creating an impenetrable force-field around the ocean shifters and saving them from the deadly breath of the Hound. But humans were still dying. After vanquishing Aquaria, Cordelia confronted the monstrous sea beast with her fire abilities. Entrusting the ring to Babette, it extended its protection to the humans too, truly uniting all three species. With Wade by her side and a glimmer of the Power of the Sea from Edward, a High Council member, they finally achieved victory, though Stephanie managed to slip away.

Back on Atlantis, Cordelia and Wade threw open their island's gates to the surviving humans, offering refuge from the radiation and nuclear chaos ravaging the mainland. Babette was entrusted with the guardianship of the Power of the Sea by the last surviving High Council member as he breathed his last, ensuring that humans would forever feel a part of Atlantis.

In a poignant ceremony honoring those lost in the attack and the venerable High Council, Stephanie unleashed her venomous snakes, poisoning Atlanteans. Jordan, Wade's devoted cousin, who had once been enamored with Stephanie, delivered the fatal blow, stabbing her through the heart and ending her reign of terror.

Only then did tranquility return to the island, with Cordelia dropping the bombshell that she was pregnant. But the pages of *The Mermaid Chronicles* never remain still for long.

RECAP OF BOOK 4 – GHOST PIRATES

During the seven years that passed since Cordelia and Wade's son, Gal, came into the world, Atlantis enjoyed a period of relative tranquility under their rule. However, Cordelia's inner turmoil festered as she battled the shadows of her past, haunted by the ever-present fear that something might befall her beloved son. As the Fountain of Youth didn't work for Gal, Cordelia rarely let him out of her sight, believing she was the only one who could protect him from harm. Despite concerns from friends and family about her mental well-being, Cordelia remained fixated on Gal's safety, pushing him to train in martial arts for self-defense.

When the pages of *The Mermaid Chronicles* began to turn, indicating a new prophecy was on the way, Cordelia's anxiety heightened, and she suspected one of her oldest enemies would return. The arrival of a reclusive shifting clan, the orcana, brought an unusual winter to the ordinarily temperate island, and the kids discovered a new sense of joy along with a fresh blanket of snow. That was until one of them went missing. Searching for the young girl in the tunnels beneath the island led to devastating land collapses. Cordelia and Gal were trapped in a cave-in and accidentally discovered a powerful elemental orb, which enhanced Cordelia's affinity with fire. While Gal recovered from a concussion in the hospital, more children went missing, leading the Atlanteans to believe there were nefarious motives behind their disappearances.

All became clear when the leader of the orcana admitted to placing a cursed stone in the Fountain of Youth, ultimately blinding Maya, the oracle of Atlantis, and stunting the prophecies within *The Mermaid Chronicles*. Ghost pirates were behind the children's disappearances, and they returned each night to steal more, lashing with their poisonous whips and scattering their venomous spiders on the island. Cordelia discovered they were not merely undead, but immortal. Only by combing all six elemental orbs could they be turned to flesh and therefore become mortal. With two orbs in their possession, a hunt for the remaining orbs ensued. When Gal was taken, Cordelia risked everything, including her own life, in her desperate search for the elemental orbs, shunning those close to her and turning the residents against her with her rash actions.

When Caol, an evil selachii from her past, appeared on the island, it confirmed Cordelia's suspicions that her oldest enemy, Zale, was after her. Caol claimed he had the last remaining orb in his possession and she killed him without remorse. The island was thrown into a deep depression as they realized the last orb was lost to them, and therefore all the children.

Cordelia vowed to make it up to her people, and with the help of her friends and family, discovered the last orb and turned the pirates to flesh once more. The Atlanteans accepted her apology, and it took uniting all the ocean shifters as well as the humans to defeat the ghost pirates in a deadly battle. Reunited with her son once more, Cordelia's joy was short-lived as Zale finally launched his attack. Protecting her son, she threw herself at Zale's mercy, only to discover he had none. With her powers depleted and unable to defeat his new megalodon size, Zale got the better of Cordelia and put an end to her life, leaving her son and husband distraught.

The entire island mourned the loss of their queen, but the story was far from over...

RECAP OF BOOK 5 – VENDETTA

For twelve long years, Gal burned with the desire for revenge. His target was Zale, the murderous selachii who had stolen his mother's life. Furious at being chained to prophecies that had done nothing to save his mother, Gal destroyed *The Mermaid Chronicles*. Yet, as the pages burned, fragments of a new prophecy caught his eye:

> *Celestial Abyss...*
> *Vorago's Trident...*
> *Parting the sea...*

The cryptic words sent a chill through him, but he shoved his fears aside as well as the information that he could now read the encoded book, and focused on his plan of revenge. On the anniversary of his mother's death, Gal set sail on his perilous quest, only to discover two stowaways aboard his boat: Ember, his cousin and the last remaining dragon king, and Una, the ever-optimistic daughter of his mother's best friend. Though furious about now being responsible for their safety, Gal reluctantly allowed them to join, unwilling to lose time returning them to Atlantis.

Their search for Zale led them to the unforgiving Antarctic, where they sought guidance from the orcana. Directed to the Lady of the Lake in England, they set course north. But before they could travel far, a brutal storm capsized their boat, plunging them into the depths. As Gal battled to keep them alive, guilt churned within him—he cursed himself for allowing Ember and Una to follow him into danger.

Salvation came in the form of Gal's reclusive grandfather, who plucked them from the storm-tossed ocean. As they sailed north, his grandfather recounted tales of Gal's parents' legendary love. To Gal's surprise, his grandfather had never disapproved of his mother but admired her courage instead. Slowly, Gal's icy demeanor thawed, and he begrudgingly admitted that his friends had made the journey less lonely. But when he caught Una casting lingering glances in his direction, he vowed never to fall in love. He couldn't risk doing to someone what his mother had done to his father—leaving them heartbroken and alone.

Reaching England, the trio entered a post-apocalyptic Lake District filled with ominous danger. Mutant dogs, known as muttwalkers, stalked their every step as they hurried toward the lake. On its shores, they presented offerings symbolizing the six elements and recited a poem to summon the Lady of the Lake. She emerged from the waters, revealing that the only weapon capable of defeating Zale was Vorago's trident, hidden deep in the Galapagos and fiercely guarded by seawolves. To charm the seawolves into submission, Gal would need to carve and play an ice flute made from the whispering ice of an Icelandic glacier.

A near-miss with the muttwalkers forced the trio to seek shelter in an abandoned house. With Ember on watch and only one bed available, Gal and Una shared the first shift of sleep. Despite his growing feelings, Gal remained too stubborn to admit the truth.

Their journey to Iceland began with Babette, Gal's uncle's on-again, off-again girlfriend and the guardian of the Power of the Sea. Babette brought them to a local couple for shelter and guided them in their search for the magical ice. Overwhelmed by guilt over the dangers his friends faced, Gal set out alone to find the ice—only to end up stranded, requiring rescue. His recklessness resulted in a polar bear attack that left Una gravely injured and missing an eye. Gal, overcome with grief and guilt, finally admitted to himself that he was in love with her.

As Una recovered, Gal resolved to accept help from his companions. He successfully found the magical ice and attempted to carve the flute, drawing closer to Una as they both acknowledged their feelings. Though still terrified of loss, Gal could no longer deny his love for her.

Frustration mounted as his first two attempts at carving the flute failed. A volcanic eruption forced an evacuation of the island, cutting short any further attempts. Before they could leave, Babette was mortally wounded in a violent storm, leaving Gal, Una, and Ember to continue their mission alone.

From Greenland, the trio journeyed across Canada, finally reaching the west coast, where they commandeered a boat. Along the way, Gal successfully carved and played the ice flute, while also learning to rely on his friends and let them in.

When they arrived at the Galapagos, they dove into the depths with the flute in hand. The seawolves attacked, wounding them all before Gal's melody subdued the creatures. Guided into a hidden cave, they discovered the ancient trident. The moment Gal picked it up, it glowed with radiant power, and all the nearby creatures bowed in respect.

But their victory was short-lived. Zale awaited them outside the cave, determined to claim the trident's power for himself. In a vicious battle, Gal defeated Zale. Though victorious, the fight brought him no solace. His heart still ached with grief, yet his newfound closeness with Una gave him a glimmer of hope.

Returning to Atlantis, Gal placed the trident in the Fountain of Youth, allowing its curative waters to heal humans as well. To his shock, *The Mermaid Chronicles* was reborn, hinting at a new prophecy on the horizon...

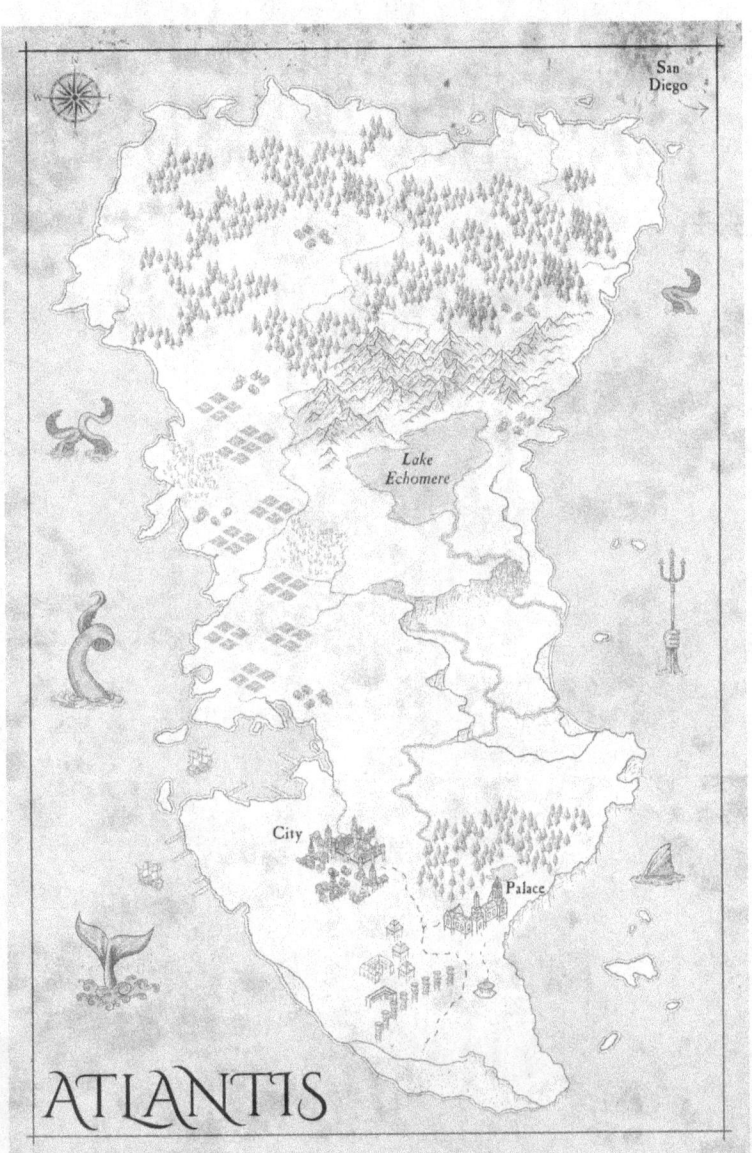

San
Diego

*Lake
Echomere*

City

Palace

ATLANTIS

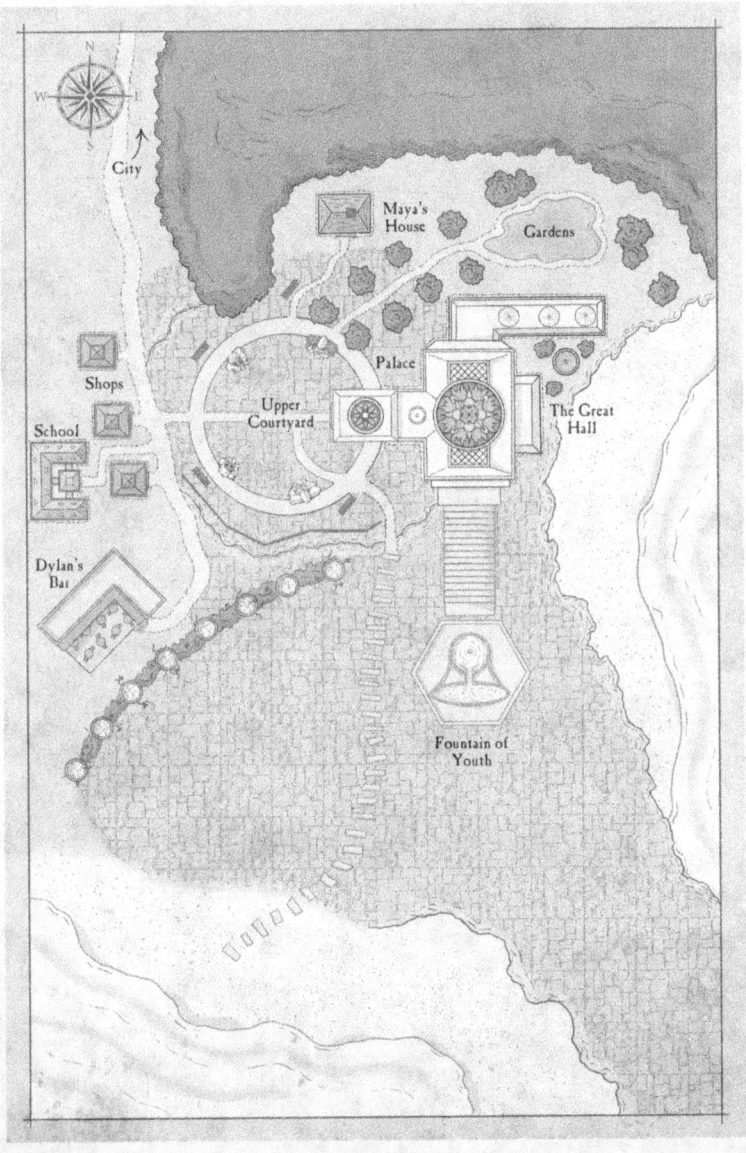

CHAPTER ONE

I jumped back to avoid the foot connecting with my chest. Gripping the glowing trident in my right hand, I carved it through the air, nearly taking off the offending foot.

Ford's eyes widened as he leaped out of the trident's path, and I couldn't help the cocky smile swarming over my lips.

"For Vorago's sake, you're getting good at that."

My grin stretched wider. "I learned from the best." It was only fair to compliment the man who'd taught me everything I knew about combat, as well as the trident's powers.

In the nine months since I'd been back in Atlantis, I'd been training with Ford every day. So far, I had only mastered three of its powers: water breathing, healing waters, and tidal control. Of the many abilities it could grant me, it had only thought me fit to learn the most basic, as if I wasn't worthy of acquiring more. Maybe I wasn't, but my frustration was growing daily.

The moment we'd returned from our fight with Zale, *The Mermaid Chronicles* had informed us the four dark gods of the depths would be coming. The Denizens. Ancient evils with insurmountable power at their fingertips. They were waiting for their chance to tear apart the world I knew. And loved. I had only ever fought a selachii before. Granted, a selachii with enhanced strength and reflexes—gifted from the very evil gods on their way to cast their dark shadows on my homeland—but still a selachii.

If I couldn't wield all the trident's powers by the time the Denizens attacked...how was I going to save my island? My people? Una?

Ford's foot slammed into my chest, knocking the air from my lungs. I stumbled backward, losing my balance, colliding with the low stone wall and toppling over it to land on my ass, the trident falling from my grip, its golden sheen dimming.

I stared at the blue sky, at the clouds scudding across it. I felt the grass under my back, the warmth of the sun caressing my face. Couldn't breathe, though.

Ford's head came into my eyeline. "You okay?"

I nodded. I still couldn't breathe, but my pride hurt worse.

Ford pulled me into a sitting position. "Never lose your focus."

He'd taught me that lesson when I was five. And again when I was six. And again, every single fucking year, and I never learned. Too caught up in my own thoughts. Unable to push the emotions away. But it was worry that motivated me. My worry over keeping everyone safe. If I, the most powerful person on the island, couldn't do that...then what the hell was my purpose?

Ford offered a hand to pull me up. As he hauled me to my feet, his gaze locked with mine. "You need to get out of your head."

I sucked in a breath. It hurt like hell, but I could breathe again. "Any tips on how to do that?"

Ford crossed his arms over his bulky chest and never moved his eyes from mine. "A few. The trident will give you more power when it deems you ready."

"So you keep saying."

"You're worried about the Denizens."

"I'm worried about Una."

I would do anything for Una. I would die for her. I almost had. But there was a tiny part of me that hated her a little bit. She'd made me fall in love with her. Okay, it wasn't entirely her fault. Feelings are feelings and they come when you least expect them, they come even harder when you don't want them. I'd promised myself I'd never fall in love. When my mom died and left my father irrevocably broken, I swore I would never do that to someone. But Una wormed her way into my heart and now it was all too late. There was no way I could live without her. And because of that, I hardly slept anymore.

"You're not in this alone, Gal," Ford said.

I sighed, raked a hand through my sweaty hair. "I know," I mumbled. And yet, no one could wield the power I possessed. I was the Prince of Atlantis. The guardian of the orb of Snow and Ice. The trident wielder. Is this how my mom felt when she became the fire mermaid? So much responsibility. So many people to disappoint. To fail.

Ford put a hand on my shoulder. The tender gesture surprised me, and I glanced up at the burly force of nature once more. "You mother and I worked with meditation. I think it could do you some good too."

I scoffed. Staring at a candle and muttering kumbaya would not take my problems away, nor how I felt about them.

"You won't know unless you try," he said, dropping his hand.

"Okay," I relented, knowing he wouldn't give me a choice. "But I'm not dancing around a fire at midnight butt naked or anything weird like that."

Ford chuckled. "I think you'd find it surprisingly freeing, but no, I won't make you dance in a circle butt naked. For now, let's see what we can get out of the trident."

Grabbing the trident, I rose to my feet. I arced it at the nearby ocean, thinking if I raised the tide high enough, I could soak it over Ford's head and finally have the last laugh. But as I swung the golden weapon over my head, performing an exaggerated circle, a dolphin leaped out of the water. It performed a flip in the air before splashing back into the waves.

Ford smiled. "You're doing something right."

"It's just a dolphin enjoying the currents."

I swung the trident once more, and this time, three dolphins leaped out of the water, followed by a surging wave that stretched toward the sky. The water spun itself into a funnel, white foam swirling at dizzying speeds, and disconnected itself from the ocean.

My grip on the trident faltered, and the funnel collapsed back into the water. I gaped at the spot where the funnel had disappeared.

Ford gave me a scrutinizing look. "Try that again."

"Try *what* again? I just did what I always do." Nevertheless, I swung the trident through the air once more, repeating the circle shape I had made before. Instantly, water leaped into the sky, spun into a large funnel, and sped across the surface until it collapsed onto the rocks. The tang of salt hit the back of my throat.

"Impressive," Ford said. "Looks like your powers are growing."

"I have no idea how I did that."

"Which is why we need to go north. Away from the main populace, where you can practice without drowning the entire city."

"One funnel isn't going to drown the city."

"I think your powers will grow quickly now. You'll be surprised what you're capable of."

I let that digest for a moment. Did the trident finally trust me? Did it sense I would need its full power? Did that mean the Denizens were finally making their approach?

"When do we start?"

"Tomorrow. We'll go to the forest cabins."

"I'm bringing Una."

Ford scrutinized my face, his expression hard to read.

"I won't be able to concentrate knowing she's so far away. And if the Denizens come while we're there..." I pressed my point.

Ford gave me an abrupt nod. "As long as she doesn't distract you."

"As you said, she's part of my team."

"Who's part of your team?" Una asked, approaching our grassy spot within the palace gardens. She wore training shorts and a crop top, leaving so many inches of skin available to feast on, that I felt an immediate stirring. But we had a training session to complete first.

"You." Dropping the trident, I smiled at her and kissed her cheek. My chest swelled, like it did every time I was with her. Her mere presence lightened my dark thoughts, eased the tension that lived in the back of my neck and coiled in my stomach. She was a miracle.

She slung an arm around my waist, then retreated when she found my back slick with sweat.

"Eww." Una danced away from me, her eyepatch dislodging to reveal a hint of the scarred socket beneath.

"Ohh, you're going get just as wet as me." I winked at her so Ford couldn't see, and her cheeks flamed immediately.

Suppressing my devious chuckle, I grabbed her around the waist, lifted her off her feet, and showered kisses on her nape. Laughing, she wriggled out of my grip. When I placed her back on the ground, I gently pulled her eyepatch back down. She caught my hand as I moved to pull away and kissed my palm, the gesture almost undoing me. I wished Ford wasn't there because I really wanted to kiss Una then. A proper kiss. And a whole hell of a lot more.

Ford cleared his throat. We both turned to look at him.

"When you two are quite done, can we carry on with the training session?"

The joviality of the moment leached out of me quicker than a receding tide. I gave Una one more light kiss, then turned my attention to Atlantis' head of security. Ford instructed us to face each other in a patch of grass. I gave a quick glance to the trident, still lying on the ground where I'd dropped it. No harm would come to it there; anyone else who tried to touch it found their skin melted from their palm and a zap of intense electricity stunning their heart into unconsciousness. It would only yield to my command.

But despite its power, I couldn't rely on it. There could be a situation when I was without it. And so I had to learn to fight with my fists. As did Una. Being the guardian of the orb of Spirit and Soul, she had no offensive abilities. Ever since we'd returned to Atlantis, she'd been joining me in the training sessions.

My job was to learn how to be rough with a woman. One of the Denizens was reported to be a female skilled in seduction, and I couldn't be taken in by it. Una was the perfect person to harden my feelings to. Except I would never do that to Una. And Una's job was to learn to take down someone twice her size. She was getting exceedingly good at it too.

Una stood a few paces away, her blonde hair tied back into a loose knot, her single eye fixed on me with that sharp intensity she always had when she was focused. Her eyepatch only added to her aura of quiet ferocity. I wiped the sweat from my brow, trying to ignore the way her lean frame glistened in the sunlight.

Ford circled around us, his hand tapping his thigh, the sword strapped to his back gleaming in the morning sun.

"Keep your form tight, Gal. Una, fists raised, balance your weight."

Focusing on Una's one blue eye, I narrowed mine at her, trying to put her off her game.

"You gonna stand there all day?" Una called, a teasing grin tugging at her lips.

"Oh, I'm coming for you, babe. But I'm taking my time. Wouldn't want to knock you on your ass too quickly."

Her grin widened, a spark of amusement in her eye. "Don't flatter yourself, *prince*."

I lunged, not too fast, giving her a chance to dodge. She sidestepped easily, slipping out of reach. Her movements were fluid, precise, but I could tell she knew I wasn't going full force. That only made her more dangerous. She hated being underestimated. But it was so much fun riling her up.

I came at her again, this time quicker, throwing a punch aimed at her midsection. She ducked under it, her body twisting gracefully as she aimed a swift kick at my thigh. I blocked it easily, catching her foot in my hand. "Nice try."

Before I could make a move, her other foot swept out, and I barely had time to react as she twisted in the air and kicked. She caught me off guard, sending me stumbling back a step. Not enough to put me on my ass, but enough to earn her a grin.

"Not bad," I admitted, dropping her foot and stepping back. Tension simmered between us, that familiar, electric hum that always ignited whenever we sparred.

Una's grin shifted into something sharper. "You're holding back."

8

I shrugged, trying to play it off. "I'm giving you a chance to—"

She didn't let me finish. She shot forward, faster than I expected, her fist aiming straight for my chest. I blocked it with ease, but she wasn't done. She spun around me, her elbow connecting with my ribs, and then, before I could take the offensive, she hooked her leg around mine and swept my feet out from under me.

I hit the ground hard, the impact causing my lungs to seize for a second time. Grass stuck to my skin as I lay there for a minute, stunned.

Ford's deep voice rang out from the sidelines. "You let your guard down, Gal."

I groaned, propping myself up on my elbows. "Thanks for the insight," I muttered, but my eyes were on Una, who stood over me with a victorious smirk.

"Thought you weren't going easy on me," she said

I laughed, shaking my head as I got to my feet. She had gotten the best of me once, but that wasn't happening again.

"Alright," I said, rolling my shoulders. "No more playing around."

"Finally," she said, eyeing me with a hint of suspicion. "Show me what you've got."

This time, I moved with purpose, closing the distance between us in an instant. She tried to block, but I was quicker, stronger. I shot out my hand, grabbing her wrist before she swung, and I twisted, spinning her around until her back was pressed against my chest, her arm pinned between us.

"Now what, Una?" Ford called. "Remember what I taught you. Use his height against him."

She struggled, but I held her tight, leaning in so my lips brushed her ear. "Not so easy now, is it?"

Her body tensed against mine, her breath hitching. I felt the heat of her skin through her clothes, the way her pulse raced beneath my fingers. The tension between us hummed, sharper now, more dangerous. Triumphant, I couldn't help the way my grip tightened just slightly, and also the way my heart pounded in my chest at the feel of her.

Una let out a low growl, twisting in my hold. "Don't get cocky, Gal."

"Do *not* get cocky, Gal," Ford repeated, his face a picture of disappointment.

With a sudden burst of strength, Una wrenched her arm free, spinning around to face me. Her fist swung toward my face, but I caught it, my fingers wrapping around her small hand. Fire ignited in her lone blue eye.

She pushed against me, but I didn't budge. Instead, I pulled her closer, so close that our faces were only inches apart. Her breath came in quick, shallow bursts, her chest rising and falling against mine. I felt her heart racing, and something else—the same tension that had been simmering between us since the start of the fight.

"You do *not* want to bring a Denizen closer, Gal!" Ford's voice dripped with disapproval, but I was barely listening.

"Still think you're faster?" I asked, my voice low.

Her eye flicked to my mouth, and for a moment, I thought she might kiss me. But instead, she grinned, that wicked, teasing grin I loved. "You might be stronger," she admitted, her voice soft but edged with challenge. "But I'll always be one step ahead."

Before I could respond, she slipped out of my grasp, ducking under my arm and twisting away. She was quick, faster than I had given her credit for, but I wasn't letting her escape again. I lunged after her, catching her by the waist and pulling her back against me.

"This is not foreplay 1-0-1," Ford yelled at us.

We tumbled to the ground, rolling in the grass, our limbs tangled together. She fought to get free, but I was stronger, and this time, I didn't hold back. I pinned her beneath me, my hands on either side of her head, holding her down.

She glared up at me, panting, her chest rising and falling with each breath. "Let me go, prince."

I smirked, leaning closer so our noses were almost touching. "Not a chance."

Her eye narrowed, but there was no real anger there. Just that familiar fire, the same one that always burned between us. Her lips parted, her breath warm against my mouth. I hovered there, teasing the line between us, waiting to see if she would push me away.

Instead, she stared up at me, her body stilling beneath mine, her lips curving into a slow, dangerous smile. "You think you've won?"

I leaned in, close enough that our lips brushed. "Haven't I?"

I pinned her wrists to the ground. Her pulse raced under my fingers.

"Not for long."

And then she was moving again, her legs wrapping

around mine, flipping us over until she was the one on top, her knee pressed against my chest, her single eye gleaming with victory.

"Damn it," I muttered, breathless.

Ford's voice cut through the moment. "Considering I felt like I'd intruded on a private moment, that wasn't awful. But next time, Gal, don't get distracted. We'll work on that when we go north."

I grinned up at Una, still pinned beneath her. "I *am* working on it."

"North?" Una asked, still straddling me.

"We're going to go the cabins in the north to practice the more...difficult powers of the trident. I need to make sure no one's around while I learn its more dangerous abilities."

Una's eye softened and she dipped her adorable, elfin chin. "How long will you be gone?"

"We."

"We?"

"How long will *we* be gone...You're coming with me. I can't fight without you."

Una planted a kiss on my lips, a soft, lingering touch that had me wrapping my arms around her even though Ford was still standing there. "You've finally learned that teamwork makes the dream work, eh?"

"Or the nightmare," I muttered, considering that's exactly what the Denizens were.

CHAPTER TWO

I plucked the trident from the ground, its shaft fitting perfectly within my grip and its golden light shimmering into existence once more.

"Gal?" Una put a hand on my arm, the one holding the trident.

I frowned when I caught the tentative look crossing her features. "What's up?"

"I don't like the idea of putting all our eggs in one basket. And I know we have the army and the explosive spears..." She looked at her feet, then brought her gaze back to my face. "What the hell am *I* expected to do?"

Surprised at her sudden doubts, I stared at her. I wasn't the type of person to suggest she stay locked up in her room— not anymore, not after she set me straight during our last adventure—but that's exactly what I wanted her to do. Stay safe. Stay alive.

I also wanted her by my side for every single terrifying moment of whatever battles were coming our way. We fought well together, could anticipate each other's movements. But if she was with me, I would be distracted by trying to keep her safe. I guess that was part of the reason for going north to train with the trident. Ford was determined to teach me how to keep my thoughts focused on the moment. And I damn well better learn how to do it, or I would be putting Una's life in danger. Which was the whole reason I hadn't wanted to fall in love with her in the first place. Around in circles I went.

I nudged her elbow. "You're the guardian of the orb of Spirit and Soul—"

"Empathy isn't going to help beat four evil gods—"

"You're an oracle. And you can beat my ass too." I slung an arm around her shoulder.

She snorted. "Only because I know how you fight. I can anticipate your movements. When it comes to it..." she shook her head. "I'm a liability."

I raised the trident so it came into her eyeline. "I haven't learned most of what this can do." My voice was quiet, the fear evident, even when I tried to clamp down on it. "And if I don't learn all its secrets before they arrive..." It was my turn to shake my head. I sighed, unable to finish the thought.

"I believe in you."

That made one of us. "Thanks."

She placed her hand on my chest, right over my heart. "I believe in Atlantis. In you. In Ember. And Blaze and your dad and my parents and Ford and Dylan...everyone. We'll do it together."

And how many would we lose along the way?

Our last journey saw the death of Babette, my uncle's on-

and-off-again, long-term girlfriend. Although I hadn't spent much time with her before then, I'd grown to care for her, and her death had left a hollowness in my stomach. I still felt guilty when I looked at my uncle, knowing she died because she'd helped me.

Una cupped my face in her palms. "I know what you're thinking, Gal Waters." She raised herself to tiptoes and pressed her lips against mine. "We put all the guilt and worry behind us, remember? I'm not going to let you revert to your previous bad habits."

I folded my arm around her and hugged her against my chest. "Worrying about people is a bad habit?"

She prodded my pec with her finger. "You know what I mean. You have a tendency to dwell. And I'm not going to allow it. In fact, I know a way to keep your mind off it."

She tilted her head back, her lips parting, and pushed her breasts against my chest. They swelled between us. I couldn't look at anything else. Why would I?

It never failed. Una, and what she could do with her body always ripped me away from my dark thoughts.

I made a parody of scanning the garden where a few people were ambling along the pathways and others had turned into their shifter forms and were swimming in the water channels. "What? Right here? In front of everyone?"

Una ran a fingernail across my chest. "Nope. I do not share well with others. Not when it comes to you."

I loved every single word. I felt the familiar pull in my chest, that magnetic force that seemed to draw me to her no matter how far apart we were. We had been training hard for weeks, barely any time to just...be. But here, in the peace of the palace gardens, everything else fell away.

Una's body pressed against mine, her warmth sinking into me as I held her close, my trident still clutched in one hand. The other rested around her waist, fingers curling into the fabric of her top.

Her breath fanned against my neck, her lips so close that it took everything in me not to close the distance.

She slid a hand down my arm, fingers grazing my hand. "I can't decide which you love more, me, or the trident."

I smirked, tightening my grip around her waist, pulling her flush against me. "Who says I can't love both?"

Her eye narrowed playfully, and her pulse fluttered at the base of her throat. Every inch of her was tense, alive, like a coiled spring waiting to snap. I moved my thigh between her legs and she let out a little moan.

She shifted in my arms, her lips grazing my jaw. "As long as you don't take the trident to bed with you," she whispered, her voice like the whisper of the ocean, soft but full of hidden depths.

I let out a low laugh, dipping my head so my forehead rested against hers. "It doesn't complain when I snore."

"But you can't sleep with all that glowing light." Her smirk deepened, and before I could react, she reached up, tugging at the hand holding the trident. I felt it shift in my grip, and before I could blink, it was gone, tossed into the grass a few feet away. She grinned, the wicked curve of her lips making my pulse spike.

"There," she said, her voice triumphant. "That's better."

I let out a breathless laugh, my hand instinctively tightening on her hip. "You're trouble, you know that?"

Her eye gleamed with amusement. "And you love it."

"I thought you wanted to be somewhere more private?"

"We'll get there."

Before I could answer, she leaned in, capturing my lips with hers. The kiss was hot, demanding, the tension that had been building between us igniting like wildfire. I pulled her closer, one hand tangling in her hair as I kissed her back with all the heat she was throwing at me. There was nothing gentle about it—it was fierce, raw, like we were both hungry for more than we'd ever admit.

Her hands slid up my chest, gripping my muscles as she deepened the kiss, her body pressing harder against mine. The feel of her, the taste of her—it was indescribable. Salt and the ocean and jasmine. Every single time. Somehow sweet and delicate when Una was anything but. Every brush of her lips, every flick of her tongue sent a fresh wave of heat rolling through me, and I couldn't get enough.

I broke the kiss just long enough to catch my breath. "We need to get somewhere private pretty damn soon," I whispered, my desire obvious.

Wordlessly, she stepped out of my embrace, caught my hand, and tugged me toward the palace steps. I grabbed the trident and jogged behind her, blood barreling through my veins, desperate to touch her, unable to stand the current gap between us.

When we entered the coolness of the palace, Una went to the stairs, placed a hand on the intricate marble post, jutted a hip.

"I need to put the trident away first." I gestured to the great hall. It was the room where all the magical artifacts of Atlantis were stored. The Power of the Sea and the five other elemental orbs. *The Mermaid Chronicles*. And my trident. Usually, at this time of day on a Saturday, tours to the public were in full swing, but since the prophecy concerning the Denizens appeared in *The Mermaid Chronicles*, tours had been put to a halt.

"Hurry up."

"Come with me." I held my hand out to her.

She grinned and took my hand, following me into the vast room.

Once inside, I closed the door softly behind us. Unable to wait to continue devouring Una, I rushed to the mantle place and lifted the trident onto its brackets. It gave a brief brighter wink of light, as if knowing it was time to sleep, then faded to its usual dim golden color when it wasn't being handled by me.

I turned, took Una's hand, yanked her against my chest, and lowered my lips to hers.

"We need to go upstairs," she murmured between kisses.

I shook my head, dragging her deeper into the room, around the corner where a small alcove looked out over the gardens and the patch of grass we'd just been training on.

"I won't make it."

She threw her head back and laughed, giving me perfect access to her delicious neck.

"We can't do it in here." She pushed against my chest, but I refused to let her go.

"No one comes in here apart from the High Council or

the senate," I murmured as I drew the lobe of her ear between my lips.

"Which is *both* of my parents."

"I've always wanted to...in here...surrounded by the orbs."

As if on cue, both of our orbs glowed a little brighter, bringing a glinting delight to Una's blue eye.

I guided her to the window ledge where a padded seat offered a comfortable reading space. It was a place Una often sat, cross-legged, with *The Mermaid Chronicles* open on her lap. Now, it would provide an entirely different use.

As she eased back onto the seat, her lips moved against mine with a practiced skill, like she knew exactly how to push me to the edge without letting me fall.

I groaned against her mouth, sliding my hand down her back, feeling the curve of her body under my palm. She arched into me, her fingers curling into my hair, pulling me even closer. I couldn't get enough of her. She was my air. My entire reason for being. Without her...there simply was no me.

With a deep breath, I leaned in, pressing my lips against the sensitive spot where her neck met her shoulder. She exhaled a breathy sigh into my ear, her body melting onto the seat beneath us. I flicked out my tongue, tasting the salt of her skin from a recent swim. Her muscles tensed beneath my touch, her body responding with a mind of its own. She whimpered, hips rolling against mine. The friction sent sparks shooting through my body.

I followed the curve of her throat with my lips, moving lower until I reached the fullness of her breast. Slipping my hand under her top, I pulled it down just enough to expose her nipple before taking it into my mouth, tugging gently and eliciting a sharp gasp from her lips.

Una moaned, her fingers weaving through my hair and holding me close as I kneeled before her. My lips drifted further down, leaving a trail of kisses along the smooth contours of her stomach. Her body arched toward me, silently begging for more.

I gave in to the urge and yanked down her shorts and underwear, exposing her quivering arousal in one swift movement. God, she was beautiful. She radiated an inner light that drew me in like a siren's song.

"Gal..." It was a feeble protest. We were both too far over the edge to stop now.

I traced the tip of my tongue across Una's hip and ventured lower until I reached the delicate bud that would send waves of pleasure coursing through her. She widened her legs, granting me access, and I buried my face between them, sucking deeply on her most sensitive spot.

Una bucked beneath me, her hips rising to meet my tongue, her breaths coming faster and shallower. I could sense her growing urgency, the need for release building within her.

"Someone could come in," she groaned.

"I don't care," I murmured into her heated core, causing her to writhe once more.

I slid a hand between her thighs, my fingers diving into her wet warmth. As I stroked her most sensitive spots, Una's breathing grew ragged. Her nails raked down my back.

"I can't..."

"Yes, you can," I said, sliding my fingers deeper.

Una's body tensed, trembling on the edge. With a cry of ecstasy, she threw her head back and clung to me. I didn't let up until the last shudder and moan left her.

As the aftershocks subsided, Una's eye fluttered open and she gave me a dreamy smile that made me grin from ear to ear. I had lost my virginity to Una. She was the only woman I'd ever known. And in the months we'd been together, we'd loved and explored and experimented. And now I knew exactly how to pleasure her.

The sound of the doors swinging open made Una flinch in my arms, and my own desire plummeted. I backed away from her, helped her pull her shorts up and straightened her top.

"Una?" Trent's voice. Her father.

I glanced at Una to see her cheeks flaming with color.

Footsteps gained on our not so hidden hiding place. "Una? Are you in here?"

I held my breath, clamped a hand over Una's mouth when I saw her about to let loose an inappropriately timed giggle. Still flushed with heat, I could smell her. Could smell what we'd just done, as well as taste her. If her father rounded the corner, he'd know what we'd been up to. Not that it was a problem. All the adults in our lives knew we were in a relationship, knew we were having sex, but it wasn't something we wanted to throw in their faces either. Especially when Una still lived at home. Which was something I had been trying to change. But her parents refused to let her move out until she turned eighteen. So arbitrary. What did age even matter? Thankfully, her birthday was only a few weeks away.

The footsteps receded and faded until the door to the great hall swung open and closed once more.

I removed my hand from Una's mouth, but she immediately covered it with both of hers, stifling a gasp. I rested my head against her shoulder, sucking in a deep breath to soothe my trembling legs.

"That was too close," Una whispered.

"Which is one of the reasons I want you to come north. No parents to interrupt us."

"There's Ford."

"He doesn't give a shit where we sleep or what we do as long as I don't lose focus."

Una pushed herself off the seat and into my arms, jabbed a finger at my chest. "Which is why I'll come, but I'm going to stay out of the way."

Taking her hand, I shook my head. "I need to learn how to focus when you are around. Because when the Denizens come, you're going to be fighting by my side. And I have to learn not to worry about you."

She smiled the sweetest smile and pressed a soft kiss to my cheek. "You don't have to stop worrying, Gal, that's not really normal. You just have to make sure it doesn't get the best of you."

CHAPTER THREE

Saying goodbye to Uncle Dylan was harder than I thought. As I nursed a drink in the bar that evening, sitting on a stool opposite where Dylan was serving, I couldn't quite find the words to tell him I was leaving for the north of the island for the foreseeable future. Or until I learned to master all the abilities the trident could offer. It had taken me nine months to learn the three most basic ones and I sensed I was running out of time.

During a pause in customers, Uncle Dylan swiped a cloth over the bar, catching drips and splatters left behind from full pint glasses. "You've been nursing that beer for an hour. What's wrong?"

When I didn't reply, he dropped the cloth, leaned over the counter, and pressed me with a look. Part fear, part curiosity, and part you-better-tell-me-what-the-hell-is-going-on.

I waved a hand, picked up my drink, and drained the contents. Completely flat. "Nothing to worry about." I wiped my mouth with the back of my hand. "Just came in for a drink...and to say goodbye to my favorite uncle."

Uncle Dylan hunched his shoulders. "I'm your *only* uncle."

I shrugged. "You know what I mean." Even if I had ten uncles, Dylan would still be my favorite.

"Where are you going?" He watched me with his hazel eyes, alert for any sense of impending doom. "Are the pages turning again?"

I shook my head. "Nothing like that. The damn book hasn't delivered any new prophecies since the day I came home. It would be good if it provided a little detail occasionally. Or a timeline."

Dylan's face relaxed and the corners of his mouth quirked in amusement. "Doesn't work that way."

"Tell me about it." I gestured for him to refill my glass. "But to answer your question, I'm going north with Ford and Una to practice with the trident. I'm hoping if we're away from the masses, I'll be able to figure out its more destructive abilities without hurting anyone."

Uncle Dylan nodded. "Makes sense."

"I might be gone a long time."

Dylan cocked his head as he finished refilling my glass. "How come?"

"Because it's taken me so damn long to learn the three most basic powers..." I trailed off, disgusted with myself. I was the sole wielder of Vorago's trident. The god of the ocean. The god who built Atlantis for us. A freaking *god*. I was bestowed with the weapon of a *god*. The responsibility alone left me brooding for days. "I haven't got to grips with it yet."

"You'll get it," Uncle Dylan said.

I snorted a laugh. "No. Nope. Do not put that pressure on me."

Uncle Dylan raised an eyebrow, concern softening his features. "What's really going on?"

The sudden heat behind my eyes took me by surprise. Tension lived in my muscles, coiled in my stomach, wound around my limbs, always there, always waiting for something to go wrong.

"I thought I'd learned a lot about myself when I went after Zale." I took a swig of beer to collect my thoughts. "But it seems I haven't learned a damn thing. I'm still afraid of losing people. And if I don't master that trident, I can't protect those I love."

Uncle Dylan puffed up his cheeks and blew out an elongated breath. "You are so like your mother."

The comment startled me and brought with it a tightening in my chest. Although her death was almost thirteen years ago, the ache inside never went away. I'd watched her die. I'd watched Zale devour her with his jaws. To save me.

"When she was alive, she was the most powerful person on the island," Uncle Dylan said, casting a quick glance at the door as new customers ventured inside. "And she too had to learn to rely on others, to learn that it wasn't only her responsibility. It wasn't until the ghost pirates attacked that she realized she couldn't do it alone. She needed us. Me. The orb guardians. They couldn't be defeated without us."

"None of that changes the fact that she gave her life for mine."

Uncle Dylan eyed me carefully. "She did what any

parent would do. And it sucks. And it hurts. But you can't be mad at her for dying."

His words hit like a sucker punch. All this time I'd thought I'd been grieving her loss. But truthfully, I was mad she'd taken such a risk and left me alone. Because the day she died, I'd lost my father too. He'd retreated into a cloud of grief. It was only since I'd defeated Zale that our relationship had improved. He was making an effort to spend time with me, to resume the duties of being the King of Atlantis. Although both of us had been ready to relinquish our titles in favor of a more democratic governance, the people voted for us to remain as figureheads and to sit on the High Council and senate. So, king and prince we remained.

But he would never be the same. Neither of us would. He even refused to drink from the fountain. He said it was because he didn't want to delay the moment he was reunited with her. But really, I knew it was because he didn't want to outlive me. With the fountain not working for me, I would die before him if he took the water and prolonged his lifespan. He couldn't take another loss. But neither could I.

"I don't want to be angry, and I don't want to be afraid," I said, clenching my hand around the glass. "And I don't want to be responsible for Una losing her other eye." The guilt gnawed at my insides like a relentless parasite.

"That wasn't your fault," Uncle Dylan said, pressing his point into my palm with a finger. "You can't keep beating yourself up over that."

I opened my mouth to argue when Uncle Dylan carried on. He laid his hands flat on the bar. "Go north. Learn the ways of the trident. Love Una. And live your life."

"What, like you're doing?" I knew the jibe was childish, and maybe I still had some growing up to do, but I didn't know how to deal with pressure, and sometimes it was easier to lash out.

Before Dylan could reply, my Aunt Marina slipped out of the office and wound an arm around Dylan's waist. He gave her a light kiss on the cheek, then turned back to me and blushed.

I pointed a finger at them, moving it back and forth between them. "Uh...when did that happen?" My mother's brother and my father's sister. Together. What the actual...?

"As I said," Uncle Dylan drew Aunt Marina closer to his side, "life's too short."

"Amen to that," Marina said, and patted my hand.

Before I could quiz them on just what the hell was going on between them, Ember slid onto the stool next to me, his dark eyes full of mischief and his wings dragging across the floor.

"I hear we're going north." He slid the drink from my hand and gulped down half of it. "To turn you into a trident master."

"No...*I'm* going north."

"I want to come."

"It's not safe."

"Let's just say I've got some tropical greenery up there that needs my expert touch." Ember had been growing cannabis in the fields north of the mountain since he was fourteen. With his dragon king wings, no area of the island was inaccessible to him. "And I could use some bonding time with my brother and sister."

27

I blanched, gaped at him. "*Brother and sister? Since when do you have a brother and sister?*"

Ember raised both brows. "Yeah, so that was the big news I was going to tell you. Turns out my dad had a little fun after he split with Mom, but the female in question didn't know he was the father until last week, when Ash and Cyra's wings developed. Well, Ash's. Cyra's haven't appeared yet, but they're twins, so..."

"Ash and Cyra?" My thoughts spun, knocked against each other, collided so hard I couldn't think straight. There were two more dragon kings in the world.

"Dad's a little thrown, obviously. Needs some time to sort things out with...Nimara...thought I could take Ash and Cyra away and get to know them. Help them...neither of them can conjure their fire."

It was only last year Ember discovered he couldn't breathe fire like the rest of his kind, but he could inhale it. It had been a sore spot for him for years. And I knew he would do anything to help his siblings, even if it was awkward.

"They're thirteen?"

"Yeah."

"It might be dangerous."

Ember downed the rest of my beer, gestured to my uncle for another. "Yeah, but just think, if I can get them to use their fire, we'll have two more powerful team members in the fight against the Denizens."

He had a point.

"Okay then." I raised my refilled glass and offered a toast. "To trident powers, fiery breath, and making sweet, sweet love under a full moon."

Ember chuckled, clinked my glass, then downed his fresh beer in one. He swiveled on his stool. "Speaking of making love..." He waggled his eyebrows and his eyes took on a glint I hadn't seen in a long time.

I followed his gaze to see a newcomer standing in the open doorway. Words fell out of my head. Thought deserted me. And coils of desire tightened in the pit of my stomach. The woman hovering on the threshold was the most beautiful fucking woman I had ever laid eyes on. A gusty breeze tunneled in through the door and billowed her clothing and hair. Soft music floated around the bar, so tangible I could almost taste each note.

"Who *is* that?" I asked, unable to tear my gaze away. The way she moved through the crowded bar with effortless grace transfixed me. There was something about her—an aura of power and allure that was both captivating and unsettling. As she drew closer, I felt a strange pull, as if an invisible force was tugging me toward her.

Ember let out a low whistle as the captivating music grew in volume. "I have no freaking idea, but I think it might be time for me to try dating again."

I barely heard him, too entranced by the ethereal creature before me. She moved with a fluid elegance that was almost hypnotic, her lithe form swaying to an unheard melody.

As if sensing my stare, her gaze collided with mine across the room. Something electric passed between us, an inexplicable pull. Like magnets. My heart raced as she inclined her head ever so slightly, the ghost of a smile touching her lips.

"And if I were you," Ember said. "I wouldn't let Una catch me with my mouth hanging open like that."

I snapped my jaw shut.

Whoever this woman was, I couldn't deny the powerful attraction I felt, the sense that our paths were meant to cross. But I loved Una. That hadn't changed. Of course not. She was the love of my life and always would be. My lobster, as we liked to joke. My queen. My forever. So why the hell was my skin turning slick at the sight of this mysterious woman?

"You see her around before?" I asked my cousin.

"Nope. Maybe she lives in one of the villages."

I turned on my stool and waved to get my uncle's attention. "Who is that?" I mouthed.

He glanced at the woman, shrugged, then turned back to his customer. By the time I turned to face the room again, the woman had ventured further inside. My breath caught, and I found myself ridiculously tongue-tied. I hoped to hell she didn't come over here.

Ember slapped my thigh. "Wish me luck."

Before I could say a word, he shot off the stool and met the woman halfway across the room. Gathering my thoughts, and my composure, I exhaled slow and measured breaths, slapped my cheek a couple times and gave myself a stern talking to.

I was in a loving relationship that I had fought against and fought for. It was Ember's turn to find love. But I couldn't remember the last time I'd been so physically affected by a member of the opposite sex. There were other beautiful women in Atlantis, Una included, so why did this woman make my breath hitch and my pulse spike?

Shaking my head, I was about to turn back to the bar when Ember returned, his expression crestfallen.

"Crash and burn," he muttered as he slid onto his stool. The music shifted, became deeper, more emotional, more...I couldn't describe it...more hypnotic. "She may have taken my pride, but at least no one can steal my wings."

I slapped his shoulder, turning my back to the room and the strange new atmosphere the woman had brought in with her. "You were brave to try, buddy. And she's crazy not to take one look at those wings and fall into an instant haze of lust."

"Nothing holding me back from going north now," Ember grinned. "I was about Cyra and Ash's age when I started smoking the funky fruit. Maybe I can chill them out with a little wacky tobacky and get their fire to come out—"

I laughed into my beer. "They're thirteen."

"So? Maybe if I'd started a year younger I'd have found my fire sooner. And besides, it will give us something to bond over."

"You don't need to be nervous around thirteen-year-olds."

Ember fidgeted on his stool. "I don't know what to say to a thirteen-year-old."

"Just talk to them like they're our age. They'll respect that more."

Ember gave me a side-eye, raked a hand through his unruly locks. "When did you get so smart?"

I planted both hands over my chest. "Una."

"Yep. That'll do it."

"Prince Gal?"

I cringed. No one called me that. No one used my title. I did my best to forget I was a prince. When I turned to greet the unfamiliar voice, my throat tightened around my vocal chords.

"I don't believe we've had the pleasure of meeting. My name is Siryn," she said, her voice like velvet brushing against my skin.

It was *her*. And all I could do was gape at her, take in the length of her flowing dark hair, the deep hue of her skin, the mystery in her dark eyes, and the obvious curves of her full figure. *Jesus.*

Una. Una. Una.

She extended her hand, and I found myself reaching out to take it, my skin tingling at her touch. Her fingers lingered on mine a moment longer than necessary, and a slow, seductive smile curved her lips.

"Prince Gal, I was hoping you might indulge me with a personal tour of the great hall where the legendary trident is kept. I've heard so much about it," she said, her voice like a song I'd been longing to hear and her eyes never leaving mine.

I hesitated, a flicker of unease rippling through me. The trident was a sacred artifact, the Denizens wanted it, and tours were on hold. And yet, the way she was looking at me, her eyes dark and inviting, made it hard to refuse. "Tours have been paused for the time being."

"Paused?" She tilted her head on a graceful swan neck. "How come?"

I frowned. Surely she would know. The entire island did. Ever since the prophecy concerning the Denizens had appeared, the magical artifacts had been locked down. But it wasn't unusual for inhabitants to take long sabbaticals from the island, to venture to the mainland searching for family or merely for a change of scenery. Perhaps she had been away. That would make sense, considering I didn't remember ever seeing her before.

She stepped closer, her hand trailing up my arm. "I'd really love to see it," she murmured, her breath warm against my ear. The words "see it" echoed in my head. Without meaning to, I stood, intending to walk her to the great hall.

"Gal," Ember said sharply, a note of warning in his voice.

I blinked, breaking free of the strange urge. "I'm sorry," I said, stepping back. "But the answer is no. The trident is not for public viewing."

For a moment, something dangerous flashed in her eyes, but then it was gone, replaced by a coy smile.

"Pity," she sighed. "But I understand. Perhaps another time, then."

She turned to go, her hips swaying hypnotically. I watched her leave, the door slamming closed on a gust behind her, my heart pounding and my mind reeling. What was it about her that had such a strong effect on me? And why did I get the feeling this wouldn't be the last time our paths crossed? The music cut out. The speakers above my head crackled as if disappointed.

Ember let out a low whistle. "You sure know how to pick 'em, Gal. That one's trouble with a capital T."

I didn't respond, still staring at the door where Siryn had disappeared. He was right. Trouble was definitely on the horizon. And somehow, I knew it was just the beginning.

CHAPTER FOUR

Goodbyes sucked.

No matter how many times I told myself this wasn't forever, the knot in my chest didn't care. I didn't love living in the palace—too many reminders of a royal status I never asked for—but my relationship with Dad was fragile, something that needed time and patience. What if he retreated into himself again while I was gone?

I grabbed my packed bag, the rough fabric brushing against my fingers, and ventured into the living area of the royal suite. The air felt heavy, thick with the scent of wood smoke and the faint sea breeze creeping through the open window. Dad stood by the fireplace, watching the flames sway and flicker, even though it was far too warm for a fire. He did this every night, a ritual that helped him remember her. My mother.

"Dad." My voice came out softer than I intended, the weight of the moment settling deep in my chest. I placed a hand on his shoulder. His skin felt warm under my palm, the muscles beneath still solid, still strong, but there was a still-ness to him that hadn't been there before.

He turned to face me, his eyes searching mine, and for a brief second, I saw all the worries he was trying to hide.

"Be safe." Just two words, but the layers beneath them were endless. A plea. A promise. A warning.

"And you." I forced the words out, even though they felt inadequate. In truth, I never worried about my father. He was the strongest man on the island—literally. His strength, granted by the Power of the Sea, had saved him when he'd been on the brink of death during one of his adventures with my mother. That strength still pulsed beneath his skin, visible in the hard lines of his muscles. But it had been a long time since I'd seen him use it. There hadn't been a reason. Yet.

I picked up my bag and turned to leave.

"Gal."

The emotion in my father's voice made me hesitate. I turned back, catching the faint tremor in his brow, the worry etched into every line of his face.

"I know you're scared."

"I'm fucking terrified," I admitted, the words leaving me before I could stop them.

Dad crossed the room in a few powerful strides, his hands landing firmly on my shoulders, grounding me. "I promised myself I would never let you fight alone again. When the time comes, I'll be right by your side." His voice wavered, and when I met his eyes, they glistened with an emotion he rarely showed.

Heat rose behind my own eyes, but I blinked it away.

"The whole island will fight," Dad said. "We've never

faced anything like the Denizens before. We will stand together."

He pulled me into a fierce hug, and I leaned into the solidity that was my father.

But I couldn't linger. I pulled back before emotion overwhelmed me, giving him one last look. "You'll be okay while I'm gone?"

Dad nodded. "I've got things to keep me occupied." He tilted his head, a faint smile tugging at his lips. "Ruling an island for one."

I smiled.

"Remember the radios in the cabin. If you need to talk."

"Thanks, Dad." I turned and left. If I stayed, fear would get the better of me and I might never venture out of the royal suite.

Closing the door softly behind me, I lugged my bag over one shoulder and made my way to the great hall. The trident caught the light of the sun, giving off a brief, glimmering wink as I lifted it from its brackets. The cool metal slid into my grip, fitting perfectly, as if it understood it was time to get serious. Time to face what was coming.

Una found me inside. She made her way to the plinth that supported *The Mermaid Chronicles* and plucked it off its stand.

"What do you plan on doing with that?" I gestured to the book, which, thankfully, was silent for once. The last thing I needed was another cryptic prophecy whispering in my ear.

"Good morning to you too," she replied, and pressed a lingering kiss to my lips.

I smiled beneath the kiss, flicking my tongue against the

seam of her mouth. "Wanna go again?" I murmured, my voice low, the invitation clear.

Laughing, she shoved me away. "Not in here, thank you very much. That was a little too close for comfort last time."

I bumped her with my hip, urging us toward the door.

Una swept a loving hand over the embossed cover of *The Mermaid Chronicles*. "Mom said I could take it with me to keep an eye on things. She's gotten so good at receiving the prophecies without the book, she doesn't need to be around it anymore."

"Jeez, that's next-level oracle badassery."

Una grinned. "So I get to keep it with me."

"As long as you don't turn into some ethereal, all-seeing, sanctimonious entity."

"The lady of the Lake I am not," she said, referring to a person we'd met on our last journey. "And besides, I prefer my corporeal comforts way too much." She cut me a sexy grin, the kind that lit a spark in my gut, sending a rush of desire straight through me.

But just as quickly as the feeling came, the memory of last night surfaced—Siryn. Guilt prickled beneath my skin, uninvited and unwelcome. I hadn't done anything wrong, hadn't crossed any lines, but the fact that I'd even let myself admire another woman left a bitter taste.

I shook it off as we stepped outside, the cool breeze off the sea sweeping over us. The salty air cleared my head, but it didn't stop me from worrying about what Una might have thought if she'd known.

Descending the palace steps, Ford joined us, his short swords crossed over his back, their hilts catching the early morning light. Guns had been introduced to Atlantis during the human rebellion, but Ford had always preferred his blades. And I had an instinct gunfire would do nothing to harm four evil, dark gods older than time itself.

Ford clapped, rubbed his hands together. "I have a good feeling about this trip. I know you're going to master the trident, Gal."

He could have been telling the truth. Ford was a member of the High Council and therefore one of the few able to read *The Mermaid Chronicles*. The High Council members experienced a special insight when it came to the prophecies. Perhaps he knew something. Or if he didn't know it, he sensed it. But I suspected it was more likely he was trying to pump me full of confidence.

I was the anomaly. I wasn't a High Council member, and yet I could read the damn book. But I never experienced the *special insight* the other members referred to. Una claimed it was all part of some wider plan, but when I tried to pin her down for details, she shrugged and said it wasn't clear yet.

What was the point of having a book of prophecies and warnings, if it couldn't give us the details?

Okay, yeah, the members always said if they gave us too much information it could alter the future for the worse. Blah, blah, blah. That was why I'd burned the book before. I didn't want to live chained to prophecies. And my attitude toward it hadn't changed. But I promised I wouldn't destroy it again.

I shot Ford a disgruntled look. There were three more known powers the trident could bestow: hydrokinesis, storm manipulation, and teleportation. If I could learn just one of them, I'd be content, confident in my ability to fight the Denizens. There was also a myriad of other abilities alluded to but undocumented. No one had any idea of its real strengths or limitations. I guessed we were about to find out.

"I'm going to focus on hydrokinesis. That sounds... useful." To be able to manipulate water at will, cause tidal waves, whirlpools...the power of it was literally awesome.

"We'll start with meditation and mindfulness," Ford said with a sly look.

I groaned. "Meditation and mindfulness aren't going to teach me how to use the trident."

"No, but they'll teach you how to keep your head when it matters most," Ford countered, his eyes gleaming with the wisdom of someone who'd seen more battles than I could count.

I glanced at Una, noted the bright blue eye patch she wore that matched the iris of her single eye. Her injury was a living reminder of how I'd failed her. I would not fail her again. And so if Ford insisted we spent time on meditation, I would give it my all.

"Let's do it," I said.

Ford hesitated, as if expecting me to argue.

"I mean it. I do. Really."

He nodded, his glance moving to Una. He knew me better than I knew myself.

"Good," Ford said. "We can start on the boat."

The three of us trailed along one of the cobble paths to the water channel that led to the north of the island. Ember was waiting for us there with two younger teenagers.

The boy hovered a few feet above the ground, his wings

beating lazily as if flying was the most natural thing in the world. His light brown skin was shaded the same as Ember's. Muscles were beginning to shape his slender frame, the telltale signs of adolescence giving way to manhood. His honey-colored eyes glinted with mischief, and his messy blond hair looked like it hadn't seen a brush in weeks. The permanent grin plastered across his face suggested he hadn't stopped flying since discovering his wings.

The girl stood beside her brother, rooted firmly on the ground. Her skin, hair, and eyes were identical to his, but there was no visible sign of her dragon king heritage. At thirteen, she was already tall, nearly eye-to-eye with Ember, and had begun growing into her womanhood with a poise beyond her years. Still, there was something hesitant in her posture, like she didn't understand where she fit in this world of wings and tridents.

Doubts flooded through me. They were too young for this. Although it was important for every dragon king to learn about who they were and what abilities they possessed, the last thing I wanted to do was thrust two young teenagers into the battle of the century. This was a bad idea.

Introductions were made, and Cyra's face brightened when she met Una, who she towered over. It seemed she was pleased to have another female in the group. And Una being Una, the eldest of four siblings, would do everything to make the girl feel welcome. That was something at least.

Ash approached me next, the grin fixed to his face as he shook my hand. His gaze drifted toward the trident, and I caught the curiosity sparking in his eyes.

He reached out, fingers hovering near the weapon. "Can I—?"

I jerked the trident away from his grasp. "Not a good idea. It'll burn the skin right off your hand."

His mouth fell open, and he darted his hand back to his side. "Can I watch you use it?"

I considered. Although I wanted these two kids far away from danger, it would do me good to practice maintaining my focus when I was worried about others. "Of course."

"Awesome!" Ash dropped to the ground, wings folding into his back as he shifted into his fully human form. His feet hit the earth with a soft thud, but he bounced with restless energy.

Cyra rolled her eyes. "Show off."

"Just because you haven't got yours yet," Ash retorted.

"That's because mine will be bigger," Cyra said with a smug grin.

Una threw an arm around both of them, laughing as she led them toward the waiting barge. "You two sound just like my siblings."

I was the last to board. It would take us two days to reach the northern forest where the royal cabin was located. While Una and Ember kept the twins occupied, Ford and I sat at the back of the barge and formed a strategy. Ford laid out a rough map, and we began plotting. Every minute was crucial, and with the looming threat of the Denizens, we couldn't waste a second. We sketched out a timetable: meditation, hand-to-hand combat, training with the trident, and—of course—various distractions.

That last part would be Una.

The trident hummed in my grasp, its power thrumming beneath the surface. It was the most powerful weapon in our realm and my gut clenched at the idea that I could harm Una with it. That led to a two-hour stewing session about the burden of responsibility.

Every time I glanced at Una, her laughter carrying back to where Ford and I sat, my chest tightened. She deserved better than the uncertainty I carried. But the truth was, this battle was coming whether I was ready or not, and all I could do was keep going, for her, for the island, for all of us.

Ford's voice broke through my thoughts.

"I could tell you to not repeat the mistakes of a parent," he said gently. "I could tell you, you are your own worst enemy. I could tell you that you must learn to let things go. None of this is new information. You know all this. It's knowing all this that has you twisted into knots. You don't know how."

"I don't know how," I echoed. I was aware of my faults. I knew I wouldn't perform to the best of my abilities if I didn't put my fears aside. I knew I would put more people at risk if I didn't overcome my insecurities. But doing it was a whole other thing.

Ford watched me for a moment, his gaze calm, steady, like the ocean after a storm. Then he spoke, his voice carrying a weight that made me sit up a little straighter.

"You're right," he said, his tone low and measured. "Knowing and doing are two different beasts. But here's the thing: Fear, it isn't something you just conquer. It's not something you erase or bury. Fear is like the ocean—you don't fight it, Gal. You learn how to swim through it."

I glanced at him, but he wasn't finished.

"Every time you face fear, it's like diving into deep water. It'll pull at you, make you feel like you're drowning. But the trick? You don't fight the current. You let it wash over you, feel it, then move with it. Because when you stop trying to control everything, you find a way to move forward despite the fear."

He paused, letting the words sink in. "You don't have to be fearless to win. You just have to stop letting fear hold you still. Fear is always going to be there, but it doesn't have to decide where you go."

I blinked, the knot in my chest loosening a little. Ford smiled faintly, as if he could see it happening.

"So stop worrying about how to get rid of it," he said. "Start focusing on how you can keep moving forward, even with it by your side. You've got more strength than you realize, Gal. It's not about being perfect. It's about finding your rhythm in the chaos."

THAT FIRST NIGHT on the barge, I slept with Una on a narrow bed as the currents rocked the boat. Pretended to sleep. I couldn't sleep. Sailing to the north of the island felt like a step on a journey I couldn't retrace. A pathway that had no return. I was setting things in motion. Cause and effect. Prophecies and battles.

Una rolled toward me, her eye searching my face in the dark. "What's wrong?"

"What happens if the Denizens get hold of the trident?"

She pursed her lips as she stared at me. "Honestly? No one knows. The book hasn't revealed much either."

"Because it can't, or won't?"

"I don't know." She drew lazy circles across my chest. "But whatever the reason, it amounts to the same."

"So what would happen?" I asked again, shoving a hand through my hair. "If a Denizen got hold of the trident?"

"I guess it would depend on what they wanted to do with it," Una replied, keeping her circling fingers in a steady rhythm. "They are gods. With their own desires and motivations."

"They want Atlantis."

"I expect so. But they're not immortal."

I frowned. "I thought all gods were immortal."

"If they were immortal, and therefore unkillable, then there wouldn't be a prophecy."

I mulled over her point.

The Denizens of the Deep crave the power of Vorago's trident. The one true wielder must remain strong.

That was the latest prophecy. I was the trident wielder. And I must remain strong. It was a warning. So it must be possible for me to defeat the Denizens. Otherwise, what was the point of the book?

Una propped herself on an elbow and swept her hand back and forth over my chest. "Although she can command wind, Nautalun mostly comes in human form, so I expect she'll be defeated any way a mortal can be."

"But she's a god."

"Gods have weaknesses," she said. "They have desires,

and they have faults. Imperfections. Weaknesses we can use to our advantage."

"I guess."

"Dagonar is the Weaver of Darkness. I don't know how you eradicate darkness. Maybe with light?"

"Well, there's a shit ton of that on Atlantis." I glanced at the trident propped in the corner of the small room. "And when I'm holding the trident, it lights up like a firework."

"Exactly." Una gave me a poke before resuming her gentle sweeps across my chest. "Now you're getting it."

"Maelstrom mostly appears as a tsunami."

"And one of the trident's powers is controlling the tides."

Fear ebbed away. My shoulders relaxed, and the soothing strokes of Una's hand matched the rhythm of my calming heartbeat.

"Karkenloth can appear as any ocean animal," I said. "Its weakness is its heart. I can beat an ocean animal. I can stab a heart. I killed Zale, after all, and he was one tanked up selachii mother fucker..."

Una chuckled. "Keep that cockiness in check, prince. Fear and courage are a balance. Too much of one and you're asking for trouble."

"Too much fear and I'm done for."

"Remember what Ford told you. About fear. He told me what he said to you earlier."

"I get it. I understand what he said. I know he's right..." I sighed. "But the knowing and doing are two different things."

"Only if you make them that way." Una dropped down beside me and rested her head against mine. "You have the trident, something to give you power. I have...nothing—"

"Una—"

She raised a hand. "I may not have a weapon. Not like the trident, anyway. But I have the book, and I have you. That's enough for me. And yes, I'm scared too. Fucking terrified if you must know. But I believe in us." She took my hand and laced her fingers through mine. "I believe in the prophecies. I believe we can win."

CHAPTER FIVE

Standing on the raft with Ford, a hundred yards into the bay, I tightened my grip on the trident. Its power hummed beneath my fingers. The scent of salt and pine surrounded me, a pleasant mingling of aromas unique to this part of the island that cleared my head.

The sea was calm, the sun high, the floating platform gently undulating, but my pulse drummed through my veins. Every time I held this weapon, I marveled at the power it commanded. The power *I* would learn to command. And that it had chosen me to do it.

I swished the trident a few inches above the water's surface, watching as the prongs sparked with golden light. The water responded immediately—a stream of bubbles floated into the air, shimmering in the sunlight as if eager to play.

The stream intensified, swirling around the raft, arcing high over my head like an obedient serpent before splashing down on the other side with a satisfying hiss. I couldn't help the pride surging inside me, my confidence growing with each second the trident obeyed my will.

I loosened a grin at Ford. "Not bad for my first try, right?"

Ford raised a brow, his stance unshaken as the raft swayed beneath his feet. "Don't get too cocky."

I waggled the trident at him. "But come on, you've gotta admit—this deserves a little praise." I let another stream of water twirl through the air like a ribbon, sunlight catching the droplets, turning them into a rainbow.

Ford's eyes narrowed, but he didn't react to the water. "The trident is giving you power because it knows the stakes," he said. "But this is only the beginning. A rainbow over your head isn't going to stop a Denizen."

I rolled my eyes, my earlier triumph deflating a little. "Alright, alright," I grumbled, then flicked the trident again, sending a spray of water directly over Ford's head.

Ford ducked as droplets rained down on him. "Real mature, Gal," he said, but there was the faintest hint of amusement beneath his words.

"I grinned, twirling the trident with a flourish. "Maybe not," I admitted, "but it was fun." The rush of controlling the water so effortlessly surged through me, filling my veins with adrenaline. It felt...right. The more I held the trident, the more in tune with it I became, as if it whispered to me, revealing secrets no one else could hear. The others might have seen the trident as a relic, a tool of slumbering, neglectful gods of the past. But to me? It was alive. I could feel its pulse, its power beating in time with mine, eager to be unleashed.

I was the one chosen to wield it. Out of all the people

who'd tried, who had ever dared to hope, I was the one. That thought alone made my chest swell with pride. I wasn't just some soldier or player in a prophecy anymore. I was the one who could change everything. The one capable of wielding the force that could shift the tides, control the storms, and take on the Denizens. It was time I started accepting that.

"You didn't even knock me off the raft," Ford said, the challenge in his tone evident. He shifted his weight, squatting to lower his center of gravity as if he sensed what I was about to do.

Irritation flared. "If you wanted me to knock you off the raft, you should have asked."

I spun the trident in my hand, pointing the prongs at the water, letting its weight shift with mine. The water beneath us stirred, and I focused, whispering to the tide. It felt alive, a living force that obeyed my thoughts. Within seconds, an enormous spout of water erupted from the ocean like a geyser, roaring into the sky.

My heart raced as I directed the spout, its power surging through me, the trident acting like an extension of my will. The spout thickened, three feet wide now.

I cast a glance over my shoulder, catching Ford's reaction. His eyes widened, and I couldn't help the rush of satisfaction that coursed through me. Then, with a quick arc of the trident, I pointed the prongs at his chest. The water responded instantly, an enormous barrel of seawater shooting forward like a battering ram.

Ford barely had time to react before the wave crashed into him with the force of a storm. He stumbled back, his feet slipping on the raft, coughing and spluttering as the water pummeled him, driving him toward the edge. His balance faltered, and with a splash, he tumbled into the ocean.

The spout collapsed into the bay with a mighty splash, leaving the water eerily calm once more. I stood there, the trident lowered, my breath coming quicker than I expected.

Ford's head popped above the surface, water dripping from his shaved head as he treaded water. "Okay," he called, his voice laced with resignation. "I guess I asked for that."

I couldn't help but laugh, offering a hand as he swam toward the raft. When he grasped it, I pulled him onto the wooden boards. His breath came in heavy pants, but he was smiling.

"That's what you wanted, wasn't it?" I asked, grinning now. "To see what I'm capable of?"

Ford shook the water from his face, his lips quirking into a wry smile. "I wanted to see if you had the focus to back up the power. And I think you're getting there."

I glanced at the trident, its prongs gleaming with a soft golden light. Fear narrowed to a pinprick. Not that it wasn't there, and not that I wasn't terrified of facing the Denizens, but whatever Ford had said on the boat, it started to stick. Because I was making progress. I was meant for this. For the first time in months, I didn't feel raw terror tugging at the edges of my mind.

Rolling the tension out of my shoulders, I glanced toward the shore. There, through the wide glass wall of the house, I spotted Una and the twins in the kitchen. The back of the house was almost entirely glass, offering an unbroken view of the bay and the narrow strip of sand beyond. Inside, they were baking something, laughing and moving in that easy way people do when they're fully in the moment. The same way Una made me feel when I was with her.

Ember had flown off to his cannabis field earlier, promising to be back later today, but right now, it was just Una and the twins. With the trident dangling at my side in a loose grip, I watched them for a minute.

Ash and Cyra had their hands buried deep in a mixing bowl, their faces filled with concentration, but there was an unmistakable mischief between them. Una, sitting on the counter, was giving them instructions, her single blue eye bright with amusement, her lips curved into a smile that sent warmth flooding through me.

My heart tightened as I watched her. I'd seen her fight, lead, and stand beside me in battle. I'd seen her fierce, determined, and relentless. But moments like this—these small, everyday moments—where she let herself relax and just be...they were the ones that got to me. It wasn't only her strength that drew me in, though I admired it endlessly. It was this side of her, this playful, nurturing warmth that made me fall a little more every time I saw it.

Suddenly, Ash grinned and, with a quick flick of his hand, launched a handful of flour straight at Una. It caught her off guard, coating her hair and turning her eyepatch white. I chuckled, the sound of their laughter drifting through the open window and wrapping around me like a melody I never wanted to end.

Una's head tipped back as she laughed, the sound soft and carefree. My chest tightened again. There was something about that laugh—it was rare and unguarded, the type she only let out when she truly felt at peace. I loved that I got to witness it, that I got to see her this way when the rest of the world saw her as an oracle in training, the guardian of the orb of Spirit and Soul, the future Princess of Atlantis. At least, I hoped she wanted to be.

But here, with flour in her hair and the twins grinning up at her like she was their favorite person in the world, she was simply Una. *My* Una.

The rush of emotion nearly knocked me sideways, and I had to steady myself on the swaying raft. When I lifted my gaze to her once more, Una was wiping the flour from her hair, her lips still curved into that irresistible smile. Ash tried to help, but she batted his hand away, shaking her head with mock exasperation. Cyra was already plotting her own flour attack, her eyes sparkling with the same playful energy.

Una looked up then, her eyes meeting mine through the glass, and her smile softened. That single glance sent a wave of calm through me.

Content, I turned back to Ford, ready to unleash another surge of water over him, but an unexpected question formed in my mind.

"Why don't you have...someone?"

Ford flinched, his body going rigid. He ran a hand over his damp shorts, smoothing them out as if the motion could iron away the sudden tension between us. "I did."

I narrowed my eyes at him, studying the lines of his face. "You've known me my entire life. You know every single one of my strengths and weaknesses. Don't you think I deserve to know something personal about you?"

Ford crossed his arms, his broad chest rising with a slow,

measured breath. Finally, he spoke, his voice low, steady—too steady. "How will that help you?"

I dipped my chin, trying to gather my thoughts, trying to find the right words that didn't feel like I was crossing a line. But when I looked again, I caught something in his eyes—an emotion flickering like a dying flame, one I couldn't name. That wasn't true. I could name it. It was regret.

"It helps because I look up to you," I said quietly. "You've taught me everything I know. I strive to be as strong, as unshakable, as you. But if it turns out you're as human as the rest of us, if you've learned how to bury your emotions somewhere deep...I need to know how you do it."

Ford's eyes darkened, a storm gathering behind his calm exterior. His jaw tightened. "Ignoring your emotions won't help you win against the Denizens. I've told you that before. I told you that on the boat."

"You're not afraid?" I asked.

"Of course I'm afraid," Ford replied, a rawness edging into his voice, "but fear isn't the emotion I'm ignoring."

I stared at him, the tension between us stretching thin. "What are you ignoring?"

His eyes met mine, a sharp glint of something like irritation—or maybe it was pain. "You're getting a little too perceptive for my liking, Gal."

"I think that's a compliment?"

Ford sighed, planted his hands on his hips. "I lost my wife during the nuclear war. She wasn't an ocean shifter. After Atlantis was rediscovered, all of us were pulled here, away from the mainland. By the time I returned to see what had happened..." He shook his head, a grim shadow darkening his face. "It was too late."

My parents had saved countless lives when they'd redis-covered Atlantis. But they'd also put into motion a war that stole countless more.

"I'm sorry." I didn't know what else to say. I'd spent my life hearing condolences for my own losses, but I'd never had to give them. Not like this. Not for something so deep, so irrevocable.

"Do you have...were there children...?"

Ford nodded. "I had a son."

The harsh reality of his words made my throat ache. I swallowed around the tightness. "It's been fifteen years since Atlantis was reclaimed...you haven't thought to...have you tried to—?"

"No." Ford's expression flatlined. "And that's all I'll say about it."

"I'm sorry." Perhaps I shouldn't have pried. Nope. I *definitely* shouldn't have pried. "I'm really sorry."

Ford gave me a faint smile, put an arm on my shoulder. "I've always thought of you as a son, Gal. You have given me that."

And just like that, he turned, diving into the water before I could respond, leaving me alone on the raft with a storm of emotions swirling inside me. When he resurfaced, he said, "That's enough for today."

While Ford swam for the shore, I remained on the raft, my thoughts and emotions competing for attention. I was *not* done for the day. How the hell would I ever speak to Ford again after a conversation like that? Part of me was filled with pride that he thought of me that way. The other half felt the burden of responsibility. He expected...he expected my best. Hell, I expected my best. But I didn't know if my best was good enough, and now there was another person on my long list of people I cared about that I was likely to fail.

I looked at the trident, its golden light glowing in the approaching dusk. Ford's words rang in my head, repeating like a mantra. *Feel the fear and move through it.*

Gritting my teeth, I raised the trident, its weight familiar now, another appendage, part of me. I swirled it above my head, focusing all my energy, all my frustration, and was startled when a massive six-foot wave barreled across the bay, roaring louder than I'd intended. It grew, towering higher and higher until I panicked, afraid it would swallow the entire island.

I yanked the trident down, the wave collapsing in on itself, crashing against the raft and washing over my feet.

Well, okay then.

CHAPTER SIX

The fifteen-foot wave crested over me, almost washing me off the raft. A quick flick of the trident and my footing remained solid, as if my feet were glued to the wooden platform. It was the last in a series of monstrous waves I had created. Sometimes I coaxed the waves into swirling vortexes, spinning them into a wild frenzy before they collapsed back into the sea or, once or twice, crashed into the trees lining the shore.

The feel of the trident in my hand, the thrum of the power streaking through my limbs, the buzz of energy flowing through my veins...it was all so addictive. Out here, on the north of the island where the population was almost nonexistent, I could finally unleash the power of the trident. The power of me. The power of our union. Is this what Vorago had felt like when he'd forged the weapon? When he'd created Atlantis?

The Denizens of the Deep crave the power of Vorago's trident. The one true wielder must remain strong.

The prophecy whispered through my thoughts. The Denizens were after the trident. But it belonged to me. I had only scratched the surface of its potential, but I believed, for the first time, that I could face them. A few more days of practice and I'd master storm manipulation, teleportation, and perfect the hydrokinesis I'd been working on all day.

"Gal!" Ford called from the shore.

I looked toward the thin strip of sand and saw him cupping his hands around his mouth, calling my name again. I waved to let him know I'd heard, though adrenaline still pulsed in my limbs, and I wasn't ready to stop. The power sang sweetly through me, whispering at me to push it further, to see what else I could create.

I glanced at the trident, still aglow with power, casting its golden light over me, the raft, and a circle of ocean. Under its light, it felt like daytime. That's why I hadn't noticed the lowering sun.

The rich, smoky aroma of grilled fish hit me, and my stomach growled in protest. I realized I hadn't eaten since breakfast, and now the moon was rising, casting a silver glow over the water. Still, the hunger I felt wasn't merely for food —it was for *her*.

I glanced at the shore again and saw them: Ford, Ember, the twins, all gathered around a campfire. But it was Una who held my attention. She sat with *The Mermaid Chronicles* open on her lap, her brow furrowed in concentration. Just one look at her, and I knew I was done with the trident for the day. Now, my body craved hers. The rising moonlight made her skin glow, and the sight of her made my pulse quicken in a way that no amount of power ever could. Eager to soak up her presence, I dove off the raft, pushed my tail into existence, and swam to shore with the trident in one hand.

As I trudged up the beach, I dropped the trident into the sand. Its glow faded the moment it left my grasp, but the buzzing energy remained swirling inside of me. I shook out my hair, water droplets scattering in all directions as I approached the campfire.

Una looked up, her eyes bright with amusement. "You're soaking wet!" she squealed, batting at my legs as I stood over her, dripping everywhere.

Grinning, I bent over and shook my head, sending another spray of water droplets over her book. "Oops."

She rolled out of the way, laughing as she snapped the book shut. "You're going to ruin it!"

"I hate that book," I muttered with a smirk, dropping to my knees and pulling her into my arms.

Before she could protest, I peppered her face with kisses —her cheeks, her ears, her throat, even the flour-dusted top of her head from earlier. Her laughter filled the air as she half-heartedly tried to push me away, her body melting into mine. Flour streaked across my chest, but I didn't care. Being with her, wrapped in her warmth, was more invigorating than any magic I could summon.

"Looks like we should move the surf competition here," Ember said from where he perched on a log. "You could make some killer waves with that trident."

"Yeah." Ash fluttered his wings over his head as he pumped his arm. "Dad promised me he'd teach me how to surf."

I chuckled, still holding Una close as she settled against me. "Maybe after the Denizens are dealt with."

"The whole island's been on edge since that prophecy appeared," Ember muttered, pulling a bone from his plate of fish. "But it's been months, and nothing's happened. I think everyone needs to chill out a little."

Ford handed me a plate with grilled fish and a generous helping of salad and potatoes, caught my eye, but he didn't give his opinion on the matter.

"I don't want to let my guard down," I said, allowing Una to feed me a bite of fish. "And isn't that why you're here? For a change of scenery, to unwind?"

Although I was here to focus on learning new powers, I couldn't deny being away from the palace had eased the knot in my chest. Maybe it was being away from prying eyes, the sense of responsibility, the complicated relationship with my father. Here, in the woods with Una and my best friend, I could be myself. I could learn the ways of the trident without feeling the pressure. Pressure that I put on myself, granted. But I knew everyone was relying on me to save Atlantis. To save them. To eviscerate the Denizens.

"Absolutely," Una murmured, her lips brushing my cheek as she pulled me closer. Her presence grounded me, chased away the storm of thoughts.

Ember grumbled, placed his plate on the floor, and removed a pre-rolled joint.

Ash's wings twitched with excitement as Ember leaned toward the fire to light it. "Can I try some?"

"No," Ember replied, taking a long drag. "I will not be responsible for burgeoning drug habits."

"But *you* smoke!" Cyra said, laughing. "And the fountain doesn't even work for you."

"Can't change the habit of a lifetime." Ember grinned through the haze of smoke. "And don't remind me about the fountain."

Ford chuckled, shaking his head. "You're eighteen."

Ember tapped his head. "I'm older inside."

"Amen to that," I added, wrapping an arm tighter around Una.

"See?" Ember nodded at me. "He gets it. Because he's my bro. We've seen shit together."

"Oh no." I shook my finger at him. "Don't you dare drag me into this."

Ford slid another grilled fish onto my plate. "You need the calories."

He wasn't wrong. Despite my exhaustion, my body craved more fuel. As I devoured the second helping, the banter around the campfire buzzed, light and familiar. It took me back to when it was just the three of us—Ember, Una, and me—hunting Zale. It hadn't been all bad, despite the danger. There had been moments like this, when the world slowed, when it felt like we could laugh and forget about the danger waiting for us. The calm before the storm.

As soon as I thought that, an eerie sense of foreboding crept up my spine. I glanced at *The Mermaid Chronicles*, half expecting its pages to be glowing with an ominous warning, but they remained as dim as the trident. Perhaps the book had felt it had given us warning enough. But something deep in the pit of my stomach knew the Denizens were approaching. Having lost my appetite, I set down my half-eaten fish, the taste turning to ash in my mouth. Without a word, I slipped an arm around Una's waist, pulling her onto my lap.

"You okay?" she whispered in my ear.

I rested my chin on her shoulder, inhaled her intoxicating scent of the ocean and salt and jasmine, hoping it would calm the appearance of my sudden nerves. "Just needed you."

She cupped my face, her thumb tracing a gentle line across my cheek. "I'm here," she said, her voice anchoring me and diluting my nerves. And that was enough.

When I tuned back into the conversation, I caught Ford's eyes lingering on me, his expression neutral. He knew. He always did. Ignoring his evaluating stare, I chose to focus on something lighter, something that wasn't a prophecy or the threat of an ancient enemy. Namely, Ash trying to breathe fire.

The blond-haired kid half stood, his fists clenched, his face bright red as he exhaled and puffed and screamed at the campfire as if it was at fault for his own lack of flames.

Cyra sat opposite him, her knees pressed together and her arms crossed. An exaggerated eyeroll crossed her face. "Dad said you have to be patient, remember?" she said, her voice dripping with sibling superiority.

"He also said to keep trying," Ash snapped back between puffs.

I glanced at Cyra, a pang of sympathy tugging at me. She had no wings and there was no sign of her fire either. That had to be hard for her. On a whim, I untangled myself from Una, walked to the house, grabbed the few items I wanted, and returned to the fire. I handed Cyra a bag of marshmallows and a bundle of small sticks.

After nodding her thanks, she tore the bag open and placed marshmallows on the sticks, resting them against the stone near the fire to roast.

Ash tumbled back to the ground with a heavy sigh, kicked at the ground.

"Give it time," I said, echoing Ford's words to me, and Cyra's.

"My fire didn't come until last year," Ember reminded his brother.

"That because you inhale, not exhale." Ash waved a hand at him. "How is that useful?"

Ember quirked an eyebrow. "Well, when your snowmobile is carrying a dozen jerrycans filled to the brim with gasoline and it crashes and explodes, I think you'll find it comes in very useful."

"Whatever," Ash muttered. "I prefer the sun."

Cyra chuckled around a mouthful of marshmallow and I shot her a conspiratorial wink.

"And what a pretty fine sight you were," I said to Ember. "Walking out of a fire storm naked as the day you were born."

"Roasted," Ash smirked, and raised his hand to me for a high-five. "I like your style."

Cyra snorted.

Ford kept his head lowered, but his amused smile didn't escape me. I was glad he was loosening up, even if he wasn't contributing much. He was never one for many words, and preferred one-to-one company to groups. I thought of his wife, his son. How hard it must be for him to smile.

"We were in Iceland." Ember glared at me playfully,

letting me know revenge was coming. "During a snowstorm. It was *cold*."

I raised both hands and grinned at him. "Didn't say it wasn't."

Ember threw a pinecone at me, but I caught it before it crashed into my nose, gave it to Una who chucked it into the fire. It crackled and spit. Sparks danced in the sky.

"Even a pinecone has more fire than me," Ash grumbled.

"Patience, Little Jackass," I said, remembering a story Babette had once told me. Once upon a time, not so long ago, I'd had to learn patience too.

Giggling, Cyra leaned over the fire, lowering her stick to the ground. "That's so what I'm going to call you now. *Jackass.*" She laughed so hard she wound her arms around her waist to support herself, snorting and spluttering. She gasped for air, once, twice, and then the entire campfire disappeared into her mouth.

The drop in temperature was immediate. Cyra snapped her mouth shut and her eyes widened so much I could see the panic building in her blown pupils. Steam poured from between her lips and her skin beaded with sweat.

"What the *fuck?*" Ash launched to his feet.

"Language!" Ember kicked his brother.

"You can inhale fire?" Ash stared at his twin.

Cyra, still with her lips clenched closed, shook her head vehemently.

I stood, put a hand on her shoulder. "Open your mouth."

She shook her head again.

I locked my gaze on her, tried to show her she was among people she could trust, who would help her. "It's okay."

"If she doesn't let it out, she's going to burn from the inside out," Ash said with a smirk.

That made her mouth pop open. The fire came roaring out, flames licking the sky as it streaked past the smoldering logs, singeing Ash's wing, and barreling into the trunk of a spindly pine, which immediately caught fire.

Cyra clamped a hand over her mouth. "That wasn't me."

"Ouch." Ash jumped from foot to foot, waving his wing, only fanning the flames higher and bringing the stench of charred leather closer.

Una swept an arm around Cyra as she started to cry.

"Don't worry," I told the young girl as I leaped over the dead campfire. I plucked the trident from the sand and swirled it in the direction of the water until I'd created a whirlpool big enough to do the job. Using the trident, I guided the whirlpool to Ash and dumped it over his head. The flames along his wing extinguished as he coughed and sputtered, complaining I was trying to drown him.

Ignoring Ash's protests, I pulled another whirlpool from the bay and sent this one to the pine tree, dousing it until every tiny flame winked out.

The trident and the full moon gave us the only light to see by as we all caught our breath. I approached Cyra where she huddled close to Una, despite being a head taller than her.

"No harm done," I said, gesturing to the tree and Ash.

Ash frowned. "Tell that to my wing! I can smell it! It *reeks*. And it *hurts!*"

"You're alive, aren't you?" Ember said to his brother. "It's better than battling a thirty-foot great white selachii with Denizen-level powers."

Ash rolled his eyes. "Yes, we know you were there when Zale was killed. So you keep telling us. Well done you."

I tapped Ash on the shoulder. "I couldn't have done it without your brother." Ash sobered a little. "And I'm going to need you too when we face the Denizens. You and your wings. Cyra and her fire."

Ash's eyes lit up. "You need...me?"

"Absolutely," I confirmed.

Ash stared at me with his mouth open.

Ford thrust a flask in Ash's direction. I was sure it contained water from the Fountain of Youth. Ash took a long swig and the protective leather of his wing immediately grew back.

Cyra stepped away from Una. "I want to help. But I have no idea what just happened. And I'm freaking terrified."

Ford cleared his throat. "Dragon king unions with other ocean shifters are rare." He nodded at Ember, whose father was a dragon king and mother was my Aunt Raina, a mermaid. "We saw the result of that with Ember—his fire power being delayed and limited to inhaling fire only. And now it appears the typical dragon king abilities are split between you both." He focused his serious eyes on Ash and Cyra. "Because you are twins. One of you got wings. One of you got fire."

CHAPTER SEVEN

"B ut that's not fair," Ash said, planting his hands on his slim hips.

Ford leaned back, arms crossed, his gaze steady as he watched Ash grumble. "Life's never been about fair," he said. "Fair is something people make up when they don't want to face the truth. The truth is, we're all dealt different hands, but what matters is how we play them. Your wings—they might not seem as flashy as fire now, but there'll come a time when what you have will save someone's life, maybe even your own. Your sister's got fire, sure, but you've got something equally important. You've got the power to rise above it all. Don't waste your time comparing flames when you've got the whole sky waiting for you."

Ford's words settled around us. They resonated deeper than I'd expected. Was there something I needed to learn in there too? I thought I'd done all my learning on the last mission, but I couldn't deny my instinct, erroneous as it might be, to do whatever I had to do to protect Una, to shield her from battle, to make damn sure she didn't lose another eye, or worse.

Love made me act like a crazy person. It made me wish I'd never been born. It did all the things I had been terrified it would do. But I wouldn't take it back. Because love—loving someone, being loved—wasn't something I'd trade for anything. Now that I had it, I would guard it with everything I had.

"What about me?" Cyra asked, raising her hand tentatively like she was a shy student in the back of class.

Ford leaned down to Cyra's level. "You know, Cyra, control doesn't come easy—especially with fire. It's wild, like the ocean, like the storms. But the thing about fire is, when you learn to guide it, it becomes the most powerful tool you have. It's not about putting it out, it's about learning to let it burn without letting it consume you."

He paused, glancing at her bare shoulders where wings would've been. "And as for the wings...you might not have them, but fire gives you something wings can't. Wings take you away from danger, but fire? Fire lets you face it head-on. You might feel like you're out of control now, but when you find your balance, you'll realize that fire doesn't need to be feared—it's part of you. And trust me, when the time comes, no one's going to be wishing they could fly when they have you to light the way."

Brother and sister stared at each other, offered the other a small, secret smile.

Una rubbed her arms. "I've got goosebumps. Ford, you are a very wise man."

He waved her off, but I caught the flush rising on his cheeks. "Just calling it as I see it."

It was the most I'd heard him say in one go in a long time.

"And on that note, I'm going to call it a night," Ford said, tossing us all a wave as he headed for the cabin.

"Me too," Ember said. "I promised Dad I wouldn't let you guys stay up too late."

Ash rolled his eyes. "We're thirteen. We don't have a bedtime."

"I'm not far behind you," I told him. "The Denizens could come any day. And we need to make sure we're rested."

He took that in with a stoic expression and followed Ember and his twin toward the cabin.

"That was kind of you." Una stood behind me and threaded her arms around my waist.

"What was?" I asked as I stared across the bay at the moonlight dancing on the gentle ripples. How calm it was now, compared to what I'd put it through earlier.

"How you handled Cyra and Ash. You're really good with kids."

"They're hardly kids."

"You know what I mean. You'll make a great dad."

I laughed, the idea of me being a father so ridiculous that I couldn't help but shake my head.

Una circled her way around the front of me, grabbed my shoulders, and stared at me with her one beautiful blue eye. "Why is that funny?"

Because the idea of losing you is sorrowful enough. Because I don't want to put any child I might have through what my dad did to me. Because I couldn't bear for there to be more people for me to protect.

"Gal?" She squeezed my shoulders.

I struggled for words. "I'm not dad material."

She placed a hand on my face, cradled my jaw. "Don't be ridiculous. You have so much love to give."

I shook my head as the sudden heat of emotion formed behind my eyes. "It's all for you. I don't want...kids...Una."

She frowned. "I assumed when I became queen—"

"Oh, you're going to be queen are you?" I attempted humor, but it fell flat.

Una flushed. "I don't want to make assumptions, but I thought we...I thought we were..."

I kissed her cheek. "Of course you'll be my queen. One day. I was only teasing. But for you to be queen, that would mean my father..."

"I'm sorry, Gal." Her face fell, and that little bit of disappointment almost broke my heart. "I didn't mean it like that. It was a poor choice of words. I meant that when we... when we..."

"When we...?"

"Married," she whispered, not able to look at me. *Adorable.*

I held her tight against my chest, kissed the top of her head. "Of course we'll get married. One day. But I won't ever have kids."

She pulled back to look at me, her eye roaming my face.

"And, no," I said. "You won't change my mind. You made me fall in love with you. You made me face fears I never wanted to confront. But I can't do it again. I can't lose anyone else. I can't worry about anyone else."

"I never made you do anything." She ran a finger across my chest, her touch warm and delicate. "You fell in love with me. You were always in love with me, you just hadn't admitted it."

True. And true.

She didn't say anything else. Stepping out of my arms, she pulled her sweater over her head, then slipped out of her shorts.

"What are you doing?" I admired the way the moonlight caressed her skin, turning it a creamy white.

She looked over her shoulder at me, a glint in her eye. "I'm going for a swim. Care to join me?"

I responded to her challenge in more ways than one and was on her heels when she dashed into the water. When I caught up to her, she laughed and allowed me to lift her into my arms, and then dove beneath the surface. Our tails flicked out, my onyx merfolk one that glinted with flecks of gold, and her gray selachii tail that parted the water as she swam.

When we reached the raft, we shed our tails and climbed the small metal ladder. With the transformation, our swimwear reappeared, and water cascaded down our bodies. I helped her onto the raft and drew her to the middle of the platform, winding an army around her waist, holding her tight against me. She'd lost her eye patch somewhere in the swim and tried to cover her scars with her hair.

"Don't hide it," I whispered, pushing her hair away from her face. "It's part of your beauty. You should be proud of your battle scars." I pressed my lips to her empty eye socket.

The starlit sky stretched endlessly above us as Una and I stood entwined on the gently rocking platform. My heart raced as I cupped her cheek, marveling at how her single blue eye sparkled with more brilliance than the entire night sky.

"You think Ford will be mad I stole you away from your beauty sleep?" Una whispered, a mischievous grin playing on her lips.

I chuckled, running my fingers through her hair. "Ford knows how much I need you."

I lowered my lips to hers, pressing my mouth against the divine lushness of hers. I teased the seam of her mouth with my tongue until she parted her lips and allowed me inside. Flicking my tongue inside her mouth, I savored her delicate tastes. The ocean, salt, and jasmine. She always smelled and tasted the same, no matter where we were.

Cupping her cheek again, I anchored her against me, pressing my thigh between her supple legs until she yielded with a breathy moan and melted into my chest. She twitched against me, an involuntary shiver that made her eyelid flutter. I pressed my thigh into her point of need, eliciting another gasp which I caught with my mouth.

"Gal," she murmured, her hands running down the muscles of my arms, stroking the definition of my back, sweeping over my broad shoulders.

My hand tightened on her jaw, the other trailing down her side, caressing her skin, exploring the shallow dips and smooth planes of her utter perfection. I drew her bottom lip into my mouth, nibbled on it lightly, then released it again as my tongue claimed hers once more and I dug my hand into her rear. I shifted her against me, pressed my thigh harder between her legs, causing a shudder to roll through her.

As we kissed, a familiar pang of fear gripped my heart. I'd already come so close to losing Una once. The memory of her lying unconscious after the polar bear attack, her face bloody and mangled, still haunted my dreams. I kissed her more fiercely, as if I could keep her safe through sheer force of will.

Una must have sensed the shift in my mood. She pulled back, her brow furrowed. "What's wrong, Gal?"

I sighed, resting my forehead against hers. "Nothing. I just...I love you so damn much, Una. Sometimes it terrifies me."

She cupped my face in her hands, her thumbs caressing my cheeks. "I'm right here. I'm not going anywhere."

"The Denizens..."

"I will be right by your side."

That's what I was afraid of. She was too stubborn to seek safety.

I covered all my doubts and further conversation with another kiss. I didn't want to dwell on the prophecies tonight. I wanted Una to myself, and I would not share her with my darker thoughts and fears.

Una's fingers trailed down my chest, leaving goosebumps in their wake and a restless burning that set my skin alight. She traced the contours of my stomach, her fingers drifting over the dips and valleys, making my sensitive muscles clench under the lightness of her touch. I needed more. So much more.

She moved her lips to my jaw, floated kisses down the column of my throat, trailed more along the edge of my collarbone. I curled my fingers into her hair as biting spasms of pleasure rippled through my body and coiled deep in the pit of my stomach. It wouldn't be long before I'd need to be inside her, inside her wet warmth, with all of her wrapped around me. I couldn't go long without it, as if making love to her was the fuel I needed to survive. Even more precious than air. Or water.

Una stepped back, her lips curling into a smoky grin, her thirsty gaze raking over my body.

I grabbed her wrist to yank her back, but she reached behind her back and untied the laces of her bikini, letting the scandalous excuse for cover fall to the floor. Moonlight caressed her breasts, highlighting the curves and swells, her nipples hardening into aching peaks. My gaze dropped to the curl of her hip, the dip in her stomach, and on to the small square triangle of material that hid her most exquisite flavors. Lust pulsed through my veins as I took a series of rapid breaths. Una had always been beautiful to me, but at that moment, she was breathtaking.

"You're staring."

I swallowed. "Of course I'm fucking staring."

Una laughed, a sound as melodious as the sweetest siren's song. She hooked her thumbs into the waistband of her bikini bottoms, sliding them down her legs with deliberate slowness. The raft rocked gently under our feet. Heat swamped my senses as I took in the dusting of light hair hiding her center, my mouth already salivating for her taste.

"Christ," I muttered, already rock hard at the sight of her exquisite nakedness.

"I've never made love on a raft."

"Una," I breathed, my voice husky with desire. One large step closed the distance between us. I fisted my hands in her hair, pulled her head back, and claimed her mouth with hard, rough kisses. It was all teeth and lips and nips and bites and oh so much wanton desire.

Folding an arm around her waist, I held her against my chest, allowing room for my other hand to palm the swell of her breast. It fit perfectly in my hand, as if made for my touch.

As she clutched my hips, I rubbed my thumb across her nipple, then dipped my head and kissed the swell of her other breast. I drew a nipple between my teeth, gave it a gentle nip which made her gasp my name and her grip tighten on my hips. Ripples of pleasure skirted through me, hardening my desire as I devoured the taste of her.

A restless burning surged beneath my skin as I lifted my lips to hers once more, claiming her mouth, making her mine. I held her tight against me, feeling the heat of her arousal through her damp skin. She raked her hands through my hair, dug them into my shoulders, then rolled her naked hips against mine.

Breathless, she pulled away and dipped her hand into the waistband of my shorts. She raised her foot, wound her toes into the waistband, and pushed them to the ground in one fluid movement.

"Cute," I said.

She grinned. "I have my tricks." Her gaze dropped to my hard length and she wasted no time circling her hand around me.

"Una," I growled her name, already so close to release, sensations rushing through me in a hot, blinding torrent.

She ran a finger along the protruding ridge and tension exploded at the base of my spine. I clamped my mouth over hers, dragging her bottom lip between mine, nipping with my teeth. Heat erupted between us. Our mouths crashed together, our tongues dancing in a skilled duet, my hands roaming every inch of her.

"I love you," I whispered between kisses, my hands greedy for her bare skin, committing every curve to memory.

"I love you too," she said, her voice catching.

I traced a pattern on her skin with my tongue, punctuating it with kisses. Dipping lower, I pressed my lips against her throat, then between the valley of her breasts, drew each nipple in turn between my lips, and dragged my tongue across the taut smoothness of her stomach. Circling around her navel, I blew a little breath of air over her damp skin, making her jerk in my arms.

As the raft swayed beneath us, I kneeled before her, trailing kisses along her hips, up her thighs, and digging my fingers into her rear. I inhaled her sweet, intoxicating scent, my arousal growing with every shiver that wracked her body. When my lips drifted to her center, she gasped and moaned my name, her hands tightening on my shoulders, fingers digging in, sure to leave marks. Marks I would cherish.

The ocean, salt, and jasmine. That was her scent. Her taste. Everywhere. From the hollow of her throat, to the shell of her ear, to the dip of her stomach, and the center of her glistening core. I pressed a gentle kiss to the sensitive bundle of nerves and she immediately bucked in my arms.

"Gal," she gasped.

I gripped her rear tighter to hold her still and licked the length of her slick folds. Once, twice, ever so slowly until she bucked to draw me deeper and tangled her fingers in my hair.

"Gal..." It was half a scream. She was close.

I felt the shudders roll through her body as I kissed and licked and nipped at her. Her taste was my nectar. A taste I would bury myself in all day if I could. My tongue delved into her, finding the sensitive nub and teasing it relentlessly. She arched her back, her moans growing louder with each passing moment. Heat radiated from her body as I ran my fingers over her thighs, her stomach, her hips, claiming her body as I did every night. And when I skated my hand from her stomach to the apex of her thighs, her body trembled with anticipation. I slipped two fingers inside her welcoming warmth.

"Gal...oh, shit, Gal," she whimpered, her hips rolling to meet my hand.

"Shh, let go, my queen," I said, flicking my tongue over her clit once more, drawing it between my teeth.

With a cry that echoed through the bay, she shattered in my arms. Her body convulsing, pulling me into her climax as if I were part of her very being. I held her upright as the orgasm tore her apart.

When her quaking subsided, I rose, capturing her lips in a fierce kiss that told her everything my voice could not.

The weight of my arousal pressed against her thigh and she circled her hand around me once more, her thumb making teasing sweeps along my ridge.

"Una..." I couldn't get the words past my throat. It was all need and heat and desire.

Una pressed a hand to my chest, guided me to the smooth wooden planks of the raft until I sat with my legs dangling in the water, and my erection painfully obvious.

Heat hummed beneath my skin as she swept a leg over me and lowered herself onto my lap, her breasts sliding against my chest. She pushed me back until I was staring up at her, admiring the way the moonlight played with her curves. I lay beneath her, my cock hard and throbbing as she straddled me, her weight pressing me into the wood.

Fuck, that felt good.

She circled a hand around my length, and began pumping it up and down, all the while her heavy-lidded gaze stayed fixed on mine.

"I can't wait anymore," I said, positioning her above me.

With a seductive smile, she lowered herself onto me with excruciating slowness. Her eye locked with mine, and in it I saw a thousand unspoken promises. This woman was my salvation, my reason for fighting.

She sank onto me, taking me fully into her tight, wet heat. We both groaned at the sudden intrusion, the sensation almost overwhelming. With her muscles clenching around me, I knew it wouldn't be long. Una began to ride me, her hips moving with a practiced grace. Each thrust of her body sent jolts of pleasure shooting through me, making my vision blur with need.

"Una...fuck, Una," I grunted, my hands gripping her hips as I tried to match her pace.

The faint sound of music drifted over the raft. I couldn't

tell where it was coming from. Perhaps one of the twins was playing music by an open window. I stopped caring when Una leaned forward, her breasts brushing against my chest as she kissed me. She moved her body in sinuous rolls as I thrust up inside her. I folded one arm around her waist, holding her tight to my chest, lowering my lips to her breasts.

"Don't stop," she begged, her voice hitching. "Please, don't stop."

I couldn't have stopped if I wanted to. The pleasure was too intense, too consuming. The music grew in volume, surrounding us in an almost physical shroud. My hands roamed her back, tracing the contours of her muscles as she rode me harder, faster. Our breaths mingled, harsh and desperate, as we clung to each other.

And when I looked up, it wasn't Una who stared down at me. It wasn't Una who sat astride me. It wasn't Una making love to me.

It was Siryn.

I flinched, tried to pull away, but Siryn's longer legs were locked firmly around me, holding me in place. And her curvier hips rolled and bucked in just the right way to almost make me not care. And musical notes curved around her naked form, caressing her body, teasing my hair and heated skin.

"Una..."

I couldn't stop. Each thrust of my hips promised an approaching release. Siryn's muscles clamped around me so tightly I could barely remember my own name. The wracks of carnal pleasure coiling down my spine were enough to make me hiss out a string of curses. The musical notes drifted over my skin, urging me on.

"Una..."

Siryn gripped my shoulders, pinning me down. She threw her head back and smiled at the sky, her larger breasts swaying in my face as she rocked her hips against me. Her waterfall of dark hair caught the light of the moon, cascaded past her shoulders, swept over my chest.

Call my name, Prince Gal.

The command entered my mind.

I gritted my teeth, but I couldn't stop my hands digging into her hips, encouraging her to increase her pace. Siryn threw her head back and laughed, followed it with a throaty groan. Moonlight spilled over her, accentuating every curve, the swell of her breasts, the curl of her hips as she bucked and rolled, the softness of her rear as she pulled my hand around her to cup it. And music serenaded us the entire time, building to a crescendo, taking me with it.

Call my name.

I cupped her ass, spread her wider, deepened my thrusts.

Una's blonde head appeared above me, her eye staring down at me, a lazy smile on her lips.

Then it was Siryn again, her hands planted on my chest, her fingers curling into the smattering of coarse hair that grew there.

Call my name.

"Siryn!" I yelled, as I bucked beneath her, thrusting into her with all my strength, musical notes exploding in my vision.

All too soon, I felt the surge of my release building, the aching spikes of pleasure spiraling out of control.

That's not my name, but you'll learn it soon enough.

I frowned, but could do nothing to stop the way she writhed on top of me, nothing to stop the way I thrust into her, nothing to stop how much I wanted this.

"Una!" I screamed her name, desperate for this apparition to disappear. This couldn't be happening. Where the fuck was Una?

You want this, Prince Gal. You know you do.

The voice filled my head, light and teasing, commanding and relentless.

"No, I fucking don't!" I screamed at Siryn as she held me beneath her. I was powerless to stop. My betrayal evident in each upward thrust of my hips and in each shudder of pleasure careening down my spine.

Siryn laughed, then quivered, her own climax cresting.

I gaped in horror as this woman, this stranger, opened her mouth and roared her release. Her orgasm caused her muscles to tighten around me further, drawing me deeper and pushing me over the edge at the same time.

"Fuck," I roared, my entire body jerking as the explosive release radiated from my core and ignited every nerve ending. The rush of intense sensations fired along my length, taking all my muscles prisoner until they spasmed with uncontrollable pleasure. I lay back, panting, surges of ecstasy shooting through me, trying to catch my breath.

Finally gaining control of myself, I wound an arm around Siryn's back and flipped us over so I was now pinning her to the raft. Still inside her, my erection still rock hard, her muscles still twitching around me.

She smiled up at me. She fucking *smiled*.

"Get out of my fucking head!" I screamed at her. The music winked off.

"Gal? Gal? What's wrong? What's happened?"

I opened my eyes. Hadn't realized I'd closed them. Una stared up at me with her one beautiful blue eye, now glistening with unshed tears.

"Gal?" she whispered. "What's wrong?"

I collapsed onto her, still inside of her. It was Una after all. Una. Of course it was Una. I rolled off her and lay on my back, pressing the heels of my hands into my eyes.

"Fuck!" I roared again.

Una's warm arm folded over my chest, reached for my wrist and pulled my hand away from my eyes. "What happened, Gal? Where did you go?"

"I don't know."

CHAPTER EIGHT

I wept into Una's hair. We sat on the raft, bobbing on the gentle current, her arms wrapped around us, and I fucking cried.

"What is it, Gal?" she whispered as she stroked my back.

The cool air wrapped around me, dousing my earlier desire, making my skin erupt in goosebumps. Thick nausea pooled in my stomach.

I pulled away from Una, wiped my face with the backs of my hands, looked around for my shorts. I didn't want to be naked. What if Siryn came back? I felt way too exposed.

While we dressed, clouds rolled over our heads, scudding across the sky and blotting out the moon. The raft rocked with the tide, small waves drifting into the bay.

Una offered her hand for me to take. "What happened? You're scaring me, Gal."

"I wish I knew." I stared at my feet, afraid to look her in the eye. What if she saw my betrayal? Because it *was* a betrayal. However Siryn had managed it. Whoever she was. I had wanted it. I didn't stop. I'd carried on until I'd leaped over the edge with her.

But how could it have been Siryn when it was Una all along?

"I think I'm losing it." I mustered a smile, which flatlined as soon as I saw my hand was shaking.

Una frowned. "You've been under a lot of stress."

"What did you see?"

"See?"

"When we were...making love."

"I saw *you*," she said, her hand floating to her hip. "What did *you* see?"

"It wasn't you," I whispered. "I mean, it was to start with, and then it wasn't."

For several heartbeats, we stared at each other.

"Who was it?" Una whispered.

I shook my head as I collected my thoughts. I didn't know how to explain this to her. That I had met Siryn before and been struck by her beauty. That I hadn't stopped fucking her when it was her riding me. That I suspected I knew who she really was.

"I don't know."

Before I could offer more of an explanation, we were thrust into darkness. The thickening clouds blocked out the moon and stars and a foreboding wind creeped around my bare shoulders. I shivered. My teeth jammed together. My legs shook.

Una wrapped her arm around my waist, guided me to the edge of the raft. "It's getting cold. Let's go back. Then we can talk."

Nodding, I watched her slip into the water. She hissed as a wave lapped over her chest. "It's freezing."

I frowned. The water in Atlantis was never freezing.

"Gal!"

I blanched at the note of fear in her voice. Searched the water. Spotted a luminous white jellyfish floating by her shoulder, its tentacles stretching at least six feet.

"Come here." It came out as more of a command than a suggestion, but that was the fear talking.

Una placed a hand on the edge of the raft. I leaned over, intending to grab her shoulders and lift her aboard.

"Gal..." Her eye was fixed not on the jellyfish bobbing by her shoulder, but on the countless others streaming toward us on the currents.

"Shit," I muttered as I hauled her out of the water. "You okay?" I asked as she clung to me.

We eyed the water together, the ominous luminescence of the creatures casting an eerie glow over the bay. As far as I could see, the surface rippled with countless disks of undulating, glowing white. Jellyfish. Their gelatinous bodies pulsed in rhythm, forming a vast, living tapestry beneath us. Each one shimmered with a soft, ghostly light, like the breath of the ocean itself. But there was nothing soothing about it. The water was teeming with them—venomous, dangerous. We both knew what a single sting could do, and there were hundreds, maybe thousands, of them swarming around our tiny raft.

The timing was all wrong for this kind of bloom. My grip on Una's waist tightened as a wave of unease slithered up my spine. Una's hand found mine, her fingers cold and trembling. She didn't have to say anything; the fear was in her eye, wide and dark as it flickered from me to the sea.

The jellyfish pulsed in unison, like they were one conscious mind. They drifted closer to the raft, their tentacles long and invisible beneath the surface.

"They're boxing us in," I muttered. It had to be the work of the Denizens.

I wasn't ready for a confrontation like this, not with Una here, not with the ocean turned against us.

"We're trapped," she whispered, her voice barely audible over the soft slap of water against our floating prison.

I glanced at the shore where the trident and *The Mermaid Chronicles* had been discarded so haphazardly on the sand. How foolish we'd been to leave them unprotected. How foolish I'd been to think that Fate, or the prophecies, or the Denizens would give us one night of peace together.

"Do you think it's...them?" Una whispered, her warm breath flushing against my chest.

With the clouds blocking the light of the moon, all I could see were jellyfish. And they were exceptional in their own evil, luminescent beauty. I'd never seen jellyfish in the bay before. Never seen them this close to the island. They reminded me of the ashrays my father used to speak of; deadly, ghostly rays that preyed on selachii flesh.

Without a doubt, I knew these jellyfish were here to harm us. And there wasn't a damn thing I could do about it. At least it was only Una and I trapped on the raft. Perhaps come morning, the others could row to us, but boats were hard to come by on this side of the island when so many preferred to swim.

"I do," I said, and drew her closer.

The wind whisked the waves higher, sending water lapping over our feet and a jellyfish sliding across the corner of the platform, its tentacles straying only a few inches from our toes.

Una shivered into my chest. "How do we get back?"

I glanced at the trident once more, furious with myself for leaving it abandoned. Ford was right. As much as I needed Una, she was also a distraction. But I didn't loosen my protective grip on her.

I scanned the water for a solution, the number of burgeoning jellyfish filling the bay until no matter which direction I looked in, all I could see were pulsing white lights and luminescent deadly tentacles drifting on the currents.

The wind whipped higher, tugging at my hair and chilling my already cold skin. Each gust seemed sharper, more ferocious, stabbing at our flesh, dragging the warmth from our bodies. Una and I clutched each other as we shivered, drawing our arms tighter as we absorbed each other's body heat.

"Why is it so cold?" she mumbled, her frozen lips pressed against my throat.

Dark storm clouds barreled across the sky, bringing with them dense, fat drops of rain. Atlantis was a tropical island and we experienced frequent rain showers, but they were always warm and welcoming. Nothing like this. Not this icy chill that flayed my flesh and wormed its way into my bones.

Dense, icy raindrops hammered against our heads as the wind tore at our hair, sliced through skin, yanked at our hold on each other. Waves rocked higher, lapping over the surface of the raft, plucking at it with foaming fingertips. My grip on the raft slickened, my feet slipping as I fought to stay balanced.

At the mouth of the bay, a darkness thicker than the storm gathered. A heaving mass of writhing inkiness that sent dread skittering down my spine. The water beneath us heaved with unnatural force, and then I saw it.

"Una." A wildfire of uneasiness surged through me.

She turned at the alarm in my voice, followed my eyeline through the punishing rain. "What *is* that?"

Blinking rapidly to clear my vision from the intrusive rain, I stared. The darkness rose from the water, dragging with it the pale, glowing bodies of jellyfish. Their deadly, luminescent tentacles floated on the choppy surface. But that wasn't the worst of it. Tendrils of pure darkness, darker than the deepest abyss, flickered and whipped from the shadowy form, stretching toward us with malicious intent.

"I don't know." My heart turned into a staccato beat, uneven and unreliable. "But you need to get to safety."

"I'm not leaving you."

"There's nothing you can do here," I barked at her.

"Without the trident, there's nothing you can do either."

We were trapped—stranded on a small raft in the middle of the bay, venomous jellyfish surrounding us like a deadly minefield, and that dark, rising monstrosity looming closer, devouring the sky. Wind screaming. Rain drilling. Balance so incredibly precarious.

Somehow, the shape managed to swallow the sky, eradicating light as if it simply shouldn't be allowed to exist.

Adrenaline coiled through my veins, fighting with the

trepidation pooling at the small of my back. I glanced at the trident, the weapon I was born to wield, and willed it to do my bidding. A spark of light flickered from one of its prongs, infusing me with a sense of hope. I held Una in one arm and raised the other toward the trident, my hand shaking with the effort of my will.

The wind barreled into my chest, threatening to knock me over, and my feet skittered over the slick surface. But I would not give up, and I would not let go of Una.

"Come to me," I whispered.

A second spark of light flickered at the trident's tip. Hope surged through me as it shimmered, golden light rippling across its surface. It shifted in the sand, then, with a rush of power, it shot through the air, slamming into my grip so hard I nearly toppled into the ocean. The instant I touched it, a gush of warmth spread through my body. A powerful light radiated from the trident's prongs, casting a protective glow over Una and me.

The storm hissed and spat as the light clashed with the shadow. The raft pitched violently beneath us, waves crashing over its edges, threatening to pull us into the sea. The jellyfish drifted closer, their glowing tendrils brushing the raft's sides, ready to strike.

Daring to remove my arm from around Una's waist, I placed both hands on the glowing shaft and aimed the ancient weapon at the water.

Una clung to my arm, fighting to keep her balance. "It's coming, Gal!"

I turned to see the darkness rising higher, towering over us like a monstrous god. Which is exactly what it was.

Massive, white eyes blinked open, glaring down at us with predatory hunger, narrowing with reptilian intensity. Black tendrils snaked from its torso, twisting through the sky, slashing the air, searching, reaching. The water churned beneath it, waves frothing with primal fury.

"I need to get you to shore," I shouted, unable to hear myself over the wind.

The raft teetered. Waves crashed over the wooden surface. Glowing white tentacles swept closer as the jellyfish swarmed our small square of safety.

Una's grip on my arm tightened. "Don't make me leave you," she pleaded, her voice raw with desperation.

I risked a glance at her stricken face, took in the terror and the love she wore in equal measures. My heart may have broken. Or melted. Or shattered. It did something that filled my chest with pain.

"I can't focus if I'm worried about you," I said. "*Please*, Una."

She searched my face, her hair a wild mess in the storm, whipped around by the howling wind. With her shoulders hunched, she gave me a curt nod of agreement.

I forced myself to face the swirling, venomous water again. I began moving it in slow, deliberate circles, my entire body vibrating with the effort to stay in control. Every instinct screamed at me to hurry the fuck up, but I couldn't afford to lose focus. The water churned under my command, slowly parting as it spiraled into a whirlpool, revealing patches of sand beneath. I had done this once before, during my fight with Zale, but that was when I had already been standing on the ocean floor.

With one hand I circled the trident, the other I used to keep my balance and guide my movements. I gestured with both hands for the water to part.

The wind roared in my ears, the raft bucking beneath me like an untamed selachii. My balance teetered, my feet slipping, and the grip I had on the water faltered. The path I'd cleared filled in instantly with glowing, deadly jellyfish, their luminescent tentacles creeping back toward us.

Panic bloomed. I glanced back over my shoulder, my blood rushing cold. The towering shadow loomed closer, its inky black mass shifting and writhing as it swallowed the sky. It was almost upon us.

I blinked. Sucked in a breath. Thought of my mom.

I twisted the trident in rapid circles, pushing away the violent waves ripping across the bay. Finally, the sea parted once more, revealing a dark, sludgy path of sand that stretched all the way to shore.

"Go!" I shouted, not daring to look back at Una.

She circled around me, gave me one heartfelt look, then scrambled down the ladder and leaped to the seabed.

Her feet sank into the sand. Panic flashed across her face as she threw me a desperate look.

"You can do it!" I yelled, my grip tightening on the trident. I couldn't let her see how hard it was, how the water screamed against my control, threatening to collapse at any second. The walls of water I held at bay were rising higher, defying gravity with every ounce of my will. Ten feet. Fifteen. Twenty. My muscles strained, shaking with unbearable pressure.

"Come on, Una," I hissed through my teeth when she reached the halfway mark.

Una ran. She didn't look back, I gave her that. I was so damn proud of her as she sprinted for the shore, her legs pumping, arms swinging wildly as the sand sucked at her feet.

Every second stretched, the distance between her and safety feeling impossibly long. My focus was on her, the walls, the trident, the crushing weight of the sea held at bay by nothing but sheer will.

When her feet finally hit dry sand, I exhaled sharply, relief flooding through me. I lowered the trident and the water crashed down with a deafening roar, slamming back into place, the path swallowed by the sea once more.

I turned just as the darkness loomed over me, its wide blinking eyes staring down at me from the blackness. Judging by its form and the way it sucked light from the world, it was Dagonar, Weaver of the Dark.

"Gal!" Una's scream pierced the storm, but I couldn't focus on her anymore.

This was it. This moment, this battle—this was what I was born for. The prophecies I had fought so hard to avoid had led me here. Although I detested them and *The Mermaid Chronicles*, I couldn't deny my destiny. If I didn't succumb to it, many would die.

"Gal!"

I pushed the sound of her voice to the back of my mind, steeling myself for what came next. Dagonar roared, his shadowy tendrils lashing, unfurling in every direction—some thin like serpents, others thick and gnarled like the trunks of ancient trees, all bristling with clawed points that could tear flesh from bone. The darkness clung to him, pulsating with malevolence, and the very sight of him sent a tumbling sense of icy fear pooling into my stomach.

I swallowed hard, gripping the trident tighter, my knuckles white as I tried to steady my trembling hands. I was glad for the light it provided, but I was unsure which of the abilities I had amassed would defeat the Denizen.

Tendrils stretched toward the sky. Others slithered down to coil around the raft and tested the boundary of the light that emanated from the trident. I slashed the weapon through the air, sending arcs of light sparking in every direction. An unnatural heat formed between my eyes, the strange sensation spreading through my body. It was power. The golden light didn't just shine from the trident itself, but it seeped from me, poured through my veins, flashed along my arms and legs, and lit up my entire body.

Power filled me with a terrifying strength, a raw, primal force that pulsed through every nerve. I opened my mouth and roared, a sound I didn't recognize as my own. Golden energy exploded from the trident, streaking across the darkness in a torrent of light aimed at Dagonar.

The Denizen reeled back, his tendrils shrinking, writhing with a newfound fury. But as soon as I felt a glimmer of victory, a scream cut through the storm, sharp and desperate.

I whipped around to see Una, suspended high above the ground, a massive tendril coiled around her like a python. Only her head and feet were visible as she thrashed and punched against the thick, black vine that held her in its grip.

"Una!" Her name tore from my throat and panic threatened to overwhelm me.

Focus.

I turned back to Dagonar, every muscle in my body screaming at me to do something, anything. "Let her go!"

The gaping mouth on Dagonar's nebulous face twisted into a grotesque grin. "A trade," he hissed, his voice as cold and dark as the void itself. It slithered through the air, chilling me to my core, conjuring images of all the worst things. Hell, he *was* one of the worst things. "Her life...for the trident."

I glanced at the glowing weapon in my hand, its light still pulsing through me. My fingers tightened around the shaft, the thought of handing it over filling me with dread. "You'll never have the trident," I spat through clenched teeth.

Una's strangled screams echoed in my ears as the tendril constricted tighter around her, lifting her higher. I could hear the strain in her voice, the fear that radiated off her in waves. Her struggles grew weaker with each passing second.

"Is your lover worth so little?" Dagonar's voice slithered across the bay, filled with dark amusement.

Fear trembled through me. A physical, viscous thing that almost took my legs out from under me. Shudders wracked my body. Part cold, part adrenaline, and a hell of a lot of terror. The last time Una had been in this much danger she had lost her eye. I had sworn I would not let harm come to her again.

Gritting my teeth, I fixed my gaze on Dagonar, fire burning in my veins. "My lover is worth more than you'll ever know," I growled, pouring every ounce of defiance I had into the words.

With a surge of fury, I raised the trident and thrust it through the air, aiming for what I hoped was the Denizen's heart. The winds howled around me, but the weapon cut through the storm, glowing as it hurtled toward the monstrous figure.

My breath caught in my throat as I watched. Was the power I wielded enough? Was I ready?

It struck me then that Una had stopped screaming. I spun around, my pulse a thundering drumbeat. Her body hung in the tendril's grip, her head slumped to one side, a deep gash marring her pale cheek. Blood dripped down her neck. There was no fight left in her. She was being suffocated to death.

"No..."

Rage poured into my chest, creating an acid burn that flayed me from the inside out. I whirled back to face Dagonar, just in time to see the trident pass through his shadowy form as though it was nothing more than smoke. It plunged into the water behind him with a hollow splash. The weapon's golden glow dimmed as it sank beneath the jellyfish-infested waves, leaving me with only a faint, flickering light.

Dagonar slithered forward, his form expanding, casting everything in oppressive darkness. He brought the tendril holding Una closer, dangling her unconscious body in front of me like bait. I could almost reach her—almost...

"A trade." His voice crashed through the wind. Waves churned around the raft, the current growing treacherous.

"Never!" I yelled, desperation twisting inside me.

My gaze locked on the faint glow of the trident sinking

below the waves. I stretched out my hand, fingers trembling, and summoned it back. The weapon responded immediately, hurtling through the water and sky like a lightning bolt. It slammed back into my grasp with a force that sent vibrations up my arm. I barely registered the shock as Dagonar's massive eyes widened, his dark form shifting, unsure for the first time.

Without wasting a second, I aimed the trident at the tendril coiled around Una, focusing on the point where it connected to the amorphous mass of Dagonar's body.

I released the trident once more, sending it streaking through the air toward the beast.

But Dagonar was quicker this time. One of his thick, writhing tendrils shot out and coiled around my legs, yanking me off balance. I stumbled, crashing onto the slick surface of the raft as jellyfish spilled over the edge, their translucent bodies rolling toward me with the next wave. I tensed, bracing for the searing pain of their stings, but even as the first venomous tendril lashed across my skin, I felt a grim smile tugging at my lips.

The trident found its mark.

Dagonar roared, the massive tendril unraveling from around Una. She tumbled through the sky, her body limp, falling too fast.

"Una!" I screamed.

She didn't reply. She hit the ground with a dull *thud*.

Summoning every ounce of strength I had left, I called the trident back once more. It shot through the air and landed in my hand, glowing with renewed power. With Una lying unconscious on the sand and Dagonar still looming over us, the battle was far from over. My body ached, my vision blurred, but I couldn't stop. Not now. Not while Una's life hung by a thread.

Panting, with sweat coating my skin, wind pummeling my chest, and stinging tentacles wrapped around my ankles, I prepared to fight.

Dagonar, however, had changed. The monstrous beast, once towering and immense, was shrinking. His shadowy tendrils retracted, thinning and curling inward, as though being sucked back into his shapeless form. The darkness surrounding him withered, collapsing inward like a dying star. The terrifying presence he exuded moments before was fading, the tendrils that had spread like a web across the bay now curling into his chest. His massive form contracted further until, without a sound, it slipped beneath the surface of the water.

The wind, which had been howling relentlessly, suddenly died with Dagonar's retreat. The violent gusts that had lashed at me only moments ago were gone, replaced by a strange, eerie stillness. I stood alone on the raft, breathing heavily, the trident glowing in my hand. Jellyfish meandered around the small platform, their stings now little more than distant pricks in the battle's aftermath.

Rain continued to fall. It ran in rivulets down my face, mingling with sweat and seawater, but it wasn't cold anymore. The chill that had once clung to the air had disappeared with Dagonar, and now there was only the distant rumble of waves breaking on the shore.

I scanned the sky, but the moon did not return. Neither did the stars. As if they too were terrified of the Denizen.

Una lay motionless on the sand, and I was still stranded on the floating raft.

CHAPTER NINE

*J*ellyfish lurked within every inch of water. Conjuring the last of my strength, I twisted the trident in my hand once more, commanding the water to part. As the water began to separate, a shout came from the narrow beach.

I risked a glance to see Ford crouched by Una. She was in good hands. But I wouldn't relax until I could hold her in my arms, until I could see she was okay for myself.

My limbs shuddered with effort as a pathway opened. I didn't waste time scrambling down the ladder and jumping to the damp seabed. It took me longer to travel the narrow path than Una because I had to keep my attention on the two walls of water towering over me, jellyfish hovering at their lips, tentacles dripping into the open space above my head. It was then I noticed the pain of my previous stings. An angry red rash circled my ankles and shins. I clenched my jaw against the smarting soreness, wincing as the tender soles of my feet scraped against jagged coral and rock.

I trudged through the collapsing sand, yanking my feet from each sucking footstep, cursing at the jellyfish threatening to drown me in a bath of pain. When I reached the shore, I almost collapsed, but the sight of Una's lifeless body spurred me on.

Abandoning the trident to the ground, I sank to my knees beside her.

"Una?"

I glanced at Ford.

"She's alive," he replied. That was all I needed to know.

"Let's get you both inside." Ford rose to his feet, Una's petite form cradled against his chest. I wanted to carry her, but I had no strength left, and there were the trident and *The Mermaid Chronicles* to attend to.

Mustering some energy, I snatched both objects from the ground and followed Ford into the house. Ember and the twins were inside waiting in the kitchen.

"I can't fight that," Cyra said to me as Ford lay Una on the couch. She paced a line behind the breakfast bar, her bare feet squeaking on the tiles.

Weary, I turned to the young girl. "You can." Only two words. I didn't have it in me for a long speech. She was only thirteen, and perhaps I was too harsh, but I'd almost died, almost lost Una, and there was no point in sugarcoating things. Either she would fight, or she wouldn't. The Denizens would come either way.

I dropped the trident and the book on the table. The book wasn't glowing. There were no new prophecies to guide us. It had left us in the dark. Or perhaps it felt that two cryptic sentences were all we needed to survive.

The Denizens of the Deep crave the power of Vorago's trident. The one true wielder must remain strong.

Strong. I had remained strong. I had used the strength of Una's love, the magic of the trident, and my own powerful muscles. But strength had limits. Power needed fuel. And my heart was empty.

I sank onto the couch next to Una, placed her head over my lap as Ember covered us both in blankets.

"Thanks, buddy."

He gave me a silent nod. It was the first time I'd seen him lost for words.

Ford gave me a bowl of warm water and a rag, pointed to Una's bloodied face. "She's okay. Breathing. Sleeping. She just needs rest."

He went back to the kitchen cupboards, opened a few cabinets, rummaged through a drawer, then returned to me and sat by my feet with a second bowl. This one was filled with...something red.

"What the hell is that?" I asked.

"Tomato juice," he replied without looking up. He lifted one of my feet and placed it in the bowl. Immediately, the worst of the pain leached out of my skin and I sighed.

As Ford worked a rag up and down my legs, I dipped the cloth into the water for Una, gently swabbing it across her face, her arms, her chest, and her torso. At all the places that evil tendril had opened wounds. The Fountain of Youth didn't work for either of us. Or Ember. When we'd returned from hunting Zale and I'd placed the trident in the fountain, I'd enabled it to heal human suffering when it hadn't before. But I still didn't know why it had singled the three of us out.

As if the island was mad at us. Una continued to scour the book for a solution, but as yet, none had been found. She wore her eyepatch bravely, embraced the scars she had received in battle, but deep down, I knew she wanted her eye back. And I would do anything to give it to her. But I was only a man. A prince. A merman with an onyx tail. The wielder of an ancient weapon I didn't know if I deserved.

When Ford finished bathing my feet, he slathered a balm over my ankles and shins. The pain was enough to make me grit my teeth still, but I wouldn't complain. It could have been so much worse.

Cyra quit pacing and slid onto a stool next to Ash, her fingernails drumming a staccato beat on the marble counter. Ash's wings were on display, but folded by his side.

"I'm kind of glad I have the wings," I heard Ash mutter to his sister. "I can fly away."

"Now I want wings even more," Cyra whispered back.

I didn't blame them. I remembered when I'd been kidnapped by the ghost pirates with Una and Ember. I had been seven. Una and Ember five. It was fucking terrifying. It was only late last year when I'd gone after Zale. I'd been fucking terrified then too. So I didn't blame the twins for wanting to hide. And I didn't expect them to fight if it put them in danger. I just wanted them to feel prepared, to be able to defend themselves if they needed to. The last thing I wanted to do was drive terror into the hearts of teenagers.

After Ford disposed of the rags and bowls of water, he crouched by my side. "We need to return to the city. The radios are down."

My head snapped up so quick I thought it might jerk off

my neck. He didn't need to spell it out, I was well versed in reading between the lines. If we'd lost contact with the city, the palace, the main populace of Atlantis, we had no idea if Dagonar's attack was isolated or not. All four Denizens could have struck simultaneously.

I clenched my hands into fists as I looked up at Ford. "We should leave now."

Ford shook his head. "You and Una need to rest. Besides, the water channels are flooded with jellyfish."

"All of them?"

"I did a quick fly over," Ember said. "All of them. At least in the immediate vicinity."

"So we can assume the channels near the palace are affected too," Ford said.

"Everyone will have to go back to carrying flasks of fountain water with them," I muttered.

"For the time being," Ford confirmed. "But now you two need to rest and heal."

I lifted Una's head from my lap, laid a kiss on her damaged cheek, then crouched in front of her to take her into my arms.

Ford laid a hand on my shoulder. "I'll take her. You're exhausted."

Even though I couldn't bear to let her out of my sight, or bear to stop touching her, I nodded. Ford was right. I was exhausted. The battle had only just begun and no fountain would soothe my aches and pains.

Ford lifted her into his arms and cradled her against his chest. Before he ascended the stairs, he gave me a look. I couldn't read everything in his eyes, but I caught the flash of pride. His approval and respect had motivated me for years. But somehow it didn't seem important anymore.

The twins followed Ford upstairs, and Ember caught me before I followed.

"I tried to go out there."

I took in the regret lining his face, the tension bracketing his mouth. "Out where?"

"To help you."

I shook my head. "I'm glad you didn't. You saw what it did to Una."

"I tried." Ember said, pressing my shoulder. "I got ten feet into the air and the wind slammed me onto the roof of the cabin."

"Shit. Are you okay?"

There was no sign of his wings, but he rolled a shoulder as if it was stiff and sore. "A few small broken bones. I'll heal."

"You should have stayed inside."

"You can't fight them alone."

"I don't have a choice."

"Just like you didn't have a choice with Zale?"

I grated my teeth against the inside of my cheek. I was too tired for this conversation. I just wanted to be with Una. "That was different."

"How?"

"Because the trident chose me."

"It chose you last time too."

The truth of his words slammed into me, but I refused to give them air. "You both almost died."

A smile ghosted his lips. "Courting death is my favorite recreational activity."

"Ember, this is serious."

"I know. I just don't want you to go all *vengeful Gal* on my ass again and leave me in the dust with no hint of glory."

I barked out a bitter laugh. "It's glory you're after, huh?"

"Obviously. How else am I going to charm the girls?"

And just like that, the tension drained out of our conversation. While nothing we'd said wasn't true, we both recognized neither of us was willing to budge on our viewpoints. Not tonight, anyway.

I slapped his back. "I'll save some glory for you." I turned and marched up the stairs.

When I pushed open the door of the room I was sharing with Una and tiptoed inside, I found her asleep in the bed, covers pulled to her chest. Light spilled from the few electric lamps in the room, but their warm glows didn't penetrate as far as usual, as if Dagonar was able to influence electricity as well as natural light. Perhaps he could, considering all our power came from natural sources.

I had intended to stride into the room, sweep Una into my arms and kiss her back to consciousness, but as I stood there staring at her inert form, I couldn't bring myself to move.

Something whispered at the back of my mind, a faint hum of unease I couldn't ignore. The whisper grew louder, morphing into a low rumble in my chest. I couldn't breathe. It was like the air had thickened, congealed, turning the act of drawing breath into a struggle. My throat tightened, and I swallowed, but it didn't help. My lungs refused to fill.

My pulse quickened, heart hammering so hard I thought it might tear through my ribcage. My hands trembled at my sides, fingers curling into tight fists as I tried to force them to stop. But the shaking spread. My legs weakened, my knees buckled, and I had to steady myself on the doorframe. The world around me blurred, spinning in a garish swirl of color. The walls of the room closed in, the edges warping and twisting like a nightmare I couldn't wake from.

I couldn't get enough air.

I gasped, desperate for a lungful of oxygen, but it felt like I was drowning. How could a merman drown? My chest constricted further, every breath shallow and ragged. My vision tunneled, black spots dancing at the edges of my sight. Cold sweat prickled at the back of my neck, rolling down my spine in icy rivulets. My heart, still pounding, now thrummed with an irregular rhythm, like it was skipping beats, stuttering in my chest.

Unbearable silence pressed against my ears. I wanted to scream, to run, but I couldn't make my body respond. The only sound was my own ragged breathing, the erratic thud of my heartbeat in my ears, and the white noise of blood rushing through my veins.

I tried to focus on something—anything—to ground myself, but Una's still form was all I saw. Her pale skin, the gash on her cheek, her limp arms splayed. She could have died.

What if it happened again? What if I failed her for good?

The fear gripped me, cold and suffocating. My mind raced, spiraling into worst-case scenarios. Images flashed in my head—Una, eyes closed forever, her body cold and unresponsive as I tried in vain to wake her. My chest tightened further, and I doubled over, clutching my stomach as if I could somehow keep myself from falling apart.

The walls pressed closer, the room shrinking around me, and I was trapped—trapped in my own mind, in my own body, paralyzed by the fear that had clawed its way into my heart. I felt tears welling, but I couldn't let them fall. I had to be strong. I had to get a grip.

But I couldn't. My body locked me into overwhelming panic. I stood frozen in the doorway, my chest heaving, tears burning at the corners of my eyes as I stared at the one person I had sworn to protect—the one person I couldn't lose.

Then, somewhere in the haze of panic, I saw her move. Una's head angled toward me and her eyelids fluttered open.

"Una." I pushed her name through my tight throat.

Her gaze settled on me, a sweet smile curling her lips. But the angry red gash on her cheek was a reminder of all the things I'd sworn to prevent.

A delicate frown wrinkled her brow. "Gal? What's wrong? You look...terrified."

A tear fell down my cheek, which I hastily wiped away. I sucked in an aching breath.

Una sat up. "You're having a panic attack." She gestured for me to join her on the bed.

I staggered toward her, dropped onto the bed next to her, buried my face in my hands.

Una threw the covers off, crawled across the bed, and draped herself around me. "Just breathe, Gal. Breathe."

"I don't fucking know how."

I felt her smile. "You just did. Sing with me."

"I can barely breathe, I can't fucking sing."

"*In the deep where shadows roam, where the sea calls souls back home, a storm was born, a mother's cry, taken by a beast that passed her by,*" Una sang, her soft voice a caressing whisper.

I recognized the song immediately. It had been written about us. A song passed around for several months after we'd returned from defeating Zale. And every time I heard it I flushed with embarrassment. But Una loved that a song had been written about her. About us. And she teased me with it constantly.

"Sing with me, Gal. *Gal, with fire in his heart, set sail to tear the dark apart. Una by his side, fierce and free, together they'd rewrite destiny.*"

I rolled my eyes at her, but a fresh hit of air swept into my lungs. Una came around the front of me, sat in my lap with her legs wrapped around my back, cupped my face, all the time singing our song.

"*With Una's heart and Gal's true aim, they claimed the trident, sealed their names. Through the waves we rise, through the dark we see, a love that blooms beneath the sea.*"

I smiled at her, finally hearing the words for what they were. The deepest level of respect. A homage to the depth of our love.

I let the words pour out of me. "*In a cave of frost, with hands so true, Gal carved a flute of ice and blue, a melody that tamed the night, put seawolves deep into their flight.*"

We finished the song together. My heart rate had slowed and I could finally breathe normally again.

I kissed the wound on her cheek, rested my forehead against hers. "I came in here to take care of you."

She hugged me tightly. "We take care of each other."

"Are you feeling okay?"

"Better now you're here."

I puffed my cheeks, rubbed a hand over my face, and flopped backward on the bed. "I'm going around in circles."

"What do you mean?"

I slammed a fist into the soft mattress, wishing it hurt more. "How can I go on a journey to kill Zale, fall in love with you, and not change at all?"

"Of course you've changed."

I shook my head, balled my fists into my eyes. "No, I really haven't Una." I sat up and lifted her off my lap, placed her opposite me. "I'm still terrified. I can't bear the thought of losing you. And now I'm having panic attacks. Like my mom..."

"Because your mom cared."

"Of course she fucking *cared*. That's the fucking point. I don't *want* to care. I don't *want* to feel terror every time something bad happens. I don't *want* to freak out when Dagonar is *strangling* you to *death*."

Una pushed herself onto her knees and grabbed my wrists. "That's normal, Gal. It's *normal* to be afraid. It's *normal* to freak out when you think the person you love most is going to die."

"But it *hurts*."

"I know."

"And it's scary."

"I *know*."

"Why can't I hold on to what Ford said to me on the barge? Why can't I bottle it? Contain it?"

Una tilted her head. "That's exactly what you did do."

I looked up at her bright blue eye, at her face full of such softness and love, at the gash marring her cheek.

"You defeated Dagonar and I'm still alive."

I shook my head. "He's not dead."

"Maybe not, but the battle ended. And we're both still here. You focused, Gal. You focused on what was important. And I'm. Still. Here."

CHAPTER TEN

entatively, I raised my hand to her face, traced the edge of her new wound, and pushed a wild strand of hair behind her ear. So scarred. So beautiful. *So. Damn. Brave.*

"You are the most exquisite being in all of eternity." I kissed her nose, then her unmarred cheek, then the shell of her ear.

Una smiled. "Don't let Vorago hear you say that."

I snorted. "If Vorago gave a shit about his island, he'd be here helping to defend it from the Denizens. No, I think he deserted us long ago."

Una placed her hands on my chest, gave the most loving smile. "We're going to be okay," she said. "*You're* going to be okay. We will survive this."

I gnawed the inside of my cheek as I stared at the determination in her lone blue eye. "You don't know that."

She moved her hand to my stomach. "I feel it." Then she

placed her hand on her own stomach. "Here." She moved her hand to her heart. "And here." Then she rested her hand against my pounding heart. "And here."

"You may be an oracle, but you can't see the future."

"No, I can't. But I'm going to make every day count. And I'm going to have faith that we will win. What's the point of *The Mermaid Chronicles* otherwise?"

She had a point. And as much as I hated that damn book, we'd be lost without it.

I sighed, raised her hand to my lips, and kissed her knuckles. "You are so much better than me."

She laughed, tilted her head. "And don't you forget it."

I lifted her onto my lap, curled my arms around her. I would hold her until I was forced to let go.

"And, Gal?" she said softly. "As much as it pains me to say it, you need to imagine the worst thing. Picture it. And then imagine yourself moving past it."

I shook my head into the crook of her neck. "Never."

"If something happens to me, you will survive."

"No, I won't," I said into her hair.

"You survived your mother's death."

I gripped her tighter, my fingers digging into her sides. "I'm not sure I did."

Una pulled away, cupped my face with her hands, that soft, believing smile all I could see. "Yes, you did. And you even learned to love again. That doesn't mean there won't be scars. And it doesn't mean you won't feel grief. But you are surviving. Better than that. You are living. And you are loving. Don't forget that."

I had no more words, and so I just hugged her and buried my face in her neck, breathed in her salty ocean scent, sucked in the aroma of jasmine like it was a lifeline.

As I held Una, her words echoed through my mind, bouncing between the walls of my fear and the truth she'd just spoken. I had always been the protector, the one carrying the weight of survival, of vengeance, of leadership. But now, as much as I wanted to shield her from every danger, every Denizen that lurked in the depths, I was beginning to see something different.

She wasn't a fragile thing I needed to keep safe. She was fierce, resilient, and brave—braver than I'd given her credit for. My instinct had always been to shield her from the battlefield, but maybe that was a mistake. Maybe, in trying to protect her, I'd been ignoring what she was capable of, ignoring the fact that I needed her too.

I looked at her again, nestled in my arms, and realized the thought of facing these battles without her was...impossible. And that was the fear, wasn't it? Not only losing her, but losing the part of me that believed we could win. I needed her there. I needed her light in the darkest moments. As much as it terrified me, I had to accept that I couldn't face the Denizens alone.

But there was still fear, so much of it. The thought of her being hurt, like my mother had been—it twisted in my gut, strangled my heart with ice. I hated the idea of failing her, of watching her suffer because of my shortcomings.

I had fought Zale, carved a flute from ice, tamed the seawolves, wielded a trident born of legends—all feats I thought I had to accomplish by myself. But through it all,

Una had been by my side. Her strength had matched mine, even when I was too blinded by my need to protect her to see it. She wasn't a liability. She was my anchor.

I needed her. Not just her strength, not just her hope—but her presence. She wasn't only part of this fight; she was part of me. A part I couldn't let go of. I had to trust her. I had to rely on her, not as someone who needed saving, but as an equal partner in war. There was a reason she was the guardian of the orb of Spirit and Soul. Her empathy. Her compassion. Her thoughtfulness. Her understanding. She knew exactly what to say to help me rise to the challenge.

I didn't have to carry this burden alone.

The tightness in my chest loosened a fraction as I accepted the truth. Our unity was what would give me the strength I needed. Not just power, not just determination, but our bond. Our love. After all, that was what had made my parents successful during their battles. Their unity. *The Mermaid Chronicles* always decreed that a battle had to be fought in unity. It would be no different this time.

"I'll be brave," I whispered, more to myself than to her. And I meant it, for the first time, in a different way. I would be brave enough to let her in, to lean on her when the weight of the world became too much.

I didn't have to be the hero all the time. I could be vulnerable too, and that didn't make me weaker. If anything, it made me stronger. Maybe that's what Ford meant. *Feel the fear and move through it.*

After a few minutes, I relaxed my grip on her. "Okay."

"Okay?"

"I'll be brave."

"You already are."

"Together?"

She raised her hand and interlocked her fingers with mine. "Together."

"Together," I repeated, and this time, I truly believed it.

CHAPTER ELEVEN

*E*mber shook me awake. "Time to move."

I'd fallen asleep curled around Una, a pile of limbs and soft hair and depthless love. The warm glow of the lamps flickered, struggling to chase the shadows into the corners. I glanced at the window where the drapes fluttered in a breeze. It was still dark outside.

Rubbing grit from my eyes, I sat up. "What's wrong?"

Ember glanced at the window, raked a hand through his unruly hair. "I don't know how to tell you this, but it's noon."

I gaped at him, looked back at the window. "What the fuck?"

Una stirred beside me, yawned and stretched. The gash on her cheek had scabbed over, but it wouldn't take much to make it bleed again.

"Dagonar is the Weaver of Darkness," Ember said with a tense tone. "He brought darkness, and Ford believes, until he is...killed, the darkness will remain."

"Holy fuck." I swung my legs out of bed, grimaced when

the sting of pain circled my ankles. "The crops...the fish life...
Atlantis will die."

"And so will the people in it."

I waited for a wisecrack, but it didn't come. During our
hunt for Zale, Ember had kept us entertained—or irritated,
depending on the mood I was in—and reduced our stress
levels with constant one-liners. That he wasn't spewing them
now spoke to the depths of our plight.

"So I won't need to apply sun block every five seconds?" I
attempted humor, poking fun at my red hair and pale skin,
but the words missed their mark.

"Nice try," Ember said. "But don't give up your day job."

"I guess it's a good thing my day job is fighting the
Denizens." Sighing, I pushed my hair into a reasonable shape
and rose to my feet. I cast a loving look back at Una's sleeping
form, my jaw hardening as I contemplated Dagonar's tactics.
"He doesn't even need to fight me. He can just suck out the
light from the world and slowly suffocate us. What a
coward." If I wanted to put an end to it, I'd have to go in
search of him.

"He's more than a coward." Ember pounded his fist into
his other palm. "He's a douchebag, asshat, dickwad...and if he
were my dog, I'd shave his butt and teach him to walk
backward—"

The laugh burst out of me. "There he is."

Ember cracked a smile.

"Thanks, buddy, I needed that."

"When this is over, I think I might retire my soldiering
duties and take a second career as a court jester."

I patted his shoulder. "Follow your dreams, buddy."

We shared a look as the fleeting lightness evaporated. Banter and jokes wouldn't change our situation.

"Ford has loaded the barge," Ember said. "It's time to return to the palace." He walked to the door, turned, rapped the door frame a couple of times. "I got your back." His dark eyes blazed with determination.

"Thanks." I wouldn't refuse his help. Not anymore. Ember might not be able to battle a Denizen in hand-to-hand combat, but I'd need him for other tasks.

A few minutes later, our small group gathered on the shore. The wind stirred my hair, cold and sharp, like the breath of something unseen lurking beyond the shadows. I searched for sources of light in the darkness, desperate for a sliver of warmth, but there was only the jellyfish throbbing with venomous beauty. The sun should've been overhead, but not a single beam pierced the eternal night. Dagonar's darkness had devoured it all.

A shiver ran through me, cold as the void, as I tiptoed along the narrow gangplank, using my trident to light a path for us all. But the trident's glow flickered, as if it, too, feared this abyss of darkness. Beneath me, the water shimmered with the ghostly glow of luminescent jellyfish, their tendrils pulsing ominously with toxic light.

Once we were settled on the boat, Ford lit several lanterns, but the source of light did little to ease the sense of foreboding. Their feeble efforts at illumination were swallowed by the thick, inky blackness surrounding us. The flames struggled for life, guttering like the last heartbeat of a fading pulse.

The twins huddled together inside the cabin with Ember,

the glint of the jellyfish reflected in their wide pupils. Ford stood at the helm and guided the barge through narrow channels of still, black water. I took my place at the bow, the glowing trident in my hand, my arm wrapped around Una's waist.

She leaned her head against my chest, cradled the arm folded around her waist, and stared at the path of pulsing venom. The jellyfish glided beneath the surface, their glowing tendrils twisting like cursed roots, brushing against the boat as we drifted through the channel.

I turned the trident in small circles, willing the water to part, pushing the jellyfish aside as we passed. Hopefully, they'd find their way to the bay and then into the ocean. I prayed they would drift away on the currents before they could bring harm to an Atlantean, but I suspected they were here to stay until the Denizens were defeated.

As the hours wore on, the darkness deepened, thickening until the air became almost too dense to breathe and reflective dots of pulsing jellyfish spotted my eyelids when I blinked. The world had been swallowed whole, and we were drifting through the belly of the beast.

A few hours later, the boat's engine sputtered, once, twice, and then fell silent. It was solar paneled, like all the electricity in Atlantis, and we hadn't even made it halfway home. Ford cursed under his breath. We couldn't swim in the infested waters. It was too far to walk. It was time to test my skills with the trident and hope I didn't fatigue before I reached the palace.

"What now?" Una asked, turning to face me, worry lines

crossing her forehead. "We need to check on everyone at home."

Ash poked his head out of the cabin. "Want me to fly home and get help?"

Ember put a hand on his shoulder. "You haven't flown for that long yet, dude. Can't have you falling from the sky into a lake of jellyfish. I'll go if anyone needs to fly."

Ash rolled his eyes but didn't retort.

"I think it's time Gal puts his trident skills to use." Ford tapped his chest, holding his hand over his heart. "You can do it."

I nodded. There would be no more delays, no more time to take stock, no more training time. It was time I proved I was worthy of the trident.

Taking a breath, I swished the trident in the air and was rewarded with eddying waves rippling through the channel. The jellyfish bobbed on the surface, undulating on the gentle crests, pressing closer to the boat.

Una gave me an encouraging smile.

I swung the trident again, its golden prongs slicing through the suffocating dark, and sparks of light flaring like dying stars. The black waves responded, surging in restless crescendos, sending the barge lurching forward. A guttural groan echoed from the hull as the boat strained against the unnatural current. Jellyfish slithered out of the water and slid across the slick wooden deck, their tentacles twisting with malevolence, pale tendrils searching for flesh. The two inches of water pooling in the boat now teemed with pulsating, toxic light. The raw stings of my recent wounds throbbed with fresh pain.

"Everyone inside!" I yelled.

Ford abandoned the rudder, casting me a fleeting, grim nod before disappearing into the cabin with Ember and the twins. The cabin door slammed closed. The twins pressed their faces against the windows, their mouths gaping at the sheer number of jellyfish already in the boat.

Una made to follow, but I grabbed her wrist, pulling her back toward me. "Not you. I need you here. I want to practice my focus with you by my side...if you're willing."

"Of course." Her gaze held mine for a moment before she moved behind me. She wrapped her arms tightly around my waist, then pressed a kiss between my shoulder blades. "I love you," she whispered, and I felt the shape of her love moving against my skin.

I leaned into the warmth of Una's arms folded around me and refocused on the water. The trident hummed in my hand, vibrating with an ancient, restless power, and I felt the ocean responding to it. We were getting to know each other, the ocean and me. In ways far more powerful and familiar than I'd dreamed of. All thanks to the trident. The weapon may not have been made for me—I certainly didn't forge it— and the responsibility it presented often filled me with terror. But as I stood there on the bow of the boat, feeling the power soak into my skin, surge through my veins, strengthen my limbs, I knew I could never be apart from it again. It belonged to a forgotten god. A god who had abandoned it, Atlantis, and his people. A god who no longer had a claim on its majestic power. The trident had claimed me, just as much as I had claimed it. We were one, and I refused to allow anything or anyone to tear it away from me.

I arced the trident through the air. Sparks of light and hope radiated from the weapon in concentric circles. The waves responded, rising higher, faster, until towering walls of water slammed against the boat, propelling us forward with savage force. The boat dipped and soared over the peaks and valleys of the churning water, each impact sending spray and glowing jellyfish slamming against the deck.

We clung to the guardrails as the boat tilted dangerously, the venomous waters threatening to swallow us. The jellyfish swarmed, their glowing tendrils multiplying with every surge, wrapping around our legs with fiery rings of pain.

"Ahh!" Una let out a pained squeal as a gleaming tentacle swept over her foot.

They didn't stop coming. As our speed increased and the waves rose, an increasing number of jellyfish swarmed over us, strangling our ankles and shins, inflicting us with new agonizing stings. My shins blistered, then bled before skin peeled under the constant assault.

Una didn't leave my side, her arms still tight around my waist, even as her legs buckled from the stings.

Summoning every ounce of strength, I raised the trident high and swung it in a broad arc. The water obeyed, parting in great, eddying swirls. Then I used my free hand and pictured a path free of toxic poison. The jellyfish moved. Not just with the waves, but with my will.

I stared, disbelieving, as they drifted out of our path, their glowing forms retreating under the force of my command. I hadn't known I could do that. Until now, I thought only the trident's physical movement could be obeyed. But it seemed the weapon had granted me more control than I realized—

power over the creatures of the sea, even those bent on our destruction.

I continued to move as the boat progressed along the channel, a dance of power as I circled my arms and shifted my weight, my will winning out against the jellyfish. After a few hours, the movements became unconscious, performed with practiced ease as I conjured waves and pushed jellyfish aside. It was almost...fun, until my legs began to fatigue.

Beneath the eternal darkness, I had no sense of time. But when the flickering lights of the palace came into view, a deep weariness settled into my body, suggesting I had been controlling the water and jellyfish for far longer than I'd realized.

Una sagged against me. "We made it."

When we docked, Ember whisked the twins back to their father and Ford escorted Una and me to the hospital. We hobbled over the cobbles, our ankles bleeding and oozing, both of us leaning on Ford for support.

"Fucking jellyfish," I muttered as I stubbed a toe which was entirely unrelated.

"I never want to see another jellyfish again," Una said.

Ford took more of our weight as we staggered toward the hospital and deposited us inside.

When we stumbled through the doors, the medic on duty was shuffling a pack of well-used playing cards. She leaped to her feet. Her pupils blew wide as she glanced at our wounds.

First, she bathed our skin in fountain water. I didn't expect it to help, but it brought the pain down a few notches. Tolerable. I could walk.

After our wounds had been bandaged, I dropped Una at

her house so she could check on her family, and found Ember loitering in the palace's entrance hall. He stood at the foot of the stairs, his gaze following the path of the polished marble balustrade as it wound its way up beside the grand staircase.

"You okay?" I asked, limping toward him with the trident in my hand. With the Denizens nearby, I refused to let it out of my sight.

Ember frowned. "Can't find my mom. Dad said she was at the palace, but I can't find her in any of the obvious places."

"Let's go ask my dad. Maybe he's seen her." I grabbed the cool marble newel post, noting the presence of extra candles and lanterns flooding the palace with light as we advanced up the stairs. And yet shadows danced in the corners, poured into crevices, and appeared in places shadows had no business appearing, as if they had a mind of their own.

Ember walked by my side, offering his arm for support as we progressed along the hallway. Neither of us looked at my legs. Neither of us mentioned I wasn't in top physical form. That I was now at a disadvantage.

I pushed open the door of the royal suite. "Dad?"

The living area was empty, a fire burning in the hearth. Darkness pressed in at the windows, seemed to slither into the room somehow. I heard a noise from his bedroom.

Without thinking about it, I limped across the polished floor, Ember at my elbow, and knocked on my father's door. I didn't wait for a response, but pushed the door open and ventured into the room.

I made it three feet into the room before I stopped abruptly and my mouth dropped open. "Dad?"

"Mom?" Ember stood at my side, his wings erupting from his back, knocking over a vase and sending it crashing to the floor where it shattered into a dozen pieces.

My dad was in bed. Naked. My aunt was on top of him. Equally naked. My aunt. My mother's sister. Ember's mother. *Holy shit!*

The four of us stared at each other. No one moved. I got an eyeful of a pair of breasts I never wanted to get an eyeful of.

Ember raised a hand to block his view of our naked parents. Our naked parents still very much attached to each other.

Heat rushed to my face and I backed out of the room, dragging Ember with me. After slamming the door shut behind me, I heard thumps and footsteps sounding from the other side.

I stared at my cousin, the heat now draining from my face. "What the actual...?"

Ember shook his head, lowered his wings. "I never thought I'd see the day..."

He sank onto a couch and dropped his chin into a hand.

I gnawed on the inside of my cheek. "I never thought my dad would..."

My mother had been dead for thirteen years. Not once had he entertained romantic interest since. He'd been crushed by my mother's death. So crushed he'd retreated into himself, barely speaking, barely ruling, barely doing anything except taking up space in front of the fire he kept burning twenty-four seven. And now...with my aunt. Was this grief talking? Were they clutching at each other to fill the holes they both nursed?

There was a small part of me that couldn't help thinking they'd betrayed my mother's memory. But ocean shifters experienced longer life spans. When they drank from the fountain regularly. I couldn't expect my father to be alone forever. But I hadn't expected him to find someone again either. Perhaps it was a onetime thing. But if it was, his choice of partner was woefully flawed.

"First I find out my dad fathered two kids I had no knowledge of when he and my mom split." Ember tapped his heels against the marble floor. "And now...and now my mom is fucking the King of Atlantis."

We stared at each other, then burst out laughing.

"I wonder why it wasn't in *The Mermaid Chronicles*," I said.

"Maybe it's not important."

"Feels pretty big to me."

Ember gave me a one-shoulder shrug. "To us, yeah. But not to Atlantis and the future."

The bedroom door opened and my dad and Aunt Raina appeared, both wearing sheepish expressions, but at least they were fully clothed.

"We should talk," Dad said.

I winced. "Or not."

"You're never going to unsee what you just saw," Aunt Raina said, her hands splayed apologetically. She wore an aqua robe, the belt cinched around her waist, the same color my mother had preferred. And looking at her now, the similarity between them slammed into me. Raina had the same tumbling curls, albeit they were blonde instead of red, the same smattering of freckles across the bridge of her nose, the same bright blue eyes. For a moment, seeing her clutch my dad's hand, it was like my mother had returned.

I gave myself a mental slap and returned to the present.

They sank into separate armchairs. I was the only one left standing. I couldn't sit, despite my wounded feet. There was too much restless energy pulsing through my veins. But I did put the trident down. I didn't want to accidently arc it through the air and take someone out.

I stood with my hands laced behind my back, examining my father. I'd only been gone a few nights, but how had I missed the new color in his cheeks, the youthful glow on his skin, the lightness in his eyes? My stomach went into freefall. How long had this been going on?

Dad cleared his throat, reached across the small gap separating him from my aunt and took her hand, clasped it in his. It brought back a flash of memory. How my parents used to sit on the same chairs like that. An acid burn crawled up my throat as I realized that would never happen again. I'd known that, of course I had, and yet something about seeing my dad with another person threatened all the memories I had stored so carefully.

"Over the last few months," Dad began. "Raina and I have found each other." He glanced at her and she gave him an encouraging smile.

My stomach churned. I looked at my cousin. His shocked gaze slid to mine.

Raina patted my dad's hand. "We've both been so lonely."

Lonely?

"And we found we were spending more time together," Dad said. "With Raina's work as the palace's press officer..."

"They don't need to know all the details," Raina said. "Suffice it to say we found we had a lot in common."

Yeah, my mom.

"That we could comfort each other," Dad said.

Comfort?

"And perhaps more," Raina added quietly.

"What about Mom?" I pushed the words through my tight throat.

Dad fixed me with a sympathetic look. Tension bracketed his mouth, and he drew his lip between his teeth. "You mom has been dead for almost thirteen years."

He delivered the words softly, but I still felt like I'd been caught in a vortex. Pain, both physical and emotional, sliced through me until I had to gasp for breath.

Ember stood, put a hand on my shoulder. "Easy, buddy."

I hated that my dad had suffered so much. For so long. That he couldn't seem to find a glimmer of happiness. That I couldn't give that to him. But to see him with my aunt...that couldn't be healthy for either of them.

"Are you...in love?" The words fell out of my mouth before I could stop them.

Dad and Raina shared a worried look.

"We don't put labels on our feelings," Dad said. "Raina knows your mom was the love of my life. She's also shown me that there are different kinds of love. We care about each other a great deal. We respect each other. And we enjoy each other's company."

Ember scoffed. "You sound like something out of a historical romance novel. Not that I've read any, by the way, they're far too emotionally draining. All sensitive feelings and arranged marriages and a distinct lack of passion."

"Passion isn't everything," Dad said.

Judging by what I'd walked in on, passion wasn't their issue.

"I don't know what to say," I said.

Dad stood, locked his gaze on me and put a hand on my shoulder. "Don't take this the wrong way, but I'm not looking for your approval. But I would love to have your blessing."

This was my father's life. I couldn't complain if he'd found a way to move on. Hell, Una had showed me I too could love again after the tragedy of my mother's death. But it still hurt. It felt like we were leaving her behind. That all her memories were being boxed up, labeled neatly, and placed on a shelf out of reach where the pain could be ignored. She deserved more than that. But so did my father.

"Are you drinking from the fountain again?" I asked.

Dad gave me a small nod. "Before I met your mother, I knew I would inherit the title. I was being prepared for it from birth, on the proviso that Atlantis would be found. Meeting your mother and ruling with her was more than I'd ever dreamed of. And since her death, I've neglected my duties. I've forgotten my dreams. It's time for me to step up. And to do that, I need to drink from the fountain."

I would never be king. *Thank fuck for that*. Because the fountain didn't work for me, my father would outlive me. *Thank fuck for that too*, because I didn't want to watch another parent die. But he would have to go through losing me. That must have been a hard decision. To lose not only his wife, but eventually his son. That's when it hit me. My father truly had climbed out of the deep, dark hole he'd fallen into. He was living again. And I would not be the person to prevent that.

"Honestly?" I said. "I don't know how I feel about it. It's a shock. I want you to be happy. Both of you. So I'll get on board with whatever you want to do."

"As long as I don't have to see you naked again, Mom." Ember raised both eyebrows. "And in compromising positions. Can you put a sock on the door handle or something when you're going at it?"

Everyone laughed, albeit a little awkwardly. My parents had had a passionate relationship. No one had hidden that from me. And it was probably why I loved Una the way I did. With my heart, my mind, and my body, over and over again. I was thankful for that. Love, for me, had to be all-encompassing. Convenience wasn't a word that entered my vocabulary. Companionship wasn't my aim, although I sought that too, as well as friendship and compassion. But without the deep well of unconditional love, that irrevocable feeling that I'd simply cease to exist without Una's presence in my life...I wouldn't settle for less.

"That went better than I thought," Dad said.

"I told you he'd understand," Raina said, nodding at me.

"I think it's time I moved to a new suite," I said. "You guys should have privacy. And so should I." Especially considering I was planning to live with Una as soon as she turned eighteen.

"Whatever you feel is best," Dad said, sadness flitting across his features. "You're always welcome here."

"There are plenty of suites in the palace, and if I'm going to propose—"

Ember slapped my stomach, threw an astonished look at me. "You're going to propose to Una?"

"I mean...yeah...eventually. Like, not today or anything. But I'm going to marry her one day so there will have to be a proposal of some sort."

Dad beamed at me. "I'm really happy for you, son."

"A royal wedding!" Raina clapped.

I threw both my hands in the air. "I haven't bought a ring or anything. Let's not get carried away. And we have other more pressing matters to deal with first."

We all glanced at the windows, at the darkness seeping into the room, and at the glow of luminescent jellyfish dotting the ocean as far as we could see.

"Has anyone been hurt?" I asked Dad.

Dad shook his head. "Not that I know of. A few needed the fountain but they're okay now." His gaze fell to my ankles. "It looks like you were, though. What happened?"

As Raina rang for food to be brought to the suite, I filled them in on what had happened at the cabin. How we had a limited amount of time to defeat Dagonar before Atlantis fell to ruin. I didn't mention Siryn. I couldn't wrap my head around what had happened. Part of me was humiliated that she had deceived me in such a mortifying way. The other part of me didn't quite believe it had been her possessing Una's body. And let's face it, Siryn wasn't her name. Her real name was Nautalun, one of the Denizens, known for her beauty and seduction. And I had fallen for it hook, line, and sinker. I wasn't ready to admit that...yet.

CHAPTER TWELVE

*D*arkness swirled around me as I stood alone in the deserted courtyard. If I hadn't seen the ghost pirates defeated with my own eyes, I might have thought the inky sky was the perfect aesthetic for them to sail onto the island in their ship of cobwebs and dust. But we had killed them. *I* had helped kill them.

The salty tang of the ocean drifted up from the beach. Lanterns flickered on the tables, battling the shifting shadows. Their flames crackled and spat as the darkness sucked at them. Wind stirred, whisking the water in the fountain into disturbing ripples and toying with the vines hanging from the surrounding marble columns.

I limped past the statues of the original High Council. Esmeralda wore her infamous mermaid brooch at her neck, Shane held the Power of the Sea in his hands, Edward stood with a smaller version of the Power of the Sea ready to hurl at the unrepresented hound, and then there was Gal, the dragon king I had been named after and Ember's grandfather. He stood taller than the rest, his stone wings unfurled, giving the impression he was flying. I wished I had met them. Although Mom and Dad said they'd been a handful.

I came to a stop opposite the statue of my mother. It had been erected after her death. She stood in the shadow of Gal's wing as if he was shielding her. She held a fireball in her hand, wild hair caught in a moment of battle, snow dusting her head. I hoped they had found each other in the afterlife. If it existed.

I soaked in the determination on my mother's face, the fierceness of her expression, showing how hard she'd fought for those she loved. Raising the trident, I trickled a warm glow of light over her immobile figure. I put a hand on the stone fireball in her hand, its coldness leaching into my palm. My father had let go. It was time I did too. I would never forget her, but I couldn't let her keep holding me back. It was time I lived my life fully, without apology. And it was time I loved Una the way she deserved to be loved.

"I love you, Mom," I said, then turned my back on her and headed up the stone steps to the palace.

As I neared the entrance, a delicate melody surrounded me. No more than a whisper, as if the notes were being kissed by the wind. I cocked my head to listen. It reminded me of the time I'd carved the ice flute on Mýrdalsjökull glacier. The sounds curled around my heart, eased some of the tension at the back of my neck, and pulsed around the trident, which glowed in gentle throbs to match the rhythm. I heard a succession of four or five notes, and then it disappeared. Another snatch of two or three more, but I couldn't discern where the music was coming from. It was so gentle, so delicate, as if spun by a glass or hope.

Shaking my head, I reached the top of the stairs. I noted the two royal guards standing sentry outside the great hall and figured the trident would be safe for one night resting in its mantle. Finding the door ajar, I slipped inside the room to find a peaceful silence. The only light came from a smoldering fire and a few candles dotted around the room. *The Mermaid Chronicles* was back on its pillar. No doubt Una had been here to return it. Pain clenched my heart. It had only been a few hours since I'd last seen her, but I missed her so much already.

"Prince Gal."

I whirled around at the sound of a voice, stumbled back a step when my gaze fell on Nautalun.

I gasped, her beauty an uncontainable thing. At least this time she was clothed, but I knew every curve that lay beneath that silky material containing her luscious form. Her long dark hair fell in a rich cascade down the center of her back, while the cut of her dress plunged so low that the inner swells of her breasts were revealed as well as her navel. I had kissed that navel. I had licked those breasts. I had dug my fingers into her rear. And I had fucked her.

The melody reemerged, louder this time, swirling around me as a physical force. It curled over my skin, caressed my arms, plucked at the hairs on the back of my neck.

Nautalun's lips drew into a seductive smile and my gaze dropped to her mouth, at the plump redness begging for my tongue. My mouth went dry as I remembered the taste of her skin on my lips, the salty sweetness of her body.

"Nautalun," I breathed, trying to clear my head of the enchanting music.

She quirked a delicate eyebrow, seemingly impressed I'd figured it out. She smoothed her dress. A red dress made to stand out, to draw attention, to hug every single one of her forbidden curves. "You know who I am?"

I nodded. "What are you doing in here...the hall isn't open to the public...?" What was I even saying? Nautalun wasn't the public. She wasn't here for a tour. She wanted the trident. The trident I held in my hand.

As if sensing my fear, the trident pulsed, golden light pumping into the room.

Nautalun swept toward me, eating up the space between us with dangerously seductive strides, her heeled feet tapping on the marble like a countdown. "I missed you."

I laughed. "Don't be ridiculous."

She stopped only a foot from me. I backed up until my butt hit the wall. She followed, refusing to give me space, the scent of arousal hanging between us. Hers or mine, I wasn't sure. "I can help you bring light back to Atlantis."

"Why would you do that?"

Her gaze fell to the trident, drawn to its alluring glow. Her hand drifted to mine, her painted red fingernails dancing across my wrist, edging closer to the glowing shaft. The heat from her touch seared my skin, sparking a primal desire.

"I have a soft spot for handsome princes."

She might as well have dug her hand into my chest, ripped out my heart, and rubbed it over her naked flesh. Such was the power of her words.

"You won't be able to hold it," I stuttered, confused by

how thick the music was. But I wasn't entirely sure. Any Atlantean who'd been brave enough to touch the weapon intended only for me had run from the great hall screaming, diving into the fountain to heal third-degree burns. But Nautalun was a Denizen. A god. An evil god, granted, but a god, nonetheless. Perhaps she possessed the power to wield the trident too.

Sweat broke out over my skin. My throat dried out and I coughed to cover an awkward silence. A silence that was only filled with fragile notes of music. I wanted to touch them, to savor them, to surround myself with their hypnotizing sounds.

Nautalun's dark brown eyes drifted from our point of contact, swept up my chest, my neck, my jaw, my lips, and settled on my eyes. The pull of her gaze left my lips parted and I found myself growing hard. Candles flickered, doing little to dispel the darkness that shrouded us in intimate privacy.

As she circled her fingers around my wrist, she inched her thigh between my legs, pressing against the length of me. Her gown parted, revealing a slit that traveled to the highest part of her thigh, allowing me a glimpse of her smooth skin and the hidden juncture between her legs. She wasn't wearing underwear. The intensity of the music increased. I could almost taste it.

Her scent surrounded me, a swirl of musk and citrus and a touch of evil. Dangerous. Addictive. And I wanted it. The sweat dried on my skin. Blood rushed to one part of my body. My erection grew painfully hard.

"I could try." She battered her lashes. An act I didn't

think would work on me, but performed by Nautalun, I was putty in her hands. She continued drawing circles with her finger on my hand. And with her free hand, she pressed it between my legs, touching my hardness, making me inhale a sharp breath, sending of a series of pleasing chords to wrap around me.

"Don't," I warned, searching for my authority. For my will. For my loyalty. They were nowhere to be found.

"You know you want this." She looked up at me through lush lashes, her eyes framed in poetic beauty. She ran a finger along my cock, tracing the ridge, making my hips buck against her. And still music played. I couldn't figure out where it was coming from. Inside or outside, or within Nautalun herself. "I so enjoyed our night together."

"I love Una," I rasped through clenched teeth.

"Love is such a trivial word." She dropped her hand from the trident, placed it on my chest, and moved my shirt aside. Pulling at the patch of coarse hairs, delicious stabs of ecstasy pulsed through me with the tiniest of movements. Her other hand grasped my cock through my clothing. I couldn't find the words to make her stop. The music held me in place, supported my weak knees as they begged for more of her carnal touches.

"You think I'm just going to hand it to you?" My grip tightened on the trident, a grip so tight my entire arm ached.

"If you like." She dropped her hand from my painful erection and pressed her body against mine. The swell of her breasts met my chest. Her gown parted, and the apex of her legs pushed against my cock, the scent of her breaking down all my boundaries. Her breath drifted over my jaw, followed by the lightest touch of lips and tongue.

Jesus fucking Christ.

She rolled her hips against me. Just once. But it was enough to send a riot of sensations skittering down my spine and for my free arm to circle her waist, drawing her closer. I dipped my head, but couldn't bring myself to press my lips to hers. This was so wrong, I knew that. But I couldn't seem to stop myself.

Nautalun claimed my lips in a ragged kiss. All teeth and biting and nipping. Hot and rough and dangerous. Oh, so deliciously dangerous. Until she drew blood. It snapped me back to my senses and I stumbled away from her, the music finally abating.

Wiping the blood from my lip, I turned to stare at her. "This has to stop."

"You know you don't what it to." She trailed a finger around the swell of her breast, tracing her smooth skin until her finger dipped past her navel. She circled her finger around her exposed stomach, and it was all I could do not to stare. Not to drool. Not to come in my pants.

Fuck.

Her hand moved to the slit in her dress, swept aside the swatch of silky material, exposing herself to me. The scent of her sweet arousal immediately hit my nose and my hips bucked unconsciously. *Double fuck.*

She pressed a finger to her clit, swirled it into her wet folds, gently caressing. Her eyes, half lidded, wouldn't let me escape.

Give me the trident, Prince Gal.

Her voice was in my head this time. And the music was back. I couldn't think straight. Couldn't tell the difference between up and down, right and wrong, lust and love.

The trident dropped from my grasp, clattered to the floor, its golden light winking out instantaneously.

Good boy.

She stalked toward me, ignoring the trident abandoned on the floor, her eyes focused on my erection. Without asking permission, without any warning, her hand dove past the waistband of my pants and circled my dick. A swell of something extra joined her hand. The music. I couldn't see it, but I felt the notes brushing past my sensitive skin, tightening her hold on me. Squeezing...

Oh, sweet Vorago.

She dropped to her knees. Yanking my trousers down, she revealed the aching length of my erection. Before I could protest, she swallowed me with her mouth, taking me deep, taking the entire length of me until I hit the back of her throat. And all I could do was grip the back of her head and draw her closer.

I threw my head back as the ecstasy washed over me. Thoughts leached out of my brain. All I could do was feel. And it felt so damn good.

Until I winked an eye open and caught the glow of pages from *The Mermaid Chronicles*.

Una.

I lurched away from Nautalun, whipping away from her so quickly she fell back, her hands planted to break her fall.

I yanked my trousers up. "No," I roared over the sound of the mesmerizing music.

We stared at each other, our gazes a mix of desire and fury. And then she lunged for the trident.

Wrapping a hand around the shaft, she yelled out in pain, releasing it immediately. I stalked over to her, grabbed the trident from the floor, and looked at her palm as it sizzled with heat.

"You might be a Denizen, but you're not worthy of the trident." I swished it in an arc, its golden light spilling hope into the room and clearing my senses. *"And get out of my fucking head."*

Pulling herself together, Nautalun rose to her feet. Somehow, her dress fell immaculately back into place. She ran a hand through her luscious locks. "What doesn't work on you, might work on your lover." She gave me a crafty smile, then sauntered past me and left the room, taking her infernal music with her.

Una.

I took a few minutes to pull myself together, to tuck my erection back into my pants, ignoring the throb of pained arousal. I paced the room for a few more minutes, trying to organize my thoughts and still the erratic beat of my heart. When I finally had the courage to leave the great hall, I crept past the guards standing sentry, afraid they could sense my guilt. Nautalun was nowhere in sight.

I couldn't go after her now, I had to protect Una from her seductive powers.

I dashed out the back entrance of the palace, scrambled down the staircase, ran across the midnight gardens, and pulled to a stop outside Una's front door. All was quiet inside. Candles flickered in every window. I planted my hands on my thighs, catching my breath, the trident still in my hand. I wouldn't let go of it again.

Nautalun would try to seduce Una. With words, with beauty, with whatever Una might fall prey to. I had to warn her. But how would I explain? My dick was still wet from Nautalun's mouth. And here I was, expecting Una to listen to me, to love me, to forgive me.

I turned to leave, but the door swung open, and Una's father stepped into the darkness, a lantern in his hand.

He closed the door softly behind him. "She doesn't want to see you."

I frowned. "Is she okay?" I thought of the jellyfish wounds. Did she blame me for keeping her by my side on the barge? Did she blame me for the wounds she'd incurred while battling Dagonar? Did she blame me for everything? Did she decide it was too dangerous to fight by my side?

Trent raised the lantern, examined my face with parental scrutiny. "She saw you with that woman, in the great hall."

Oh. *Oh, shit.*

CHAPTER THIRTEEN

othing would ever be the same.

I had betrayed Una.

Everything I had fought for. Everything I had fought against. Gone.

The Denizens of the Deep crave the power of Vorago's trident. The one true wielder must remain strong.

I hadn't been strong in the slightest.

It was then I realized being strong wasn't just about physical strength or how much magic I could wield. It was about the strength of my will, the power of my love...the weakness of my mind.

I blinked, suddenly finding the dim light of the lantern way too bright. A heated flush crawled over my skin.

Trent stared at me, a frown marring his brow, his golden eyes searching my face for answers I wasn't sure I could give.

"I can explain," I muttered, my throat tight.

Trent gestured to the dark gardens. Shadows shifted at

the edges of my vision, spiraling tight with an unusual density. "Let's walk."

With my heart in my mouth, I followed who I hoped would be my future father-in-law deeper into the palace gardens, hoping this conversation wouldn't end in disaster. Hoping the shadows wouldn't eat us alive.

The oppressive silence between us was only broken by the subtle crunch of gravel beneath our feet. I couldn't shake the feeling that Trent already knew too much. His steps were measured, but there was a weight to them, a heaviness that made me uneasy.

Una and her family lived in a secluded part of the gardens, their house nestled against the dense woodland that bordered the palace lawns. The deeper we went, the darker it became. Even with Trent's lantern and the trident casting faint light ahead, the shadows pressed in around us. I had no idea what time it was, whether it was day or night. There was no sound, as if the darkness had stolen it. No insects rustling beneath our feet, no birds nesting in the trees above our heads, no whispering wind. Even our footsteps were muted.

We stopped at the edge of one of the water channels. The shallows glowed with the ominous light of jellyfish, their pale forms drifting beneath the surface, their tendrils swaying in slow, deliberate movements. Looking for a victim?

"We're going to have to take care of that."

"I will," I promised, gripping the trident a little tighter. "I'll get rid of them all."

Trent turned to me, his expression unreadable, studying me with a long, appraising look. "You can do that?"

I glanced at the trident. I was no longer sure where the

power came from, whether it was the weapon, me, or a combination of the two. The weapon hummed with energy, pulsing in time with my heartbeat. "I can."

His brows lifted, but he didn't question it further. Instead, he pointed to a nearby stone bench. We sat, the cold, unyielding surface pressing against my back, the night heavy around us. The lantern flickered between us, casting wavering shadows over the glowing water.

I couldn't stop thinking about Una, about what she might have seen. The thought of her witnessing even a fraction of Nautalun's actions was like the lash of a jellyfish tentacle across my heart. I wanted to rush back to her house, take her in my arms and kiss away her pain. To show her how little Nautalun meant to me, to worship her body with my devotion. But there I was, sitting with her father, my mind spinning with uncertainty.

"When we were on our journey to find Atlantis," Trent began, his voice shredding the awkward silence, "I almost slept with your mother."

I choked on my breath, nearly toppling off the bench. The trident flared with a sharp pulse of light. "Excuse me?"

Trent's lips twitched into a sheepish grin. "Yeah, I'm guessing no one ever told you that."

"Uh...that would be a *no*."

He leaned back, crossing one leg over the other, looking far too casual for the bomb he'd dropped. We watched the ebb and flow of the jellyfish for a moment. If I didn't know they were venomous, I'd think they were stunningly beautiful.

"The quest to find Atlantis got pretty hairy...in so many

ways." He shook his head as if fighting ice demons and dragon kings were fond memories. "Maya was still human, pissing everyone off with her demands to be a mermaid. *I* was pissed off. I was a selachii and she didn't want anything to do with shark tails."

"Well, she is the oracle for *The* Mermaid *Chronicles*."

Trent eyed me. "That was her point exactly. But it still hurt."

"I get that." I placed the trident on the grass and rubbed my hands along my thighs. I wasn't sure where this conversation was going, but I wished it would get there faster so I could explain things to Una.

"Your mom and dad, they were fighting back then."

I frowned. "They never fought."

Trent smiled. "They did. In the beginning. There was so much against them—neither knew who to trust."

"But they trusted each other."

"Eventually. But they had to go through some rocky periods to get there."

I bounced a knee impatiently. "So...?"

"So," Trent continued, "I was pissed at Maya. Your mom was pissed at your dad. And then his parents started throwing Stephanie in his face—"

"The sea witch?"

"The very one." Trent's face darkened. "Your dad caved. He kissed her. And your mom saw everything."

"Oh...*shit*."

"Indeed." Trent placed a hand on my knee to stop its relentless bouncing. "I was mad at Maya, your uncle was threatening to turn her into a mermaid because he had a crush on her, and your dad was screwing things up with Stephanie." He shook his head, lost to memories for a moment. "Anyway, I went to your mom's house, found her drowning her sorrows in a bottle of tequila. Thought I'd join her. One thing led to another—"

I winced, already seeing where this was going. "And you slept with her?"

"*Almost.*" Trent corrected. "There's a huge difference. We kissed. There may have been some touching—"

"I don't need details."

Trent chuckled. "My point is, I married Maya. Your mom married your dad. It all worked out in the end, in spite of the mistakes we made."

"So, you think Una will forgive me?" I asked, hope clawing at my chest. There wasn't an alternative. I simply couldn't do this without her.

"I'm not going to speak for my daughter," Trent said, his tone softening. "But what I am saying is that these things take time. Give her space. Let her process."

Trent's words hung in the air, thick and suffocating, like the shadows that clung to us. I attempted to absorb his words, but the urgency in my chest didn't wane. Space? Time? How could I do that when every second apart from Una felt like drowning? "You don't understand. We don't have time for space. That woman, Nautalun...she's a Denizen."

Trent stiffened beside me. His golden eyes darkened, hardening into stone. "The Denizen of seduction?"

"Yes." I swallowed, the memory of Nautalun's twisted beauty searing into my mind. "I would never cheat on Una. Not willingly. But Nautalun got inside my head, made me think I wanted her...it..." My voice cracked as the guilt of my recent endeavors swarmed through me. I could still feel the invasive tendrils of Nautalun's power wrapping around my mind, choking my reason. I shuddered. "And if Una saw that...I don't blame her for being hurt, pissed off...furious..."

"She wants to skin you alive."

I winced. "It was out of my control. Nautalun brainwashed me. And now she's after Una."

Trent spun to face me, his expression sharp. "What do you mean, *after Una?*"

"Her seduction will work on anyone. When it failed on me—and it did fail, you can tell Una that—she said she'd go after Una."

"Una's not...gay, or bisexual...that I know of."

"She's not, but it won't matter," I said. "Nautalun's power transcends that. Her beauty, her manipulation—it's all-consuming. No one's safe from it. Not Una. Not anyone. So I'd really like to see Una and explain all this to her."

Trent's hand gripped my shoulder, his expression softening a fraction. "I know you want to see her. To explain. And you deserve to. But give her tonight, Gal. Just tonight."

My stomach twisted. It felt as though the world was closing in, the dark, venomous shadows of Dagonar's curse suffocating me. If I could talk to Una I would make her understand. But then I put myself in her shoes, tried to imagine what she'd witnessed through the windows of the great hall. The way I must have appeared completely enraptured by Nautalun. Her beauty was overwhelming, would make any female insecure, and any male feel as though it was his lucky night. Hell, lucky year. If she saw Nautalun's mouth around my dick...*Fuck.*

The thought of leaving Una alone with Nautalun out there—hunting her—it was unbearable. I looked at the sky, the shadows creeping around us, the pulsing jellyfish. "You don't understand," I whispered, my voice hoarse. "There's no time. There are two Denizens here that we know of. Una and I need to be united now. If we're divided...we'll both be vulnerable."

Trent stood and picked up his lantern. "I understand. But I'm asserting my fatherly right. Give her the night. I'll explain to her when I get back. But give her the night."

I had no choice. Trent would not let me into the Summers' family home until tomorrow. And I wasn't going to beg. I could always creep through her window later.

Feigning acquiescence, I extended my hand. "I'm sorry."

Trent took my hand, his grip firm. "I know you are."

"*The Denizens of the Deep crave the power of Vorago's trident. The one true wielder must remain strong,*" I quoted the prophecy to him. "I need Una to do that. Like my parents needed each other. The way you and Maya need each other."

Trent's sigh sank into the night, as heavy as the shadows that cloaked us. "Unity is the key to all the prophecies. Una is aware of that. But she has to feel united in her heart. And to do that, she needs time."

The words dug into me. There was no fighting against them, no sharp retort that could break the truth of what he said. Defeat slithered through me, and so I accepted Trent's wishes, wishing Una's eighteenth birthday would hurry the fuck up so I could move her in with me and I wouldn't have to deal with parents presenting obstacles. I mean, I loved Trent and Maya, they were great people, they had made Una after all, but my relationship with their daughter didn't concern them and I wanted her all to myself. Needed. Craved. Yearned. Longed for. How many words were there to express the depth of my love? And yet, none of them were enough.

Grabbing the trident, I trudged away from Trent and made my way through the gardens without falling into a water channel and enduring a litany of new stings. As I approached the courtyard, the familiar warmth of Uncle Dylan's bar beckoned. If anyone could make sense of the clutter in my head, it was him.

I used the trident like a lantern to guide my way through the haphazard clusters of deserted chairs and tables dotted around the courtyard. It seemed most people had taken to their homes to sit out the darkness and wait for me to do my thing. *No pressure.*

A soft sound caught my attention as I followed the meandering path through the marble columns—a rustle, followed by a muffled gasp. I paused, the trident raised as if it could ward off whatever lurked in the shadows. I scanned the area, my eyes catching on something...a foot. A bare foot sticking out of a bush. My pulse quickened, the worst possibilities flashing through my mind. Had someone been stung? Attacked? Was there a body tangled in the greenery, lifeless and pale?

But then the foot moved. A gasp—a very different kind of gasp—emerged from the bush. Another foot appeared, followed by a third halfway up a column. The realization hit me like a slap. Two people were going at it...in the middle of the courtyard.

I smothered a laugh as I tiptoed away, almost wishing it was someone I knew so I could grill them about it later. But then, barely ten steps away, I stumbled upon another couple. This time, it was the baker, but the woman he had bent against the column wasn't his wife.

What the...?

I picked up my pace, the air growing thick with the unmistakable sounds of pleasure, and not just from one corner. I rushed toward Uncle D's bar, veering past three more couples in various stages of undress and ecstasy, before I hurled myself inside and slammed the door shut behind me.

The scene inside was even worse. The low hum of seductive music filled the room, vibrating in my bones and sending a wave of unwanted heat coursing through me. I recognized the sound instantly—Nautalun's melody. The notes were delicate, haunting, and powerful, a siren's call to every base instinct.

A quick scan of the bar revealed she was not present, but she must have been here recently.

Couples were tangled in each other's arms in every corner. Not only couples, but groups—threes, fours, all touching, kissing, moaning. My uncle's bar had become a den of lust. There was even a half-naked couple sprawled across the seawolf rug in front of the cold hearth, their bodies entwined like vines. I averted my eyes as I stepped over them.

But the worst of it? My uncle. Uncle Dylan stood behind the bar, his hands all over my Aunt Marina, in places no hands should be in public. The sight was enough to make me want to bleach my eyes.

I charged forward, slapping him on the back hard enough to jolt him out of his daze. "What the hell?"

He blinked, shaking his head as if he were waking from a dream. "What the fuck?" he muttered, looking around as if seeing the scene for the first time. His mouth fell open in shock as his gaze swept the bar, finally taking in the debauchery unfolding around him.

Aunt Marina, flushed and disheveled, tried to pull him back into her arms, whispering something into his ear that I really didn't want to hear. He hesitated, his eyes glazing over again as he leaned toward her.

I shoved him. "Focus! Was Nautalun here?"

"Who?" He looked confused, his eyes still clouded with whatever spell she had cast.

"Oh so high." I indicated her willowy stature with a hand to my forehead. "Beautiful, long dark hair, you'd give up your worldly possessions for just one fuck."

"Yeah, there was someone like that here. Sang us all a beautiful song."

"She's a Denizen, Uncle D. A dark god of seduction. Her music is her power, or sounds when she uses it...hell, I don't know how it works. But there are people out there—" I pointed toward the front door. "—doing things with people they should not be doing things with."

Uncle Dylan's eyes widened as Aunt Marina's fingers slipped back under his shirt, her touch slow and deliberate. His face flushed deeper, like he was fighting against his own body, but it was clear Nautalun's spell still had its grip on him. Aunt Marina leaned closer, nibbling on his ear, and whispered a sentiment that made me blush.

Uncle Dylan kissed her. I cleared my throat to regain his attention. But he completely ignored me and kissed my aunt like it was their wedding night.

I slammed my palm on the bar, rattling the glasses. "Uncle D!" His head snapped toward me, his pupils blown wide, still lost in the haze.

"Can you make it stop?" he asked.

"I don't know." We couldn't have an island of sex-craved inhabitants getting themselves off with whichever person happened to walk by next. If Una...the breath left my lungs so quickly I thought I'd been punched. Picturing Una with another person...no...I couldn't bear it. It made my vision blur with rage.

I glanced at the trident. Many of its abilities had been documented in *The Mermaid Chronicles*, but there was so much about the ancient weapon that remained undiscovered. The island was drowning in lust, in desire twisted by dark magic.

"Be good to me," I whispered to the trident, then gently swirled it in the air. Golden sparks of warm light spiraled into the bar, following meandering paths to booths and tables, touching people lightly on their skin, casting hopeful glows. The golden embers twirled into the hearth and up the chimney.

Slowly, the room shifted. People blinked, dazed, their movements slowing. Shirts were tugged back into place, embarrassed glances passed between lovers and strangers alike. Faces flushed with realization as the spell's grip weakened.

The door burst open.

Ember staggered inside, his wings dragging behind him. His trousers were hanging low on his hips, and his cheeks burned with a crimson that rivaled the setting sun. "Don't ask," he muttered, heading straight for the bar.

I snorted, despite everything. "Rough night?"

Ember collapsed onto the stool beside me, wiping a hand over his face. "You have no idea." He shot a glance at Uncle Dylan, who was hastily buttoning his shirt.

"I'll have a beer," Ember said to Uncle Dylan. "Biggest one you've got."

Uncle Dylan, still dazed, poured beers for everyone without a word. His hands shook as he slid them across the bar, his eyes flicking nervously toward Aunt Marina, who, despite her disheveled appearance, still hadn't fully shaken the spell's lingering touch. She was watching him with hungry eyes, her hand twitching toward him again before she pulled back, shaking her head as if trying to clear the fog.

"You okay, buddy?" I said to Ember as he took a long pull of his beer.

Ember pulled at the collar of his shirt. "Let's just say I found myself in a situation I never want to be in again."

Aunt Marina rubbed her forehead. "Tell me about it. Not that hanging out with your uncle isn't fun...but not in the middle of the bar for everyone to see—"

I raised a hand. "I get it."

"What are we going to do about it?" Uncle D asked.

I rested the trident against the bar. "I'm hoping it's been

taken care of for a while. But Nautalun is lurking on the island, using her song and seduction on everyone. Me too."

Ember grasped my shoulder. "I can't imagine too much harm was done if you and Una—"

"It wasn't Una," I said flatly. "It was with Nautalun herself."

Uncle Dylan raised both brows.

Ember's hand gripped my shoulder, his eyes softening. "But you resisted, right?"

I clenched my jaw, the memory of Nautalun's hands on me, her voice in my head, tightening like a vice. "Not entirely." My voice cracked. "I didn't sleep with her, but...it was close. Too close. And Una saw."

I dropped my head into my hands. I should have been stronger. I should have resisted. I was the trident-wielder. I was the only one strong enough to defeat the Denizens and at the first sign of trouble I had my dick wrapped in Nautalun's mouth.

Aunt Marina touched my hand. "She'll understand."

I laughed, a bitter sound that felt hollow. "If Una had been with someone else...I don't know how I'd get past that. So why should she?"

Uncle Dylan frowned, his brow furrowed with concern. "Because this wasn't your fault. You were under Nautalun's spell."

I shook my head. "I should've been stronger. I'm the trident-wielder. The prophecy says I'm supposed to be strong. But I failed. At the first sign of trouble, I let her get to me."

Ember leaned back, staring into his drink. "Man, you're human. You're not invincible."

"But I'm supposed to be." My voice broke, frustration boiling under my skin. "This is bigger than me, bigger than all of us. The Denizens want the trident, and I'm the only one who can stop them. But I need Una by my side for that. And now..."

"Don't be so hard on yourself," Uncle Dylan said. "People make mistakes. Forgive and move on."

"You make it sound so easy." But he had a point. The sentiment echoed Trent's words. He'd almost slept with my mom and Maya had forgiven him. Mom had looked past Dad's cheating with Stephanie. But it took time. And time we didn't have.

CHAPTER FOURTEEN

There was nothing I could do about the glow of the trident spilling into the back windows of the Summers' house as I threw pebbles at Una's window, but I had to hope she'd wake up and let me in before anyone noticed.

As I bent to gather more stones, the window swung open and I was met by Una's furious face. The hard expressions crossing her features were new to me and filled my chest with ice.

I straightened, jostling my weight from foot to foot, suddenly wondering if this was a good idea. I could hear the distant sound of waves crashing on the beach, the night air sharp with the tang of salt, but all I could focus on was the coldness radiating from her. "I'm sorry?"

Why did it sound so weak and pathetic?

"You're sorry for hooking up with another woman and allowing her to give you a blow job? Are you going to tell me your dick happened to fall into her mouth?" She hung out the window, her face as stormy as thunder clouds.

"Didn't your dad explain?"

"What's my dad got to do with this?"

"He knows why—"

"I fell asleep." As if to confirm her point, she rubbed her eye and yanked her blonde hair over her scarred eye socket.

"Can I come in?"

"No."

"It's dark out here."

She laughed. "You have the trident."

I took a breath. I wasn't getting anywhere. I hadn't even practiced a speech. "The woman you saw was Nautalun. You know one of her powers is seduction."

Una's frown deepened. "I thought you were stronger than that." Her voice—so small and broken—made something inside me crack wide open. I had faced Zale, tamed seawolves, wielded the trident in battle, but standing here now, looking up at her, I had never felt so powerless.

"We're talking about dark magic, Una. From one of the most powerful gods in our world. Everyone on the island has been going at it in bushes..." I splayed a hand as if she might be able to pick out grinding couples in the shadows, but I'd put an end to that with the trident, and when I cocked my head, there was no sound of Nautalun's seductive melody. "I didn't *let* her. I didn't *want* her. It was the magic—dark, twisted magic—and I fought it as soon as I could. But she got inside my head."

Unshed tears glistened in Una's eye. "I thought our *love*

was stronger than that." Her voice was quiet and croaky, revealing that she had been crying.

My shoulders sagged and I almost dropped the trident. Laying it on the ground, I rested my hands on my hips, searching for the words that would bring her back to me.

I stared up at her, my mind scrambling for something—anything—that would make her trust me again, but all I could feel was the cold weight of her disappointment pressing against my chest. It wasn't my fault. But it wasn't *not* my fault. I had managed to turn Nautalun away. Why didn't I do it sooner?

The silence between us stretched, thick and uncomfortable, only broken by the sound of the stones clinking together when I toed the path. I could hear Una breathing, shallow and uneven, as she wiped at her eye again, refusing to look at me.

"Una..." I swallowed, my throat tight. "Our love *is* strong—".

She scoffed, but it wasn't sharp. It was tired, defeated. "Doesn't feel like it," she whispered. "I saw you. I saw your eyes roll back into your head. I saw the look of pure bliss on your face. You didn't even fight it. You let her..." Her voice broke, and she turned her head away, staring into the darkness beyond the yard, her hand gripping the window frame like it was the only thing keeping her grounded.

"I *didn't* let her. I stopped her." My words came out harsher than I intended, but I was desperate. Desperate for her to understand. I stepped closer, my hand brushing the cold stone wall of the house, the rough texture grounding me. "I stopped her, Una, because I love you."

I gnawed on the inside of my cheek as I waited for her to say something.

"You've only ever been with me."

"I know."

Her eye flashed with anger, a tear slipping down her cheek despite her attempts to hold it back. "Maybe a part of you *wanted* it. Maybe you wanted something...different. Someone more beautiful—and god dammit, she is beautiful— or someone with two eyes."

"Una," I gasped her name, startled at the suggestion. Although I still carried guilt over the way Una had lost her eye, I'd never once thought it diminished her beauty. She was different to Nautalun, all blonde, wild curls, hard angles and compact muscles, but she was still fucking beautiful. The thought of wanting anyone else—especially Nautalun—made me sick to my core. But Una's words hit deeper than mere accusation. They dug into the cracks of her own insecurities, ones I hadn't realized were there. I laid a hand over my heart. "You know that's not true. You were the one who unlocked my heart. You were the one who made me feel. It's always been you. You know that, Una, despite what you saw. You *know* that."

Una's gaze snapped back to me, warring emotions fighting in her beautiful blue eye. "That's the problem, Gal. I thought I knew who you were. I thought we were...I don't know..." Her voice wavered. "Stronger. Clearly, I'm not enough. Clearly our love isn't strong enough. Or not enough to make you fight harder. To make you stop her."

"I *did* stop her," I choked out, my heart pounding in my chest. "Didn't you hear me? I stopped her because of you,

Una. Because even under her spell, even when everything in me was screaming to give in, I thought of you. I thought of us. And I fought. I swear I fought."

She shook her head, but I could see the crack in her armor, the way her shoulders sagged, the way her breath caught.

"I *am* stronger," I said, the words coming out rough. "Not because of magic or power or any of that." I stared at her with everything I had. "Because of you. *You* make me stronger, Una. You're my reason. Every day, I fight for this, for us, for what we have. I never wanted to hurt you. And I swear to you, I will never let something like this happen again."

"Don't make promises you can't keep." She fell quiet, her face unreadable in the low light of the trident, which cast long shadows across her features. Her silence gnawed at me, pulling me apart piece by piece.

"I love you," I said, my voice cracking, the vulnerability raw in the space between us. I reached out, my hand hovering just below her window, aching to touch her, to bridge the gap between us. "I love you in a way that makes me terrified because the thought of losing you, of not having you in my life, is like losing everything. You are *everything*, Una." Both hands were holding my heart now. I thought it might break. Or shatter. Or simply melt away.

Tears spilled over her cheek. Her lips pressed into a tight line as she blinked them away. She glanced at the trident lying on the ground, then back at me, her expression softening, but still clouded with hurt.

"I don't know how to trust you again," she whispered, and

the words were like knives, sharp and precise. "I know it's not your fault. I do. I know how evil Nautalun is. But it...*hurts*."

"It hurts me too." When I'd imagined Una with someone else...and knowing Nautalun was planning on playing some cat and mouse games with the woman I loved...anger burned through my pain. "She will stop at nothing to tear this island apart. And that starts with you and me. She's driving a wedge between us. And it's working. Don't let her, Una. Don't let her come between us."

"But what if it happens again?" She pushed her tousled hair away from her face. "I can't face seeing you like that again..."

"I can't guarantee Nautalun won't try, and I can't guarantee I won't succumb, or you won't succumb, but we're going to come out the other side of it. And to do that, we have to stick together."

Her gaze met mine, searching, conflicted. "I do love you, Gal." She blinked, more tears slipping down her face, and for a brief moment, I thought I saw a glimmer of the girl I had fallen in love with—the girl who had smiled at me with a brightness that rivaled the sun, the girl who had fought by my side, who had believed in us enough for the both of us.

"I know."

Her gaze hardened again, and she stepped back from the window, her hands shaking as they gripped the frame. "I don't think I realized how much until now. Because it hurts. It really hurts. It tore me apart. I'm not even sure where my heart is right now or how to put it back in my chest. I think I need to protect it until this is all over."

I stood there, the trident dull at my feet, the night closing in around me, and all I could feel was the ache of losing her inch by inch.

"Una, wait—"

She raised a hand. "I know we need to be united. I know it's going to take everyone on this island to defeat the Denizens. I know you need me. But please give me tonight."

I hung my head. How could I refuse her that one small request? The heat of emotions built behind my eyes, but I wouldn't give into it, not until Nautalun was dead.

"Okay," I said, raising my gaze to take her in once more. "Okay."

For a moment, I thought Una might say something, but she pulled back from the window, the distance between us turning into an insurmountable chasm. For the first time, it felt like no amount of magic in the world could fix what I had broken.

"Goodnight, Gal," she whispered, and the window creaked as she closed it, the soft click of the latch mirroring the emptiness in my heart.

When Una pulled the curtains closed, I snatched the trident from the ground and stormed away from her house. This was why I had never wanted to be in a relationship. Why I had never wanted to fall in love. All the heartache that went with it just wasn't worth it. If Una and I had never gotten together...

...I would never have known the blessing of true love. As painful as it was now, I couldn't turn my back on it, couldn't ignore it, couldn't pretend I would have been better off without her. That was the old Gal. The new Gal would shoulder his responsibilities as well as his mistakes. At least, that was what I was going to try to do.

Following one of the narrow water channels back to the palace, I watched the jellyfish float on the currents, their tentacles pulsing in rhythmic movements. I may not be able to heal Una's heart, but I could take care of the jellyfish.

Skirting around the palace, I walked through the courtyard and headed to the beach where the water channels spilled into the ocean. I stood on the sand gaping at the rolling, luminescent waves. Jellyfish filled the ocean as far as I could see, surrounding the entire island. There was no way I could rid Atlantis of them all.

I looked at the trident. It gave me a wink of light, as if encouraging me to try. I had nothing to lose—not with the venomous creatures blocking every channel of Atlantis. So, with a deep breath, I turned my back on the ocean, gripping the trident tighter, the grooves of its handle press reassuringly into my skin.

I focused on one of the narrower channels, the stagnant water thick with the mass of jellyfish. Their transparent bodies floated lazily, but I knew better than to underestimate them. They were deadly, their venom capable of paralyzing people and creating severe reactions. Una and I had been lucky. With every ounce of energy I had left, I raised the trident high above my head, muscles screaming in protest as I swung it forward, directing the prongs toward the water.

A sharp jolt of power shot through me, and the trident hummed with energy. The jellyfish reacted immediately. Each one began to glow, not the usual soft bioluminescent light, but a deep, angry crimson, as if they were seething with fury for disturbing their sinister mission. The sight sent a chill down my spine. Did jellyfish even have brains? I wasn't sure, but right now, they seemed more alive—more aware—than ever. The glow intensified, their bodies pulsing like throbbing veins, staining the water in a sickening red hue.

My arms trembled as I swung the trident again, sweat beading on my brow and sliding down my face. The jellyfish darkened further, their glow fading to the color of blood, plunging the channels into an eerie darkness.

With a third, exhausted sweep, the jellyfish finally began to move. Slowly at first, their gelatinous bodies reluctantly shifted toward the open ocean. I gritted my teeth, pushing harder, forcing the creatures into the waves. My entire body ached, the strain of holding the trident and controlling its magic like dragging boulders through sand. But I couldn't stop. I wouldn't.

The tide carried them away, their dark forms blending into the ocean, but it wasn't enough. More jellyfish clogged the tributaries, their numbers depressingly endless. My muscles screamed for relief, but I kept going, whipping the trident through the air with every ounce of strength I possessed. Power vibrated up my arms, through my shoulders, but it took everything in me to stay upright.

Again and again, I pulled the venomous creatures from the channels, sending them into the waves, watching as the tide dragged them out to sea. Time lost all meaning. My hands were numb from gripping the trident, fingers cramping from the strain.

Finally, after what felt like an eternity, the last of the jellyfish spilled into the ocean. I collapsed to my knees in the sand, the trident slipping from my grip and landing with a dull thud beside me. My whole body shook with fatigue, my muscles twitching uncontrollably. The waves lapped at the shore, a soft, rhythmic sound, lulling me to sleep. I closed my eyes and let darkness and the shadows have their way with me.

a piercing shriek yanked me from sleep.

I opened my eyes. Nothing but darkness surrounded me. I blinked, trying to clear my vision. More screams ripped through the night. Or was it day? The events of the past few days slammed back into my awareness. Dagonar. The jellyfish. Nautalun. Una. *Una*. My chest clenched.

I pushed myself into a sitting position, realized I'd fallen asleep on the beach. Panicking, I felt for the trident, found it half buried in the sand. As soon as my hand connected with the hilt, its warm glow spooled across the beach.

And that's when I saw them. The jellyfish. Dotted all over the beach. Scattered like landmines along the shore. Barely a speck of sand was visible. All the jellyfish I'd moved away last night had found their way back with the incoming tide. The beach was covered. The water channels were filled. All the good I had done...evaporated.

Another scream. Agonized. Pained. *Hurt.*

I leaped to my feet, performed an accidental jig as I narrowly avoided stepping on a crimson jellyfish, its tentacles stretching in all directions.

Holding the trident above my head, I scoped the beach for a path free of the toxic creatures.

The scream cut off. I caught the sound of rasping breath.

I spun in a circle, looking for the person responsible for the scream. There, on the edge of the path only thirty yards away, a figure lay crumpled among a horde of jellyfish. A teenager, her arms wrapped around her waist, gasping for breath.

"I'm coming!" I called.

As far as I could see in the darkness, it was just the two of us on the beach. The trident guided me, cutting into the inky blackness for ten feet or so. I picked my way over to her, fighting the urge to run. I'd already incurred countless stings and didn't want to test my body's limits to how many more it could take.

By the time I made it to the girl, she was unconscious.

My knowledge of CPR was extremely limited. Only Ember, Una and I ever needed aid of the doctor or hospital. The fountain worked for everyone else. There was nothing I could do for her here, but it would take precious minutes to carry her to the fountain while avoiding the jellyfish littering the path. Just how far had the tide come in last night? The jellyfish had made it further up the beach and pathways than the tide ever did, which made me think they possessed some sort of dark power. Well, of course they did, Dagonar had put them here.

Shutting down the frantic swirl of thoughts in my head, I crouched and scooped the girl into my arms, draping her limp body over my shoulder and balancing the trident in my other hand. Her breath was shallow, and her skin pale beneath the angry red sting marks that crawled up her leg. I felt her labored breathing against my neck, each rasp sending a jolt of urgency through me.

I hurried around the venomous jellyfish. My pulse quickened as I stumbled in the darkness, the air heavy with the stench of saltwater and fear. A searing pain shot up my foot when I stepped on a tentacle, the venom prickling through my unbandaged skin. I hissed through clenched teeth, biting back a string of curse words, but I couldn't afford to stop. The girl needed help.

The trident cast a faint light on the bodies of more jellyfish, their opaque forms blending into the darkness. Their new color made them invisible, hidden traps in the sand. My stomach twisted with guilt—this was my doing. I'd made the situation worse without realizing it.

Finally, the fountain came into view. A throng of people crowded around it, their faces tense and their voices sharp as they fought for space to dip their hands into the water. Some stood knee-deep in the shallows, cupping the healing liquid to their lips or pouring it over sting wounds. As soon as they caught sight of the trident, the chatter stopped, and a wave of hostility rolled toward me.

They glared at me, their eyes narrowed, full of accusation and anger. I didn't need to hear their words to understand what they were thinking. I had turned the jellyfish opaque. I had made them invisible in the darkness. And now, more people had been stung, more people needed the fountain. Even as I looked over my shoulder, several more clumps of people were making their way here.

Ignoring the venomous glares, I pushed through the crowd. Murmurs rippled through them stronger than a tide, their muttered curses stinging like the jellyfish in the sand. I laid the girl on the cool stone rim of the fountain, her limp body barely stirring.

"Excuse me," I muttered. It took everything in me not to shrink under the weight of their stares.

Feeling like I should ask for permission, but ignoring all the withering looks, I poured healing water between the girl's parted lips. She coughed, then her eyes fluttered. Someone helped her to sit up.

I exhaled sharply, the relief I felt a transient thing. The tension in the air was almost thicker than the surrounding darkness. The murmurs grew louder, and the crowd closed in. My father had always taught me it was best to admit my mistakes, to get out in front of it before emotion got the better of everyone.

But I had to wonder, if Una and I were more united, would the jellyfish have come back, or would I have been able to banish them forever?

"I'm sorry," I said. "I'm sorry for your pain. I too have been stung. Several times. And as you know, the fountain doesn't heal me."

"Flint died when he fell into a channel last night," someone said.

Flint had a reputation for drinking and falling into water channels. And yet, my stomach knotted with guilt.

"How are we supposed to protect ourselves if we can't even see them?" another voice added, their words laced with anger.

The trident came with an enormous amount of responsibility. I hadn't figured out all its powers. People expected me to keep them safe. They also expected me to know how to use it and not make any mistakes. That wasn't fair. But that was the price of being prince. To be the person they loved when things were going well, and to be the person they could blame when it all went wrong.

"This is a time of war," I said. "You all know the Denizens are launching their attacks. And war time mandates that you all carry a flask of fountain water."

A gentle touch landed on my shoulder. I turned to see my father standing behind me.

"My son is right." Dad addressed the growing crowd, standing tall, his unrivaled strength on display. "Our lives in the human world never ran smooth, and there is no difference here. We are lucky to have the fountain, to not be afflicted with common colds or terminal illnesses. That is a luxury no one left on the mainland can claim."

Hushed murmurs of agreement swept through the crowd.

"When Cordelia and I started our journey to find Atlantis, we didn't have the fountain. We faced ice demons, persecution, unfathomable depths, the death of parents...we almost died, for you. My son is doing his best...*for you*."

Heat sprung to my eyes. I'd never heard my father speak

so openly, so emotionally, and it stirred an uncontainable passion inside my chest.

Dad's grip on my shoulder tightened. "I have every faith that Gal will master all the powers of the trident. He is his mother's son, after all. And he *will* make mistakes. That is the human side of us. But so far, I have not seen him make a single one."

I whipped around to look at my father to find his eyes glistening. He pulled me into a tight hug, his strong arms anchoring me. "I believe in you," he whispered in my ear. "And I've got your back."

I leaked a couple tears onto his shoulder, swiped at my eyes. Behind me, the crowd cheered, then called apologies and offers of help.

I turned to face my people. "God knows I'm not perfect—"

"We left God behind, it's Vorago now," someone called.

The crowd chuckled.

I raised the trident above my head. "Vorago knows I'm not perfect." I waited for the laughter to subside. "But I love my island and I love my people. And I will lay down my life for yours. I will do what I can to protect you. But I also need your help. Please, stay inside, keep the fountain water with you at all times, and don't do anything...that I would do."

Another chuckle was followed by a loud, resounding roar. People pumped their arms into the darkness. I swirled the trident over my head and its glow touched everyone, lighting their passionate faces, skimming over the tops of their heads, and pooling into the courtyard.

Dad gripped my shoulder again, gave it a reassuring squeeze. "You've got this."

I looked at him. "*We've* got this."

Dad hadn't been with me during my mission to take down Zale. At that time, we'd not had much of a relationship. Now, with him standing by my side, I knew I could do this.

Before I could disentangle myself from Dad, the sound of wings swept overhead. I glanced up to see Ember coming into land at speed, his feet skidding across cobbles as he screeched to a halt. The soles of his boots smoked, sending an acrid scent into the air to mix with the salt.

"Gal?" he called, glancing frantically over his shoulder. "Gal?!"

"Here!" I pushed through the crowd to him, elbowing people out of the way. "What's wrong?"

His gaze collided with mine. He didn't need to say anything. Una. Una was in danger.

"Grab onto my wings," Ember said.

I shook my head. "You won't be able to carry me." I glanced at the trident. It had been granting me more power every day. If there was ever a time...

I squeezed my eyes shut, thought of Una, and before I could take a breath, I was launched over the roof of the palace. Holding onto the trident for dear life, I flew through the sky. Flecks of fire hung where the stars should have been. But I didn't have time to contemplate that now. Una was in danger.

The trident guided me to the palace gardens, and before I landed, thick swirls of musical notes surrounded me. The rhythm pulsed through my body, penetrated my mind, whispered temptations until I grew aroused.

Gritting my teeth, I landed on the ground just as Ember appeared in the sky. I would not allow Nautalun to gain control over me again. My dick might get hard, but that was as far as it would go.

I spun in a circle, holding the trident aloft to light my view. My pulse hammered in my ears as I scanned the trees, desperate for any sign of Una. Then I saw them—Nautalun, her form clad in her figure-hugging red dress, and Una, standing rigid at the tree line, almost indistinguishable from the inky blackness that threatened to swallow them both.

Nautalun's eyes met mine, her lips curving into a seductive smile that slithered over my skin, heating the blood in my veins. A shiver of something dangerously close to lust crawled into the pit of my stomach. The throbbing ache between my legs intensified with every sultry glance she threw my way, my body betraying me in ways I couldn't control. I gritted my teeth, determined to fight it, even as the music rose and temptation grew.

I marched toward them, swinging the trident, willing its power to give me strength.

Musical notes swirled around my ankles, whispered in my ears, tugged at my hair with promises too sweet to ignore. The notes were intoxicating, each one vibrating through me, trying to unravel my resolve. My muscles tensed, resisting the pull, but the heat of desire was there, simmering beneath the surface.

Focus. I screamed at myself. I couldn't afford to get lost in the melody.

My heart skittered when I took in the blood smeared across Una's face, her split cheek reopened. Fury burned through my chest, momentarily eclipsing the lust Nautalun stirred in me. Sprinting the last few feet, I didn't hesitate. I grabbed a fistful of Nautalun's dark, lush hair, yanking her away from Una. She gasped, her body crashing into mine, her scent wrapping around me, all spice and heat, igniting a dangerous fire in my core.

Her music surged louder, pressing against my mind, soft and sensual, the notes trickling over my skin like a lover's touch. My breath hitched as the desire flared again, the line between rage and lust blurring. The weight of Nautalun's body against mine, her scent, her heat—it was almost too much. My grip on her hair tightened, but not in anger, not entirely.

The trident flickered in my hand, reminding me of who I was, what I was fighting for. I forced the haze from my mind and shook off her hypnotic influence.

I glanced at Una. She was panting, her fists raised, her hair falling over her eye. Sweat coated her body and blood dripped from the wound on her cheek. Ice and fire washed over me.

"I get it now," Una said, affording me a quick glance. "She got in my head too."

"We don't have to talk about this now," I said, struggling to keep my focus on the dark goddess tangled in my grip.

Nautalun's hands moved with a languid grace, trailing up my arm, her fingers cool against my hot skin. She toyed with my wrist, the one still buried in her hair, and purred, her voice a soft, sultry croon. "Now, now, Prince Gal," she teased, her lips brushing my ear as she leaned in. "That's not very nice? Unless you'd rather wrap my hair around your throbbing cock instead?"

Fire rushed through me, unbidden and fierce. For a heartbeat, the thought of doing exactly that flashed through my mind, my body aching for release. Her words struck deep, teasing the desire I was trying to crush. But I yanked her hair again, harder this time, tilting her head back so her throat was exposed to me. My jaw clenched as I leaned closer, my voice low and harsh. "As I made it abundantly clear last time, my cock only throbs for one person."

Nautalun pouted, her lips curving into a cruel smile, as though my resistance only excited her more. Her music shifted, growing louder, digging into my skin, attempting to find a way past my mental barriers. The trident wavered in my hand. Each note was a caress, each beat a promise of pleasure that gnawed at my resolve. My legs trembled, muscles taut as I fought the growing urge to let go, to fall into her embrace.

Ember dropped out of the air and skidded to a halt beside us, narrowed his eyes at Nautalun. "I'm rather insulted she hasn't tried anything on me yet."

Nautalun's gaze slid over him, her eyes widening with amusement. "Didn't you have fun with your friend last night?"

Ember turned crimson.

Before he could respond, Nautalun extended a long, lithe leg, slipping it through the parting of her dress. "Or perhaps you're waiting for someone with a little more...experience?" She flashed a predatory smile.

"Sorry, I'm allergic to desperate," Ember growled.

Undeterred, Nautalun slid her hand down my wrist, her fingers slimming over my skin, leaving a trail of fire in their wake. She coasted down my side, her touch a soft, seductive whisper, until she found the bulge pressing between us. I hissed as her fingers grazed the sensitive skin through the fabric.

"Get your hands off him," Una yelled, swinging a fist.

I pulled Nautalun to one side, released my grip on her hair, and raised the trident.

Music battled my aim, pushed the trident to the side, swirled around my sensitive skin, lighting small fires of ecstasy.

The intoxicating music whirling around me was almost unbearable. My body betrayed me, pulsing with want despite the fury burning in my chest. Each note of her song slithered deeper into my mind, coiling around my willpower, making every movement feel sluggish, like wading through a bog. The trident wavered, struggling to obey my command, the magic in it tangled with the seductive pull of Nautalun's influence.

"Fight it," I muttered to myself through gritted teeth.

Una lunged at Nautalun, but the dark goddess side-stepped her with a graceful flick of her wrist, sending a gust of wind that knocked Una off her feet. The wind struck Una like a physical blow, knocking her back into a nearby tree with a grunt. She winced and gripped her head as she scrambled to get back to her feet. The air howled, whipping through the trees, carrying the notes of Nautalun's haunting song along with it. The wind coiled around me like a snake, tugging at my clothes, pushing me toward her, pulling me deeper into her thrall.

I glanced at Una, momentarily distracted, and that was all the opportunity Nautalun needed. Her lips brushed against my ear, her breath warm, sending a velvet shiver down my spine.

"You want me, Gal. You can't deny it. You can't fight it," she whispered, her voice as smooth as silk. Her hand slipped lower, teasing along my thigh, her fingers playing precariously close to the edge of control I clung to.

My grip on the trident faltered as a wave of pleasure and disgust surged through me, both emotions colliding and making my head spin. I wanted to shove her away, to end this, but every fiber of my body craved her touch. It was maddening.

"Don't listen to her!" Ember shouted, his voice cutting through the haze like a blade. Out of the corner of my eye, I saw him charge at Nautalun. She flicked her fingers in response, her music rippling through the air like a barrier, flipping Ember over and landing him on his ass.

She laughed, a low, throaty sound that sent a restless fire burning through my veins. "You're all so weak," she purred, her hand sliding back up to my chest, her nails dragging across my skin through the fabric. "Why fight me when you could have everything you desire?"

Her words washed over me like a drug, pulling me under her influence. My knees buckled, my grip on the trident loosening as the fires of desire raged through my veins. For a moment, I could almost see it—a future where I surrendered to her, where the struggle ended and I gave in to the temptation of power and pleasure.

But then my gaze slipped to Una. Blood stained her cheek, her face twisted in pain as she battled to stay upright, refusing to give in. Ember flapped his wings as he regained his feet.

A flash of rage tore through me, burning hotter than any lust Nautalun could stir. *No.* I would not let her control me.

With a roar, I shoved Nautalun away, tearing myself free from her grasp. Her salacious smile faltered as I steadied the trident, my focus sharpening, the fog of lust dissipating. The music still clawed at my mind, but I pushed it aside, concentrating on the pulse of magic in the trident.

Nautalun's eyes darkened, the seductive veneer slipping as she realized I was no longer hers to control. "You'll regret this," she hissed, her voice dropping an octave, taking on a sharp, dangerous edge.

She lifted her arms, summoning a surge of wind that howled through the clearing, whipping around us in a violent spiral. The gusts lashed at my face, pushing me back, while tendrils of her music wrapped themselves around me like vines, trying to drag me down. The wind picked up speed, swirling around Nautalun like a tempest, the trees groaning under its force, branches snapping and flying through the air.

I dodged the first strike of wind, the force of it enough to knock me sideways, but the second gust slammed into my chest, sending me crashing to the ground. My lungs seized, and the trident slipped from my hand and skidded across the grass.

Ember wasn't as lucky. A fierce gust hit him square in the

chest, lifting him off his feet and slamming him into a nearby tree with bone-crushing force.

Nautalun laughed, her voice a cold, mocking sound. "Did you think you could defeat a god, little prince?" she sneered, her eyes glowing with dark power as the wind screamed around us, trees uprooting and flying across the clearing like minnows. Her music had only been a starter. The power she wielded was incomprehensible.

Una held herself upright, blood dripping down her cheek, but her stance was solid, determined. She charged at Nautalun again, this time moving faster, more calculated, acting on all the hours she'd spent training with Ford. Nautalun turned, but Una was quicker, landing a solid punch to her stomach. Nautalun staggered back, fury flashing in her eyes.

But her anger only made her stronger. She flicked her wrist, and a tornado of wind blasted Una backward again, sending her skidding across the ground.

I had to end this.

I staggered to my feet and called the trident back to my hand. Nautalun's wind and music ricocheted into a deafening crescendo. I pushed through it, focusing on the magic coursing through the weapon.

"Not today," I growled, and with a roar, I leaped into the air, using her wind to carry me toward her.

Nautalun saw the movement too late. She turned, her eyes wide with surprise and fury, but I was already there. I carried the trident through the swirling winds and plunged the three prongs deep into her chest.

She gasped, her face crumbling as her body convulsed,

dark energy and wind spilling out of her like smoke. The storm abated, the winds dying as her power unraveled.

She looked up at me, her eyes filled with shock, as if she couldn't believe I had done it. Her lips moved, as though she wanted to say something, but no words came out.

And then she wilted, her body going limp, the surrounding winds dissipating into nothingness.

I withdrew the trident, watching as Nautalun's body hit the ground, her once-powerful presence reduced to nothing more than a dark stain on the earth.

CHAPTER SIXTEEN

$\mathcal{U}$na limped to my side. With the trident in one hand and my arm draped around her, I supported her against me as we staggered to the trees to check on Ember. He was out cold, but his chest rose and fell with life's breaths.

I helped Una to the ground and used my shirt to blot the blood seeping from the wound on her cheek. She winced as I dabbed at it.

"We should get that cleaned. I don't want you getting an infection," I said.

"And you." She indicated a gash on my thigh I hadn't noticed. I couldn't remember when it was inflicted. Or how.

I dabbed at Una's cheek once more, but she circled her hand around my wrist and brought my palm to her lips, kissed it gently.

"What was that for?" I asked against the hope blooming in my chest.

"For doubting you." She raised her watery gaze to meet

mine. "I knew the Denizens were powerful. I've studied *The Mermaid Chronicles* for years. I know what they are capable of, and yet I expected you to be able to withstand Nautalun's most aggressive advances." She shook her head, allowed herself a fragile smile. "That was foolish. I was too caught up in fairytales and happy ever afters—"

"Hey—"

She raised a hand. "Our love *is* like a fairytale, Gal. I'm not saying it's not. But because of that, it also comes with dark moments out of our control. I should have realized that. I shouldn't have put so much pressure on us. I've loved you for as long as I can remember and the thought of you being with someone else..." her gaze trailed into the dark woods. "It was too much. My soft heart just couldn't take it."

I cupped her wounded cheek, pressed a gentle kiss to the edge of her ear. "Your soft heart is the thing I love most about you." I lowered my palm so it fit snuggly over her chest. "Silver lining? We've both learned so much from Nautalun being here and messing with us. We've learned that sometimes mistakes are out of our control. We've learned that love can hurt even when it's strong. And I've learned that sometimes my dick acts before it thinks."

Una laughed, a surprised chuckle that rolled from deep within her throat. "And I've learned that I need to trust you. Knowing how hard it was for you to open up after losing your mom, I guess part of me expected you to turn your back on me. To decide that one day you just couldn't bear it anymore, that you were better off alone."

I shook my head. "Never. You've opened me up. Cracked me wide open. I'm as gooey as an egg."

"Oh my goodness. An unconscious guy can't get a word in edgewise with you two swooning all over each other," Ember said, his voice raw. "This is reminding me far too much of being stuck with you lovebirds in Iceland."

The three of us laughed as I helped Ember to a sitting position.

"How are you feeling, buddy?"

"Like I need a nice spin on a yacht with some freakin' sunshine to heal all my cuts and bruises. Oh, and did I mention the rather large egg-shaped bump on my head? Eggs are not actually that gooey when they're attached to your head."

"All for a good cause," I said.

Ember's eyes widened, his gaze sliding between me and Una. "We got her?"

I nodded. "Nautalun is dead. In some ways, it wasn't as hard as I thought it would be. Bit of stabby-stabby right through the heart. Easy as."

Una scoffed. "Tell that to your...unmentionables."

Turning serious, I slid my gaze over her beautiful face. "It was also a lot harder in other ways."

"Speaking of unmentionables," Ember said. "And I never thought I'd say this, but they need a spin on that yacht too."

I raised an eyebrow. "Just who was it you found yourself locked in an amorous tryst with last night?" I couldn't keep the humor from my tone.

Ember glared at me, but his smile told me he was laughing too. "I'll never tell."

Una and I helped him to his feet.

"Where is she?" Ember asked. "I need to see her body to believe it."

The three of us turned, and wearing our various injuries, limped back to the patch of dark grass where we'd left Nautalun's body. Part of me expected her to have disappeared or turned to ash and floated away on the wind. But her body lay there, as beautiful in death as it was in life, her open eyes still shining with seduction, her lithe form still somehow tempting. But there was no music. The night was as still as a tomb.

Before any of us could comment, a star fell out of the sky and engulfed her body in flames. At first I thought it was some kind of delayed act that occurred when a god was killed, but when I glanced at the sky and saw several more fireballs hurtling toward us, I knew this was something else.

A second fireball tore through the sky, slamming into the earth with a deafening roar. The ground trembled beneath our feet as flames erupted from the point of impact, sending a wave of heat rolling toward us. For a heartbeat, I stood frozen, watching the blaze consume everything in its path.

Ember's wings snapped tight against his back as one fireball shot past us, so close I could feel the heat singe my skin. It hit the ground with an earth-shaking thud, knocking over a massive tree and setting its branches ablaze. The fire spread quickly, flames licking up the trunk, smoke filling the air.

Screaming sounded from the other side of the courtyard. More fireballs fell from the sky, thudding around us, smashing through windows, eviscerating the lawns, and leaving behind fiery trails of mayhem.

The next fireball careened through the sky on a collision

course with Una's head. I swung the trident, but there was no safe water nearby to command, all the water channels were clogged with the venomous jellyfish. Before the fireball struck, I threw my arms around Una and cradled her as we dove for the ground, hands over our heads. The heat singed the back of my neck, and the air crackled with energy. We hit the ground hard, the impact knocking the breath from my lungs, but we were alive.

Out of the corner of my eye, I saw Ember step forward, his wings still pressed to his sides as he opened his mouth wide. His chest expanded, and in a single powerful breath, he inhaled the fireball whole. The flames disappeared into his body, leaving only a faint trail of smoke curling from his lips.

I scrambled to my feet, pulling Una with me.

"Thank Vorago for your unusual power," I said to my friend.

Ember stumbled as another fireball crashed into the ground nearby, sending a shower of sparks into the air. "There's too many. I can't be everywhere at once."

There was no time to rest. The sky was full of fireballs, more than I could count, each one hurtling toward the island with terrifying speed. Ember stepped forward again, inhaling another ball of fire. But his face was pale, sweat pouring down his brow.

The ground rumbled as yet another explosion rocked the island, sending shards of stone and debris flying in every direction. Shrapnel nicked my face, seared my skin, sliced open cuts on my legs. Oppressive heat scorched my lungs. The air filled with the reek of smoke and things that shouldn't burn. My eyes stung, and I couldn't hear anything over the roaring flames and the terrified screams surrounding us.

"Gal!" Una pointed toward the horizon, where more fireballs were descending, each one on a collision course with Atlantis.

My grip tightened on the trident, but what good was it now? Every water source I could have used to douse the flames was tainted, infested with venomous jellyfish. My mind raced, trying to find a solution, but all I could see was fire and destruction.

A shadow passed overhead, followed by the unmistakable sound of dragon king wings. I looked up to see Ash swooping down from the sky, his wings stirring freshness into the smoke-filled air. He landed beside us with a thud.

"We're here to help," he said, barely catching his breath before another fireball crashed dangerously close.

A moment later, Cyra appeared, running toward us, her hair wild and face flushed from the heat, smoke curling from her mouth.

"Let's go!" she shouted.

Without wasting a second, Cyra inhaled deeply, just like Ember, sucking a fireball from the sky and spitting it back toward the ocean, where it fizzled harmlessly in the waves. But even she couldn't keep up with the sheer number of them falling around us.

The blazing sky filled with fire and death. Ash took to the air again, darting between the flames, swooping to pull people out of harm's way. His wings cut through the smoke, his movements quick and precise, but for every person he saved, three more were caught in the chaos.

"Gal, we can't do this alone!" Una called as she danced away from approaching flames.

"I know!" I shouted, frustration boiling in my chest. I swung the trident desperately, trying to find a way to fight back, but every strike remained futile against the onslaught of fire.

Another fireball slammed into the ground near Ember, and he staggered as he inhaled another blaze. He coughed, doubling over, unable to keep up with the relentless bombardment. "I can't...there's too much..." he gasped.

Cyra was beside him in an instant, inhaling another fireball seconds before it reached them. She spat it back out with a fierce growl, but her face was twisted in pain. "We need to put the fires out!"

"There's no water available!" I yelled. Unless I risked everyone getting stung. Which was worse, jellyfish stings or fire?

"We'll figure something out!" Ash called from above, dodging another ball of heat.

Scattered thoughts crashed through my brain as I sifted through them for a solution.

As I dogged another blazing ball of fire, I almost took Cyra's feet out. She stood frozen, her mouth hanging open, staring at something over my shoulder. Dread strangled me. I stole myself, and then I turned around.

I'd known fear. I'd felt it when my mother died. I'd felt in when I'd fought Zale. What I saw now filled me with new unfathomable depths. Terror.

I reached for Una, folded my arm around her, and drew

her to my chest. She slumped against me, her entire body trembling.

"What are you all looking at?" Ember gasped as he leaped over a line of fiery grass. He turned, saw what had frozen us, and sank to his knees.

I had one arm around Una, the other held the trident.

Water I could handle. Fire I couldn't. A combination of the two? I had no idea.

A tsunami approached from the east of the palace, towering into the sky, lit up by the fireballs streaking through the darkness. But it wasn't an ordinary wave. Not merely a regular terror-inducing tsunami. This one had eyes. Eyes of fire that teemed with murderous intent.

"It's Maelstrom," Una muttered.

I searched my memory for the information concerning the third Denizen. He was the keeper of currents and possessed an otherworldly fire. He was responsible for the current predicament of Atlantis. And he always appeared as a tsunami.

"What do we do?" Ember asked. "Because it's getting closer, and it's bringing all the jellyfish with it."

I turned to look at my friends. "Ember, Cyra, Ash, I need you to handle the fire. Ember and Cyra, inhale as much as you can, spit it into the water. Ash, I need you to get to people to safety. Get a flask of fountain water and fly over the island. Give it to anyone you find injured."

The young teen gave me a solemn nod. Cyra and Ember were already dealing with more fireballs. I moved to turn away, to face Maelstrom, but Una grabbed my arm.

"You can't do this alone." Her eye brimmed with emotion.

Even though my body could barely contain the terror streaking through me, I couldn't let her see that. She had to believe I was capable of this. "This is what I've been training for. I'll will be back."

She shook her head. "Don't say that. I told you not to make promises you can't keep."

If I had to return from the dead to be with Una, then I would find a way. Nothing, not even Maelstrom or the terror he instilled in me, would keep me from her.

"I *will* keep this one." I wound my hand around the back of her neck, pulled her close, kissed her. There was no time for more. "Get to safety. There is nothing you can do here."

"The orbs..."

I shook my head. "They're too small to be useful. We used all their power fighting Zale."

"The Power of the Sea." Una referred to Atlantis' most powerful magic. Vorago had used it to create our island. It powered Atlantis, it leaned its magic to the fountain, it had given my mother her fiery powers, and it had helped to defeat the hound. Maybe. Maybe it could help.

"Okay. Go to the great hall. But don't come out unless you need to. Stay *safe*, Una."

She squeezed my hand and then darted away.

I turned to face the writhing ocean, startled to see how far Maelstrom had advanced. His fiery eyes settled on the glowing trident in my hand. I gritted my teeth, preparing to meet his strength, knowing I wouldn't come out of this unscathed. I limped forward, the gash on my thigh pulsing with pain, singes on my skin burning from the onslaught of fireballs, my sting wounds tightening my skin.

Maelstrom advanced toward the palace and gardens where I stood. People ran through the lawns, leaped over the dangerous water channels, their screams surrounding me, competing with the crackling of flames. The courtyard was still crowded from when I had addressed my people. So many had been caught in the open. Not that a wooden roof would do too much to protect them from otherworldly fire. I needed to draw Maelstrom away.

In the human world, fire and water never mixed well. But in my world, a dragon king's breath could tear through water. And Maelstrom himself was composed of both. My only choice was to draw him toward an isolated space and use the trident against him.

The teleportation I'd used to launch myself over the palace to face Nautalun was new. I had no idea how it worked, only that it had done so when I'd been worried about Una and desperate to find her. And if the location I had planned went wrong...I would die an extremely fiery death. But I was out of options and time. And Maelstrom's towering wave was only yards away from the cliff.

I cast a quick glance over my shoulder. The shadow of Ash's wings arced through the sky. Ember and Cyra stood together battling fireballs. Una's small form sprinted across the grass toward the palace. My friends. My family. I locked their images into my mind and drew on their strength.

Squeezing my eyes closed and gripping both hands around the trident, I pictured the lava lake in my mind. Lake

Echomere. Several years ago, it had been a lake of fresh water where many had taken vacations or sought more solitary spaces to live. Now it was a vast pool of lava. That had happened during the fight against the ghost pirates when an uncharted cavern had collapsed and revealed a pressured volcano. No one went there now. It was the perfect playground for a battle.

Ember caught my eye. "Gal, wait! You can't go alone. Wait—"

Without warning, I whipped through the night, cold air rushing past my cheeks, my eyes tearing and fireballs narrowly missing me as I sped by. Keeping a firm grip on the trident, I kept my gaze trained on Maelstrom. His fiery eyes followed every movement I made, and slowly, the tsunami turned.

My plan was working. But I still needed to land, and the margin for error was rather narrow when trying to find a safe spot at the edge of a volcano.

I swung the trident, hoping it would know what to do. But my descent came too fast, the lava too close, the heat stripping the hair from my limbs. *Shit*.

I plummeted toward the fiery lake. Una's face shot into my mind. I was going to die. I was going to die and leave her all alone. I was going to do the thing I'd promised I'd never do. The pain that sliced me in half was too much to bear. Guilt made me choke. Love made me cry.

I swung the trident, trying to slow my fall, fighting against it and myself. This couldn't be the end. *The Mermaid Chronicles* said I needed to be strong. I *was* being strong. Wasn't I? What more could I do?

Wings above my head. A strong grasp on my shoulder. My feet skated above the licking flames.

"Got you," Ember called.

Thank fuck for that.

I was yanked into the air, but we were too close to the surface of the lava. Ember banked, his wing dipping low, skimming the fiery lake.

His grip on me faltered. He cried out as he clawed his way higher, flapping his one wing furiously, the other leaving a trail of fire.

"Let me go!" I yelled. "I'll use the trident."

"You almost burned yourself to death using it!" The flames on Ember's wing died out, leaving behind a smoking, charred, ruined smell. Flesh and leather and bone scalded and scorched and burned away.

A minute later, we tumbled onto a rocky outcrop, both of us rolling into a large boulder and accruing a myriad of fresh cuts and bruises.

I pushed myself to my feet, ran to Ember's side.

He cradled his burned wing. "That fucking hurts. A thousand time worse than the bump on my head."

"You shouldn't have come after me."

"You'd be dead if I hadn't."

Quite possibly true.

We stared at each other.

"I'm sorry about your wing."

"It's not your fault."

It kind of was.

With a grimace, he peeled away a mass of charred skin and yanked it from his wing. "What were you thinking going after a Denizen alone?"

"I was trying to draw Maelstrom away from the palace," I said.

"You succeeded." Ember pointed over my shoulder.

I turned. Maelstrom's fiery eyes appeared. The tsunami was taller than ever, dwarfing the island, belittling the puddle of lava I stood beside.

I wasted no time raising the trident. "Stay back!" I called to Ember.

Tension sang through my muscles as I arced the trident over my head and focused on the advancing mountain of water. A watery fist appeared from the wall of ocean, stretching over the land, edging toward the trident I held.

The trident slipped in my grasp, water making it slick in my hand as the evil god showered us in waves. I slipped on the rocks, going down on a knee, almost burning my foot in the lava. Ember sucked some of the nearby fire away, and now not only was smoke curling out of his mouth, but his pores steamed with heat too. And he'd lost a wing.

"You can't keep doing that," I said to him.

"I'll do what I have to."

That sounded familiar.

I arced the trident again, but it was yanked from my hand. It flew through the air and crashed into the wall of Maelstrom's foaming torso, disappearing into its dark depths.

Maelstrom formed two giant fists, punched them through the water, scrabbling for the lost weapon. I scrambled back to my feet, raised my hand and called to the ancient trident. It flew out of the water and slammed back into my palm.

Two fiery eyes zeroed in on me. I thought I detected a

frown forming between them. He didn't speak. I couldn't see a mouth. But his intentions were clear.

Firming my grip on the trident, I raised it above my head, spun it as fast as I could in my slick grip. The water Maelstrom had made himself from churned. The jellyfish imprisoned within his watery body pulsed with crimson light.

An opposing force tugged at the trident, caused its hilt to slip through my hands. I grabbed it before it was yanked from my grasp and spun it again. Faster and faster, churning the tsunami into what I hoped would be a funnel. What I would do with it, I had no idea.

Another tug on the trident. Stronger. More forceful. But I refused to let go.

I was lifted off my feet, and then I spun through the air, following the trident into the dark, writhing body of Maelstrom.

"Gal!" Ember screamed.

There was no time to pray. There was no time to think of Una. There was no time for regret.

I crashed into the wall of water, the force of it hammering against my body. Maelstrom's power surrounded me—icy, crushing, and alive. Venomous jellyfish pulsed in the dark water, their tentacles trailing through the currents. They latched onto my arms, my legs, sending waves of searing pain through me as they stung, over and over, a hundred tiny explosions of agony.

I hung onto the trident as it sped toward the rocky depths, fighting the pull of the dark god. Maelstrom wanted it—his hunger for its power radiated through the water, a magnetic force trying to tear it from my grasp. My legs had already shifted into my ocean form, the sleek muscles of my tail thrashing against the powerful currents, but it wasn't enough. The Denizen dragged me deeper, into the abyss where no light reached.

I couldn't drown. I could breathe underwater in both my ocean shifter and human forms. But that didn't matter. Maelstrom wasn't trying to drown me—he was trying to *break* me. To starve me. To make me weak, so that when I was finally drained, he could take what he wanted.

I can't drown, I told myself as currents battered my bruised and broken body. *Then why does it feel like I am?*

The currents slammed into me again, brutal and unforgiving, sending me spinning in the churning chaos of Maelstrom's body. My gills flared, fighting for oxygen as I twisted through the water, every muscle in my body burning with effort. The jellyfish clung to me, their venom working its way through my veins, dulling my senses, clouding my thoughts. The weight of Maelstrom's presence pressed in on all sides, suffocating, like the entire ocean had come alive to swallow me whole.

Through the inky darkness, I saw them—*his eyes.* Twin orbs of fire glowing from within the heart of the wave, their burning gaze locked onto me, seething with ancient fury. His voice rumbled into my head, a deep, guttural growl that reverberated through my bones.

"You are nothing without the trident, boy. Give it to me, and I may spare you from oblivion."

The trident thrummed in my hands, its magic singing with defiance, but the pull was stronger now. My grip wavered as Maelstrom's current wrapped around the weapon, tugging it, demanding it.

The darkness closed in, tightening like a vise around my chest. My arms screamed in pain as the jellyfish tightened their hold, their tentacles coiling tighter and tighter, leaving trails of burning welts across my skin. Every second felt like an eternity, my strength draining away, inch by inch.

"Give it to me!" Maelstrom's voice roared in my head, the force of it sending shockwaves through my body.

I gritted my teeth, fighting the pull with everything I had left. I kicked my tail against the current, propelling myself upward, away from the abyss. But the dark god's relentless pull dragged me back, deeper into the crushing depths. The trident wrenched in my hands, slipping, inching toward his grasp.

"No!" I growled at him in my mind, pushing my rage through our joined telepathy.

With a final surge of strength, I slammed the trident into the depths of Maelstrom's wavelike body, the tip piercing the dark water with a brilliant flash of light. The trident's power exploded outward, a pulse of energy that sent a shockwave rippling through the god's form. The jellyfish scattered, their hold on me breaking as the blast tore through them, and for a moment, Maelstrom's pull weakened.

I kicked upward, using the momentum to break free, my tail thrashing against the water. But the dark god wasn't done with me. His eyes flared with rage, and the currents surged again, harder this time, trying to pull me back into the abyss.

"You will not escape me!" His voice thundered, and the water surrounding me swirled with violent intensity.

With a burst of strength, I wrenched the trident from his grasp, the force of it propelling me upward. My body shot through the water like a merfolk spear. The dark tendrils of Maelstrom's pull clawed at me, but I was already out of their grasp, surging through the water before they tightened around me.

I broke through the surface with a gasp, the cool night air hitting my face like a slap. My tail gave way to legs as I hauled myself onto the jagged rocks, my body trembling with exhaustion. I collapsed onto the stone, still clutching the trident. I clambered over the rocks to safety, finding the rocky outcrop where I'd left Ember.

He lay next to the pool of molten lava, his face pale, his wing crumpled. Heat radiated from the lava, mixing with the cold sting of the ocean spray, creating a disorienting clash of sensations.

"Ember..." I croaked.

He didn't respond, his chest rising and falling in shallow, labored breaths. I forced myself to my feet, my legs shaking as I stumbled toward him.

"I need your help," I murmured, dropping to my knees beside him.

Above us, the sky churned with fireballs, Maelstrom's arsenal taking the sky hostage. The wind howled, carrying the scent of salt and fire, and the distant rumble of thunder echoed across the island.

As I struggled for breath, the twin orbs of fire appeared once more, and Maelstrom bared down on my small rock of safety.

CHAPTER SEVENTEEN

*P*ain exploded in every part of my body. Had the venom from the jellyfish seeped into my bones? Was that possible? Because that's what it felt like. Every breath I took caused fire to surge up my spine, and each movement made my muscles scream. The welts covering my arms and chest throbbed, pulsing like a second heartbeat—angry, red, and raw. Poisoned.

"I think I know what to do," Ember said, his voice thick with pain. He staggered to his feet, using the rocks for support, almost tipping over into the bubbling lava next to him. I grabbed his arm, ignoring the pain it caused me, and pulled him back to safety.

The ledge we stood on was impossibly small. Molten lava bubbled on one side, spitting and hissing, while on the other side, Maelstrom loomed—a massive, towering wall of water, circling with deadly intent, eyes of fire glowing in the dark. I could feel his pull, even from here, trying to claim my mind along with my body.

"But I can't do it on my own," Ember rasped, his pain-filled eyes meeting mine. His mangled wing was no more than a shredded mess of bone, sinew, and charred skin. "I need Cyra."

"You can't fly," I said, glancing at his ruined wing. It was unrecognizable now, a twisted shadow of what it used to be.

"I need you to go for me."

Pain pulsed through my body. It streaked along my skin and ate at me from my poison-filled veins. Angry red welts decorated my arms and legs. My stomach and chest. My back and neck. They were everywhere. And the moment I noticed them all, I collapsed to my knees.

"I don't know if I can," I breathed, my vision blurring as Maelstrom's shadowy form loomed closer. The pull of the god and the poison, twin forces dragging me to the edge of oblivion.

"We don't have a choice." Ember reached out with his good arm, grabbing my wrist, his touch sending a fresh wave of agony through the pulsating welts. I clenched my jaw, barely suppressing a scream. "I know it hurts, Gal. I know you think you can't. But I know you can. You're strong."

The Denizens of the Deep crave the power of Vorago's trident. The one true wielder must remain strong.

The prophecy echoed in my mind. Every muscle in my body rebelled against the idea of moving. It would be so easy to give in. To let the poison take me, to let Maelstrom pull me under. The thought flickered in my mind, but then Ember's grip tightened, and I saw the determination in his eyes—determination I needed to find within myself.

I nodded, the smallest of movements, and forced myself

to my feet. I glanced at the advancing wall of water once more, attempting to estimate how long I had until Maelstrom launched another attack. I couldn't leave Ember here on his own.

"Please, Gal." Ember said, pulling on my arm. It made me wince when he connected with a tender welt, but I gritted my teeth against the pain. "Trust me."

I met his gaze and nodded once more. I gripped the trident and imagined Cyra. I didn't know where the younger dragon king would be, so I pictured her like the last time I saw her, running through the palace gardens with her cheeks flushed and her hair tangled. The memory of her filled my mind, and then I was gone.

My stomach gave way as the trident launched me into the air with brutal force, my body cutting through the wind. The world blurred beneath me, mountains, rivers, and forests flashing by in a dizzying whirl. There were a few seconds of cold as I passed the mountains, almost wishing I could pause there and gain fortification from the elements I was most comfortable with, but I couldn't afford to leave Ember for a second longer than necessary.

The moment the trident dropped me into the courtyard, the world swayed beneath me. The heat of the battle had driven the crowds away, leaving the place eerily quiet. I scanned the darkness, searching for any sign of Cyra. She came running up the beach path, her mouth full of fire, spewing flames and sparks. Ash flew above her, his wings slicing through the smoke, narrowly avoiding a streak of fire that shot across the sky.

Cyra almost ran into me. The gleam of the trident fell over her and she skidded to a halt.

"I hate to ask this, but I need your help," I gasped, each word clawing its way out of me. The venom was relentless, pushing through my body, dragging me closer to the edge with every heartbeat. My vision blurred, and for a moment, the ground tilted beneath me.

Cyra blinked. Her hands twitched at her sides. Ash's wings flapped above us, a thick leathery sound.

"Your brother needs your help," I said. I hated putting this kind of pressure on her. I had a vague idea of what Ember was planning. Had no idea if it would work, if he and his sister were even capable of such a feat, but I didn't have another plan. And I didn't know if I would survive it either. How much more could my body take before I gave in to the poison completely?

Cyra gave me a solemn nod. "I'm exhausted, but I'll do what I can."

"I'm coming too," Ash said. He swooped over the fountain, scooped water into a flask, and had the lid screwed on tight before I could think about ditching him.

"I'm not sure how many I can teleport with the trident," I said, hating his crestfallen look. "And there isn't much space to land on. And I'm so, so very tired..."

Ash flapped his wings with strong beats. "I don't need to land. Just get us there."

"You're going to be okay, Gal," Cyra whispered. Her words pierced through the fog of pain, calming me enough to focus.

I didn't have the luxury of hesitation. I offered them an

arm each, and as soon as they curled their fingers around my biceps, I hissed in pain and almost dropped the trident. Gritting my teeth, I spun the weapon in a wide arc. The magic gushed, yanking us into the air, rocketing us over the island in a blur of wind and smoke.

A few seconds later, I was reenacting my earlier fall, but this time I had two passengers to protect. Ash flapped his wings as we careened toward the rocky outcrop, slowing our descent and bringing us into land. We made it to the rock, Ember tugging us to safety as a wave of lava bubbled dangerously close to the edge.

Cyra's face paled as her gaze fell on Ember's wing—or what was left of it. "What happened?"

Ember mustered a smile. "War stories later. Action now."

Ash remained in the air above the rocks. "What's the plan?"

Ember's eyes flicked to the towering tsunami of Maelstrom, now advancing with renewed fury. "Gal is going to hold Maelstrom back with the trident. Meanwhile, Cyra and I will inhale the lava...and exhale it onto him."

Cyra's mouth dropped open. Her terrified gaze slid to the bubbling lava. "There's too much."

Ember planted his hand on her shoulder. "A little bit at a time. But as much as you can handle. You're a dragon king, Cyra. It's what we're made for."

"If anyone gets injured, I've got fountain water." Ash raised the flask. It wouldn't help Ember or me, but hopefully it would reassure Cyra.

Exhaustion and pain took hold of me. I planted my hands on my thigh, trying to draw breath through the heated air. My legs spasmed and the trident shook in my hand.

"Ember..."

Ember saw the tremor in my hands and moved to my side, placing his hand over mine, steadying my grip. He wasn't in any better state than I was.

"I don't know how long I can hold him."

Ember's face was pale, slick with sweat, but his eyes were fierce. "Long enough for us to take the shot."

Together, we lifted the trident, its power flickering weakly, but enough to push back against the Denizen. I focused all my strength—every ounce of will I had left—on keeping Maelstrom at bay.

But it wasn't enough. The force of the dark god's pull intensified, an unstoppable current crashing against me, bending the trident in my grip. My arms trembled, the muscles burning with exhaustion, as Maelstrom's icy tendrils coiled tighter, dragging me toward the roiling wave that was his body.

Cyra shot me a look, her lips trembling as she prepared to inhale, then turned toward the lake of molten lava. Ember mirrored her, his chest puffing as he exhaled all the air in his lungs.

The trident vibrated violently, the sheer power of the god trying to rip it from my hands. My fingers slipped against the slick surface, my palms raw and blistered. With each heart-beat, the pull grew stronger.

Together, Ember and Cyra stepped forward, standing at the edge of the bubbling lava. Cyra's mouth opened wide, her throat glowing with a reddish hue as she sucked in the scalding air. Ember did the same, their bodies steaming as they inhaled the searing heat of the lava in bursts, their cheeks bulging with each fiery intake.

My knees buckled, legs collapsing under the pressure, and for a split second, the trident wavered, almost slipping from my grasp. Panic surged through me. If I lost the trident, we were all doomed. I gritted my teeth, growling through the pain, and with a desperate yell, I dug my heels into the rock, forcing the trident upright once more.

The air crackled. Heat radiating from the dragon kings, oppressive and suffocating, even from where I stood. The dark mass of Maelstrom loomed closer, tendrils of water lashing out toward them, but the trident's power held him mere inches away.

Ember cut his arm through the air, indicating it was time to release their fire.

In unison, Cyra and Ember exhaled, their jaws snapping open as streams of molten lava shot from their mouths, glowing and fierce. The streams collided with Maelstrom's watery form in a violent hiss. Steam exploded into the air, thick and choking. The wave of heat from the lava met the god's chilling waters, sending scalding mist spiraling into the sky.

Another inhale, another burst—this time, the lava spewed in torrents, engulfing Maelstrom's towering wave. His roar cut through our minds, emitting pulses of concussive power, but I kept the trident raised, refusing to let his fury overwhelm me.

The lava cascaded over him, sizzling and bubbling, hardening on contact. With each surge, the water solidified, turning black, cracking as it cooled. Maelstrom's form buckled, his once fluid mass now slowed, immobilized by the growing layers of igneous rock. The waves collapsed inward, the tendrils of his body shuddering as he tried to push back, but the molten streams kept coming, turning him to stone.

A final burst of lava, a massive cloud of steam erupted into the sky, and then—silence. Maelstrom's immense body, once a raging tsunami, was now a solid, jagged mass of blackened rock, frozen in place like a statue. His fiery eyes dimmed, flickering once before being snuffed out, encased in the stone.

Cyra collapsed to her knees, panting heavily, her body shivering from the strain. Ember stumbled beside her, the charred remnants of his wings hanging limply as he fought to catch his breath. I let out a shaky exhale, my hands shaking as I lowered the trident. My body ached, the jellyfish stings still burning through me, but for the first time since the battle began, I felt hope stirring.

But hope wasn't enough to keep me conscious.

CHAPTER EIGHTEEN

The pressure of soft lips against my cheek stirred me from sleep. The sound of a monitor beeped regularly. I opened my eyes to see Una peering at me.

"Gal?"

Una leaned over me, scanning my face. I blinked. The gash on her cheek had been cleaned and treated, butterfly stitches holding the skin together. Her blonde hair was freshly washed and held back in a messy bun. She wore her pirate eyepatch. It brought a smile to my face. She'd never looked more beautiful, despite the litany of burns dotting her arms and legs.

"What happened?" I stretched my arms above my head, shifted my weight, expecting there to be pain. But I felt refreshed, like I'd woken from a deep sleep, muscles singing with new energy. And yet, by the looks of things, I was in a hospital bed attached to a multitude of wires.

Una smoothed my hair back. "You fought Maelstrom."

The tsunami. The lava. The jellyfish. The darkness.

I sat up, the beeps increasing as my heart rate picked up.

"How did I get here?"

"Ash and Blaze," she said, laying another gentle kiss at the corner of my lips. "Ash flew back and told everyone you and Ember needed help. He flew me to you with the Power of the Sea. I gave it to both of you."

I threw the covers off, intending to charge out of the room and...I didn't know what...but before I could swing my legs out of bed, they started trembling. "I inhaled the Power of the Sea?"

When the Power of the Sea was used to save someone's life, it often granted them with an extraordinary ability. Fire power for my mother, a Herculean strength for my father, the ability to command water to Babette. But these gifts were bestowed only if the person was found worthy. Were Ember and I worthy? I already had the trident.

"I arrived just in time," Una said, her voice filled with complicated emotions.

I slid my gaze back to her. Her eye filled with tears. I wrapped an arm around her and drew her against my chest. "I'm here now."

"You almost weren't. All those jellyfish stings..." Her words were muffled against my chest. "If it wasn't for the trident."

"The trident?"

She pulled back. "The trident protects its wielder."

The trident had saved me. There was no way a normal person could incur that many stings. "Where is the trident?"

Una smiled, pointed to the floor where it lay at a haphazard angle. "You wouldn't let go of it even when Blaze flew you back. It only fell out of your hand when you were put in bed. And as no one else can touch it...here it remains."

I sank back against the pillows, bringing Una with me, pulling her onto my lap to cradle her against my chest. I would never let go of her again.

"It was so hard to leave you." I pressed a kiss to the top of her head.

"You should have seen what you looked like by the lava lake, Gal. I've never been so terrified." Her voice cracked.

I closed my eyes, squeezing them tight against the pain of loss, against what might have been. But we had survived. Just. And we still had two more Denizens to face.

"How is Ember?" I asked.

Una jutted her chin at the next bed where I'd missed Ember's sleeping figure. He lay in his human form, no sign of his wings. "He's going to be okay."

"Can I put in a request for a vacation before I have to battle another Denizen?" I wasn't so worried about myself. Physically, I was perfectly healed. Emotionally, I was a mess. And Una could use some time for her wounds to heal.

Giving in to the burst of emotion, I squeezed Una tight and showered her with kisses. Cupping her chin, I turned her head to face me, met her lips with mine, and claimed what belonged to me. Took what I couldn't live without.

"Why is it every time I wake from unconsciousness, I find you two kissing like there's no tomorrow?" Humor laced Ember's voice.

Maybe there won't be a tomorrow. I shook the dark thought away. Right now, we were alive and looking a damn sight better than when we were fighting Maelstrom.

Una laughed, pushing herself off my lap and settling onto the bed beside me. "How are you feeling?"

Ember frowned, looked at his arms, then raised both legs, one at a time. He wiggled his toes. He lifted the sheet and checked on things in a more private area. "I seem to be intact. Weird. Thought I'd at least have a cool scar."

"You might get an ability from the Power of the Sea," I told him.

Both Ember's brows quirked. "Holy shit."

"My thoughts exactly," I said. "And your wing?"

Ember blinked, and a second later, one enormous leathery wing shifted into view. The right one. The left one remained hidden. He glanced at his shoulder where his wing should be, frowned, rolled the joint. "That's weird."

"It didn't heal your wing." My voice faltered as guilt raced through me. He'd come after me, prevented me from fighting alone, saved my life. And because if it, he'd lost his wing.

Color leached out of his face. "I can't fly with one wing."

Una walked across the small gap separating our hospital beds. "If I can live with one eye, you can live with one wing."

His expression didn't change. He stared at his shoulder. His eyes glistened.

"It's going to be okay." Una reached out to touch him, but Ember shrugged her off.

"It's *not* okay. What's a dragon king without wings?"

"Tell that to your sister," Una said. "She's doing pretty well without any wings at all."

Ember shook his head, refusing to listen, then pinned a glare on me. "If you'd have waited. If you'd given me half a minute. If you'd stopped thinking you had to do everything alone...I'd still have a wing."

"You don't know that." I cleared my throat, not liking the rasp in my voice.

"This isn't Gal's fault," Una said.

Ember bounced his gaze between us. "Then whose is it? I told you to wait—"

"Teleportation is faster than flight!"

Ember ignored my interruption. "I told you not to go at it alone. But you always think you know better than everyone else."

I lurched forward, swinging my legs to the floor, sending the heart rate monitor into a meltdown. "Ember, that's not fair. I didn't go off because I didn't think you could help. I did it to protect you. I'm the one with the trident. I'm the one expected to save everyone. I'm the one who's supposed to have all this power—"

"And how did that work out for you?" Ember got out of bed, his hands fisted at his side, and his wing shifted away. "United, remember? That's the key to all the prophecies."

I hung my head and sat back on the bed. Rubbing my face, I let out a weary sigh.

"Ember—"

He yanked out his wires, brushed past me, and headed out of the room.

"Shit."

Una came to my side, folded an arm around my shoulder. "He'll come around."

I shook my head, raked my hands through my hair. "He was right. I thought the trident's new powers would be all I needed. I acted recklessly. If he hadn't followed me...I would have broken my promise to you."

Una stood, shifted until she was standing between my legs and her arms resting on my shoulders. "Ember has confidence issues. He didn't know he could inhale fire until early this year. You were there. He can't conjure fire like the rest of his kind. He hates it. It makes him feel...less. And so he tries to make up for it with daring acts of courage. He wants you to need him—"

"I *do* need him!"

"Let me finish." Una kissed me to shush me. "He wants you to need him. He wants to believe he's an integral part of this battle. And he is, don't get me wrong, his bravery and powers are awesome. We do need him. But he's also human. He makes mistakes. He says things he doesn't mean—"

"Oh, I think he meant it alright..."

"Gal," Una said patiently. "What I'm trying to say is that he just lost a wing. He's a dragon king and he can't fly anymore. It's shitty. He lashed out. He's not perfect. None of us are. So he lashed out at you, his closest friend and cousin, because he can, and you'll forgive him, because that's what best friends do. And I know you feel guilty. And I know there are a million other ways you think you could have handled that situation. But Maelstrom is dead. The fireballs have disappeared from the sky. If one wing is all we lost...then I say that was a damn successful fight."

I placed my hands on her hips and squeezed, digging my fingers into her skin, grasping the solid surety of her. I rested my head against her shoulder. "You are so damn wise."

"That's why they call me an oracle."

"Don't let it go to your head."

She laughed, curled her fingers through my hair. "I'll leave the arrogance to the testosterone-wielding men."

I chuckled. "I need to make it up to him somehow."

Una lifted my chin with her finger. "Stop that. You have nothing to make up for. You'll hug, he'll get over it, and then we'll battle the next Denizen. *Together*."

I squeezed her arms. "Together. Although how I'm supposed to fight a bunch of shadowy tendrils that the trident sails right through...I have no idea."

"We'll figure it out. *Together*."

I stood, crushed her to my chest, and kissed her.

After the doc gave me the all clear, Una and I left the hospital and we wound our way toward the palace. An absurd part of me missed the fireballs. At least they had lit up the sky and provided light. Now darkness shrouded the island once more. So thick that I could feel it encroaching, a vicious entity that seemed alive with intentions all to itself.

"Cyra and Ash? Are they okay?" I asked.

"Little bit of fountain water sorted them out," Una replied. "And now that the danger has passed, they're throwing their weight around, telling their story to everyone who will listen. Which happens to be the entire island."

"Hey, Gal!" a voice called from the air.

"Speak of the devil," Una chuckled.

I looked up to see Ash sitting on the roof of the palace working his teeth around an apple, a lantern by his side.

"How you feeling?" Ash called.

"All fixed." I patted my sides as if looking for a lingering wound. "You?"

He cocked a shoulder, his wings fluttering high. "Takes a lot more than a Denizen to keep me down."

I smothered my laughter as I mounted the stairs. Oh, the bravado of youth. The intrepid foolishness. I'd have to make sure he didn't do anything stupid.

"He did require a large hit of fountain water," Una whispered to me. "Several times."

"At least he's not traumatized."

"Plenty of time for the nightmares to come."

We shared a grimace.

When we reached the palace foyer, Una brushed her lips against mine before pulling away. "I'm going to check on my family."

I frowned. "I made myself a promise I'd never let go of you again."

She laughed. "You can come with me."

I glanced at the closed doors of the great hall. "I want to check the book. I'm hoping to find something useful about how to defeat the last two Denizens."

Una ran her fingers down my arm, squeezed my hand. "You go. I'll be right back. I want to let them know you're awake."

"Okay. But hurry." I tucked my hands behind her neck and pulled her head toward my lips, gave her a gentle kiss. I couldn't find the will to release her, so hugged her against me, and slid my hand down her back in smooth strokes. "I love you. After everything with Nautalun...I need to tell you that. I need to show you—"

"And I love you," she said. "It's okay, Gal. It's in the past. I can't say I'm ever going to get those images out of my head...

but I'm not wasting time on anger and regret. I love you right back. That's all that matters."

"I *fucking* love you." I stared at her, marveling at this woman who was utterly perfect. "How do I say *I love you* and make it mean more than that? Why aren't their bigger words? Because what I feel inside..." I shook my head. "There are no words to describe how you make me feel."

She smiled, and her face bunched like she was about to cry.

"That was supposed to make you happy."

"I am happy," she croaked as she patted a few tears away. "And you're making it so damn hard to leave right now, but I really need to check on my family."

I nodded, touched her hand. "Go."

Una turned away, but I pulled her back, tugged her against my chest and kissed her like there was no tomorrow. There almost wasn't.

I tightened my hold on her, one hand sliding up the curve of her back, feeling the warmth of her skin through the thin fabric of her shirt. Her body molded to mine, as if she belonged nowhere else but in my arms.

The taste of salt and sea lingered between us. Utterly intoxicating. I kissed her deeper, greedier, and her hands fisted in my hair. Heat bloomed where our mouths met, spreading through my chest and down my spine until every inch of me was alight, buzzing with the need to be closer, to have her.

The edges of my vision blurred as I sank deeper into the kiss, like time had stretched, and all that existed was this moment. I could exist in this moment for eternity. Every touch of her lips sent electric sparks through my body. Her fingers scraped my neck, leaving a trail of heat in their wake, and I groaned into her mouth.

This wasn't just a kiss. It was a lifeline. A promise. A moment stolen from the surrounding madness, and I was drowning in it, in her.

I was breathless when she pulled away. "Give me ten minutes."

I watched her disappear down the hallway. Unwilling to move, I stood there for a few minutes, gathering the courage to enter the great hall. While I hesitated, memories of the battle came back to me. I smelled the smoke of the fireballs, felt the heat as they singed my skin. I glanced at the trident in my hand. Maelstrom's pull on it had been so strong, and yet Nautalun wasn't able to pick it up.

Needing answers, I walked past the guards stationed outside the great hall and pushed the doors open. I slipped inside, my focus on *The Mermaid Chronicles* where it rested on its plinth. As I strode across the room, the elemental orbs pulsed as if confirming I was on the right path.

I rested my hands on the book of prophecies. I'd half expected the pages to be glowing with a new insight, but they remained dim. I didn't bother opening the book, I'd already read everything inside pertaining to the Denizens. I knew all their strengths and weaknesses—what little was written, anyway. Nautalun was the master of seduction and always appeared in human form. She could be killed as though she were a mortal. Dagonar was the Weaver of Shadows and had thrust our island into eternal darkness and sent a plague of jellyfish upon us. I had discovered his torso was amorphous, but his tendrils could be severed. That was all I had to go on. The gods were so old that even *The Mermaid Chronicles* had little information about them. Maelstrom was the Keeper of Currents and usually appeared as a tsunami. We had been lucky to happen on the correct way to end him. But Karkenloth was the largest and most powerful of them all. Lord of Leviathans, the book referred to him as. A titan among gods. Whose form was a merging of all the creatures that dwelled in the darkest recesses of the ocean. Whatever that meant.

Hope leached out of me as I stared at the book, willing it to impart a secret message. Although the trident glowed in my hand, it had no answers to reveal either.

"I know what you're thinking."

I spun around at the voice. Ford stood by a window, darkness pressing in, the glow of a candle casting just enough light to decipher his form.

"I'm thinking that I don't know how to use this trident well enough." I threw the trident onto the couch, its glow immediately dimming and casting the room in semi-darkness. "I'm thinking I almost broke my promise to Una, and I should never have made it in the first place. Ember hates me. Blames me. And he's right to. I'm thinking there are two more Denizens to defeat and I almost died fighting the last one. The entire population of Atlantis is relying on me, and I don't know if I can do this."

Ford glanced at the trident lying on the couch, the dull metal now cold and distant. He took a step closer to me.

"You think Ember hates you? That you almost broke your promise to Una?" His gaze softened, cutting through the guilt and the darkness buried in my chest. "Gal, you saved his life.

You saved all our lives. He's alive because of you. And if you weren't there, he'd have lost a lot more than his wing."

"He was only there because he went after me."

Ford nodded. "That may be true. But without you, Maelstrom wouldn't be dead."

"He wouldn't be dead without Ember and Cyra either."

"United," Ford said. "But that's not what this is about, Gal. This is about your guilt. Your grief. And your love."

I couldn't deny his words.

"They have tangled together into a huge knot that you can't untie yourself from. And for some ridiculous reason, you believe you should suffer." He paused, stepping into the pool of faint candlelight. "Life is just...life. Random, chaotic, painful, joyful...and so many other things. Yes, we have the prophecies, which is a damn sight more warning than most people get—"

"Most people don't have to fight monsters."

Ford raised a hand to quieten me. "Even with the book, what happens is out of our control. We can fight. We can love. And we can do the best we can do. That is *all* we can do."

I clenched my fists as frustration burned through me. I wanted to argue, to scream that it wasn't enough. That trying my best had almost killed me, almost cost Ember his life. But no words came.

"Did you intend to hurt Ember out of maliciousness? Of course not," Ford said. "Is it wrong to believe you have the most power of anyone? No. The truth is, you do. You are the trident carrier. You must rely on the support of others, but without you, we cannot defeat the Denizens."

"I..." I started, but the words died in my throat. He wasn't wrong, but the pressure was unbearable. The weight of Atlantis wasn't just resting on my shoulders—it was crushing me, suffocating me. How could I ask them to keep helping me when every time they did, they paid the price?

Ford's gaze didn't waver. "I get it. You feel like you're not enough, like the future of Atlantis depends on you, and you're carrying it alone. But here's the thing—you've already done it. You've faced more than most would even dare, and you're still here."

I stared at the trident. It had chosen me, but what if it was wrong? What if I wasn't the one meant to see this through?

"Atlantis was lost for hundreds of years, and yet ocean shifters survived. We will continue to survive whether we defeat the gods or not."

I shook my head. "You don't know that."

"I do. It's the pattern of humanity." Ford leaned in. "But you're right, it's going to get harder. But you've been staring death in the face since this began, and yet, you're still standing. You've faced gods, Gal. Do you think Maelstrom would've let you live if you weren't stronger than him?"

I looked up at Ford, his words cutting through the fog of doubt. *Stronger than a god.* That couldn't be what *The Mermaid Chronicles* had meant when it had implied I needed to stand strong. I'd taken it to mean physically, emotionally, magically...the idea of being stronger than a god seemed ridiculous, but here I was, alive, holding the trident. So what did that make me?

Ford gestured to the golden weapon. "That thing doesn't glow for anyone else. Not for me, not for anyone on this island—only for you. It chose you. And maybe it's because you're not perfect, because you question whether you're strong enough. But you are. You've always been."

I'd never strived for perfection. But I also refused to fail. But maybe it wasn't about that. Maybe it was about surviving, about pushing forward even when everything felt impossible, about gathering my loved ones close and doing everything I could to see the next sunrise...together, however messy it was.

Ford stepped back, leaving space for me to breathe, his eyes holding mine with quiet resolve. "Atlanteans aren't relying on you because they think you're invincible. They're relying on you because you're the one who never gives up, no matter how many times you fall. That's what makes you strong."

I swallowed hard, staring at the trident, its golden metal flickering with promise. Maybe Ford was right. Maybe the strength wasn't in being invincible, but in accepting help, in pushing through the pain. The trident glowed for me for a reason.

My family carried a legacy, one I had often denied. My parents had broken a centuries-old curse and rediscovered Atlantis. It was a hell of a lot to live up to. A hell of a burden to carry. But I had defeated Zale when everyone thought I couldn't. My mother lived on inside me. She had fought in the face of fear. There was no reason I couldn't do that too.

CHAPTER NINETEEN

*L*ooking for Ember, I ventured into the palace gardens where the air was thick with shadows swirling in the murky darkness. Coils of inky blackness snaked across the ground, drifted ominously over the stagnant water channels, wrapped around every surface, and coated the plant life. Fluid vines strangled the trunks of trees and weaved across the lawns, wilting under the suffocating presence of Dagonar's curse.

The island wouldn't survive much longer in the darkness. People needed sunlight to survive. And ocean shifters needed water too. With no one able to swim in the channels or surrounding ocean, a thick depression was setting in, only enhanced by the permanent night. The island's heart was drowning in shadows, and I couldn't help but feel the curse was feeding on our collective despair, growing stronger with each passing day.

I found Ember sitting on the ground beside a water channel with a joint in his hand, the smoke curling into the darkness, and staring at a crimson jellyfish. The venomous creatures remained blood-black in color, but occasionally pulsed with a toxic red light. Ember was in his human form, his one wing nowhere in sight. It was strange seeing him like that—grounded, motionless. He was always so full of fire, so vibrant. But now, with his wing gone, there was a heaviness to him I hadn't seen before.

Bracing myself against the persistent nag of guilt, I laid the trident on the grass and sat beside him. "I'm sorry. Truly."

Ember didn't look up, but I caught a slight movement in his shoulders. His silence was worse than any sharp words he could've thrown at me. Desperate to bridge the gap between us, I laid a hand across my chest. "I do understand how you feel. If I lost my tail..." I trailed off, the thought too horrifying to finish. The sea was my life, my essence. If I couldn't swim again...I shuddered. "When this is all over, I'll find a way to get your wing back."

Ember snorted, finally glancing at me with an incredulous look. "There you go again."

"What?"

He shook his head with a small smile, though it didn't quite reach his eyes. "You can't bring my wing back. No one can. And I don't expect you to try. You may be the trident wielder, Gal, but you're not a god. And I'm not even sure the gods have that kind of power."

"If they created an island, I'm sure they can recreate your wing."

"Yeah, well, when they decide to show themselves and help us fight for our island, I'll ask them," he said dryly. "But in the meantime, stop thinking everything is your fault."

"You told me it was!"

"I was angry!" Ember said, his tone softening into something almost apologetic. "I'd just found out I'd lost a wing. Forgive me for not being all calm and collected."

We both fell into silence. I glanced at him, studying the way his brow furrowed, the lines of tension bracketing his mouth. Despite everything, he still had a mischievous spark in his eyes. It was comforting, in a way, knowing he hadn't completely lost himself in the darkness.

"You saved my life," I finally said, breaking the quiet.

"Yeah," he nodded, taking a hit on the joint. "And I'm not planning on letting you forget it anytime soon. But you did save my life too." He tossed the smoked joint into the water, watching as it drifted aimlessly. "You're right though—if you hadn't drawn Maelstrom away, things would have been much worse."

"I didn't know you could spit lava and fire back out," I said, raising an eyebrow.

Ember gave a low chuckle, the sound breaking the tension between us. "Neither did I. Figured it out in the heat of the moment—literally. I saw Cyra do it and thought, 'Hey, why not?'" He shrugged, his grin widening. "Turns out I'm a lava-spitting genius."

"Talk about a half-cocked plan..."

"Yeah, well, I learned from the best."

We shared a smile.

"You have an awesome power, Ember. I can't do anything without the trident." I splayed a hand.

"Oh, don't sell yourself short. You can make magical ice flutes."

"I *can* make magical ice flutes. That is true. Not sure how they'd help me take down a Denizen though."

"Hey, don't knock it! You could start a whole new movement in music." Ember waggled his eyebrows. "Think of the market potential. Limited-edition ice instruments that only last a day..."

"I'm sure they'd sell like...well, like ice in Atlantis," I said, my laughter softening as I glanced at the surrounding darkness. The relentless shadows clung to everything, shifting in the air with unsettling fluidity. Each breath tasted of damp earth and faint saltwater. "Not so warm right now, though."

Ember's face sobered, his eyes scanning the inky darkness. "No. It's getting colder every day. Feels like the shadows are closing in on us. Like they're choking the island."

"And that's why I need your help," I said, standing and brushing the dirt off my pants. "I don't just need to practice my teleportation with the trident—I think you and I need to figure out if the Power of the Sea granted us new abilities. They might be useful."

Ember raised an eyebrow as he stood beside me, rubbing the back of his neck. "New abilities, huh? Well, if I start turning into a fish, I'm blaming you."

I smirked, giving him a playful shove. "A fish with one wing? That I'd like to see."

He shoved me back.

"Too soon?"

"*Way* too soon." He flicked my shoulder. "Alright then, let's do this. No oversized god with shadows for limbs is gonna get the better of me and my cousin."

I slapped him on the back, the tension between us now

nonexistent as we embarked in familiar banter. "Thanks, Ember. And seriously, I'm sorry about everything."

He waved me off with a grin. "Shush already." Then, without warning, he swept my legs out from under me, sending me stumbling. "Consider that payback for the wing."

I laughed, steadying myself. "Oh, that's how it's gonna be, huh? You do know I've been training with Ford since I was five, right?"

"Yeah, yeah," he said, eyes gleaming with mischief. "You've been training, but I've got this whole 'lava-sucking, fire-spitting' thing going for me. We'll see who comes out on top."

"Oh, we'll see alright," I said, shaking my head but feeling lighter than I had in days. Maybe everything wasn't fixed. Maybe the shadows were still looming. But at least I wasn't facing it alone.

And that made all the difference.

With Ember by my side, I gripped the trident and took a deep breath. It was time to master teleportation. And hopefully I wouldn't end up back in the lava lake. Which, I had heard, was now a giant crater since Ember and Cyra had drained it of all its molten liquid.

"Alright, let's see what that fancy excuse for an oversized garden implement can do." Ember winked.

I smirked, adjusting my stance, the weight of the trident grounding me. "Just make sure you're not standing too close. Don't want to accidentally teleport inside you or something."

Ember barked out a laugh and took a few steps back. "Ewww...gross."

I focused my mind on the far side of the garden, where

the shadows appeared thinner, and closed my eyes. The trident pulsed in my hands, responding to my intent. With a deep breath, I summoned the power within it, willing myself to disappear from where I stood.

The world shifted.

For a moment, everything went weightless, the shadows swirling around me as if they were alive, trying to pull me into their depths. Then, with a snap, I was across the garden, standing in the same spot I'd envisioned. The sudden change in air pressure hit me, and I staggered for a second before regaining my balance.

"Not bad!" Ember called from behind me. "You didn't explode. Or, you know, end up in the lava lake, so I'd call that progress."

I grinned, turning to face him. "Yeah, small victories."

The shadows rippled as a new figure approached, his silhouette sharp against the gloom. Ash stepped into view and came to a stop beside Ember. "I was watching from the roof, but I needed to get a better look at this. That was awesome!" Ash flapped his wings, stirring the shadows.

"It went better than I expected," I admitted, though my heart still raced from the sudden shift in space. "I'm going again." I focused my gaze on a spot farther down the path, near where a crumbling walkway wall met the cursed water.

This time, the teleportation was smoother, as though the trident and I were syncing. I didn't lose my balance when I reappeared. The air remained heavy with the weight of darkness, the black coils of shadow a constant reminder that Dagonar could return any moment. But I'd done it.

"So cool!" Ash cheered from across the garden. "But how's that going to help defeat Dagonar?"

I have no freakin' idea.

Before I could respond, Una emerged from the shadows, a spear slung over her back, a quiet smile on her lips. "Looks like I'm not the only one training tonight."

"Since when did you carry a spear around?" I asked as I walked toward her. I ran a hand down the smooth metal shaft of the slim spear, admiring its lightness, then stole a kiss.

"It was supposed to be a surprise," Una said. "While you've been at trident practice with Ford, Rob has been training me with the spears. I was going to give you a little performance on my birthday."

Una's birthday was still a couple months away. Not long before Christmas. And always during the two weeks of Atlantis' cold season when the snow would settle over the palace and the kids made snowmen and pelted passersby with snowballs.

I gaped at her and ran my fingers lightly over the healing wound on her cheek. "You've been keeping secrets."

"Only the good kind." She unsheathed the spear from the holder on her back, twirled it in her hands, the motion fluid and practiced. "Rob's going to make them explosive. Should come in handy when the last two Denizens arrive."

"Holy shit," I said. Rob was the head of the Atlantean army. And Babette's father. Having survived a nuclear war on the mainland, he'd taken over the role when he and his daughter had moved to Atlantis looking for sanctuary. The army had limited firepower in terms of the more traditional human weapons of guns and explosives. The senate and

High Council decided long ago that such weapons wouldn't be permitted in Atlantis, and so the old ways were left behind. And they wouldn't have done much against the gods anyway. Since then, Rob had taken it upon himself to train his army in spears, swords, and knives, but adding modern flares such as explosive blades gave us a much better advantage.

Something loosened in my chest. A knot of tension. I knew Una was capable in a hand-to-hand, one-on-one combat situation, but against a god, there was little she could offer. Now, if her aim was accurate, she would be a huge asset, and perhaps I wouldn't worry about her so much.

"There's something about a woman with a spear." I winked at her.

Una slapped my stomach. "You concentrate. Remember you need to be focused even when I'm in the vicinity."

"Oh, I'll be focused alright." I shot an obvious stare at her chest.

Ember cleared his throat. "Please. Not in front of my little brother. He's far too young to witness such traumatic acts."

"Oh, no. Don't you dare," Ash said with a grin. "This is just getting good."

Una waved her spear between Ember and me. "It's good to see you two getting along again. But don't you have new powers to unearth?"

Ember rolled his eyes, but I caught the glint of a smile on his lips as he turned back toward the twisted darkness curling around the trees. "Fine, fine. Let's see what else I've got in the tank," he muttered, his tone nonchalant, but I knew him well enough to catch the undercurrent of curiosity. He'd lost a wing and couldn't conjure fire, could only inhale it and then exhale it. Having a new power might make up for what he felt were deficiencies.

Ember took a breath. "Any idea on how to find it, exactly?"

"Reach inside?" I suggested.

"You have to feel it," Una said.

"You have to connect with your inner emotions," Ash offered. "Try singing a song, emptying your mind, meditating with a candle...you know, the usual."

Ember flipped him off, then drew in another breath. He extended his arms out to his sides, as if reaching for something unseen. The shadows around him rippled in response, like they were drawn to an energy building in his core. His hands glowed, a warm radiance spreading from his fingertips and along his arms, like veins of liquid amber.

The shift in the air was almost imperceptible at first, but then the temperature rose. The cold shadows recoiled, a faint sizzling sound reaching my ears as if the darkness was burning away from his presence.

A low rumble echoed from Ember's chest, and with a sudden flick of his wrist, flames burst into life, encircling him in a blazing ring. The fire was unlike any normal flame—it was deep, almost crimson in color, with gold threads lacing through it like liquid sunlight. Heat rolled off him in waves, the sharp scent of burning ozone filling the air as the shadows recoiled further, their inky tendrils retreating like wounded snakes.

"What the—?" Ash's voice was full of awe as he stepped forward. "You're doing that? *All* of it?"

Ember didn't respond, his focus sharp as the ring of fire pulsed outwards, forming a protective barrier. I felt the power in it, the intensity of his control, as if the flames weren't merely fire but something ancient, something raw. He stood at the center of it all, his eyes blazing with the same light, his one wing beginning to twitch with excitement. His whole body vibrated with the energy coursing through him.

I exchanged a glance with Una. Her expression was as nonplussed as I felt.

"Not bad," I called, shielding my face from the heat as I stepped back, sweat beading on my forehead despite the ever-present chill of the shadows. "Looks like you've got yourself some kind of pyro shield."

Ember grinned, his teeth flashing in the light of the flames.

Una took a step forward, her spear held loosely at her side as she surveyed the shield with a thoughtful expression. "You could use that to hold off Dagonar," she said, her eyes flicking between Ember and the glowing ring of fire. "Look at the way it's eating the shadows. It's more than just a defense. You could burn right through his shadows."

The fire surrounding him flared higher, as if responding to Una's words, licking the air with hungry tendrils. The ground beneath his feet sizzled, the shadows continuing to peel away as the light from the flames spread out in concentric waves. Even the cursed darkness thinned, revealing pockets of gray light.

Ash whistled, his eyes wide as he inched closer to my side. "You could probably barbecue an entire army with that."

"Let's hope we don't get hungry," Ember joked, but the intensity in his gaze didn't waver.

As the flames dimmed, Ember let out a breath, the glow fading from his arms as he relaxed. The ring of fire dissipated, leaving only faint scorch marks on the grass and a circle of singed shadows, still smoldering where they had been repelled.

Una smiled, stepping forward with her spear twirling in her hands. "Looks like we've found a way to turn the heat up."

"Yeah...but I'm exhausted," Ember said. "I can't hold it for long."

"But can you make it bigger?" I asked. "Could you protect us all?"

CHAPTER TWENTY

*E*mber's pyro shield was incredible. The way a circle of fire radiated from his body, the liquid lines of flames pushing against the darkness, scorching the shadows... it was more power than my mother ever had. And maybe it made up for his lost wing.

"I think I'm developing an inferiority complex," I said to my best friend.

Ember scoffed, waved a hand at the trident. "Says the guy who can teleport."

Una rolled her eyes. "Put the testosterone back in your pants, boys."

Ash tilted his head, prodded a finger into his chin. "It's reverse testosterone, I think."

Una swept a hand down my arm. "Your turn. Let's see what you've got."

I shrugged, kicked at the grass, causing shadows to wriggle over my feet. "I may not have another ability. The Power of the Sea might have decided the trident is enough."

"I feel that you do," Una said.

"Is that an oracle thing or a girlfriend thing?" I asked.

"An oracle thing."

Her words sent a shiver through me. Another ability. Could I handle it when I'd only recently learned how to teleport? I wasn't sure I wanted it. But then, if it helped me defeat the remaining Denizens, I'd embrace it.

After placing the trident on the ground, I took a breath, closed my eyes, and searched inside myself. I felt a knot in my stomach, an ache in my tight throat, tension hovering at the back of my neck. But nothing new. Nothing powerful.

"Ember?"

"Yeah?"

"How did you find your power?"

"Search inside." I sensed his laughter. "Meditate, sing yourself a song. What Ash said."

I opened my eyes to see him laughing. Ash pumped an arm and offered me a cocky grin.

"You've got this," Una said. Her hand swept over my arm again and she laced her fingers through mine. "Just...focus."

"You might want to stand back, just in case."

"It's going to be icy," Ember said.

"Huh?"

"Dragon kings are known for fire, right?"

"Yeah," I murmured, wishing he'd get to the point.

"My new power relates to fire." He swept a hand across his body, flexed his wing. And suddenly he seemed more powerful with just the one. "You're the guardian of Snow and Ice. So, as much as I'm going to hate it, because you know I detest the cold, I reckon yours will relate to something icy."

I gnawed on the inside of my cheek. When did Ember get so clever? I was used to him spewing wisecracks, drifting away on a cloud of weed. His insight surprised me, and I was left wondering if I was the only one still scrambling for answers.

I took Ember's words to heart, letting them roll around in my mind. Something icy. It made sense. Snow and ice had been part of me since the elemental orbs had been discovered during the ghost pirates' attack. Still, standing in the eternal night of Atlantis, where even the stars refused to break through the dark coils of Dagonar's curse, I wasn't sure how ice could help.

The trident lay on the ground, humming in time with my heartbeat, but it wouldn't be the source of my new power. Una took a step back, Ember and Ash following suit. I closed my eyes again, trying to reach down into that cold place deep inside me.

Nothing.

"Focus," I muttered, as though saying it aloud would make it happen.

"Try harder, bro," Ember called, a smirk evident in his voice. "Or maybe you're just not destined to be as awesome as me."

My eyes snapped open. A laugh burst out of me. "Oh, I think I surpassed you a long time ago." I winked at my friend. But my hands were clammy with anxiety. What if this didn't work?

I took a breath, inhaling the thick, damp air around me, and thought of meditation and candles and relaxing sounds and...Una. Una always calmed me. I looked at her now, through the shadows twisting and coiling like living things, drawing on her love. I fisted my hands and willed something, *anything,* to happen.

For a moment, there was nothing. Only the stillness of the cursed garden, the faint rustle of dark leaves shivering in the cold. Then I noticed water vapor in the air. Dagonar may have stolen our sunlight, but he hadn't changed the consistency of the air. Moisture hung in front of me, almost whispering, nearly as thick as the drifting shadows, begging to be used.

I raised a hand, calling it to me. Atlantis was born from water. And we were all ocean shifters. Then it hit. A cold so sharp it pierced every bone in my body.

The air around me shifted, a chill creeping up my spine. Frost bloomed from the tips of my fingers and spread across my body, like an unstoppable wave of ice. My breath fogged in front of me, a puff of mist in the blackened air.

And then, in a snap of raw instinct, I thrust my hands forward, gathering the nearby water molecules and transforming them into something else.

A sharp crack split the air. Ice shot from my fingertips like an avalanche, a wild blast of freezing water and jagged frost exploding outward. I didn't have time to aim—just react —and the next thing I knew, I heard a yelp, followed by the crunch of ice encasing something solid.

I scanned my surroundings and found Ember trapped in a block of ice, frozen mid-grin, his hand half-raised like he'd been about to wave.

"Oh, shit!" I gasped, rushing over. His entire body shimmered beneath the layer of frost. "Ember! Can you hear me?"

Ash burst out laughing, clutching his sides. "Dude! You *froze* him. That's one way to win an argument!"

"Not helping!" I jabbed at the ice, watching Ember's frozen expression. "Hang on, Ember, I'll get you out."

I refocused, trying to figure out how to reverse the effect. With the cold power still swirling within me, I willed the ice to retreat, watching as the frost melted, leaving Ember soaked but free.

Ember blinked, his teeth chattering, a look of utter disbelief on his face. "You *froze* me, you asswipe!" He shook himself off like a drenched dog, ice shards falling from his hair. "Of all the people..."

"I told you to stand back?" I said it like a question, sincerely hoping frostbite hadn't gathered in unmentionable areas. I remembered how much Ember had hated the cold during our journey to find Zale.

"Try it again," Una said. Ember took a few steps back, while Ash flapped his wings and flew to the palace roof. "Go bigger."

"That wasn't enough for you?"

"Karkenloth's size is undetermined. Imagine what you could do if you could freeze him."

I conceded her point. Personal shields and tiny blocks of ice would do nothing to win our war. Ember was fire. I was ice. Together, if we learned to maximize our powers, we could be an unstoppable force.

I jogged a few steps backward, leaping over a water channel, eager to try again. This time, when I took a deep breath, I felt it—a delicate mist wrapping around me, the scent of the ocean mingling with the crispness of winter air. Tiny water vapors drifted through the darkness, shimmering like stars lost in an abyss. So easily they came to me. I waved a hand, gathering a cluster of particles, their temperature dropping rapidly.

Glancing at the shadow-choked tree line, I couldn't help but feel a twinge of sympathy for the struggling flora. They were suffocating under the weight of darkness, their leaves wilting like forgotten memories. I thrust my hand in their direction. They would be better off frozen than left to wither. Before I could blink, the line of trees spanning over five hundred yards transformed into a stunning landscape of frost. The rich, earthy browns of bark were now coated in glistening white, and a hush fell over the area, thick and secretive.

Icy tendrils crept across the trunks and frost glimmered in the dim light, each flake catching what little gleam of light managed to seep through the encroaching shadows. Gentle cracking and tinkling sounds echoed through the air as ice split and fell from the branches. I closed my eyes for a moment, letting the peacefulness wash over me, the coolness of my breath mixing with the frigid air.

"It's...beautiful." Una said, coming to stand by my side.

I frowned. Beauty wasn't what I was going for. I could freeze my friends, freeze trees, but how would it help me defeat the last two Denizens?

Staring at a drifting spiral of shadows, I raised my hand once more. Gathering vapor in my hand, I twisted my arm and shot my frozen power at the shadow. Immediately, a block of ice formed in the air, and hung there, defying gravity.

Before a smile could form, the ice split and the shadow slithered out of the cracks.

Perhaps this new power would work on Karkenloth, but I'd need Ember when Dagonar appeared.

Wanting to test the limits of the ability, I raised my hand once more, but before I could gather vapor into my hand, my knees buckled.

I slid to the grass, but didn't lower my hand, keeping it raised as I searched deep for the cold power inside me. It refused to rise, no matter how many times I willed it.

"It's okay, Gal," Una said. "You've done enough for tonight."

I shook my head. "I need to know what I'm capable of. I need to know it will come when I call it."

I gritted my teeth, trying to summon it again, but nothing came. The cold inside me was gone, replaced by an empty ache, like I'd burned through something vital.

Una put a hand on my raised arm, pushed it down to my side. She moved to stand in front of me, cupped my face with her hands. "You've done enough for one night. Both you and Ember. The fountain won't replenish you and powers always take a toll."

"Not with the trident."

"Even with the trident," she disagreed. "I saw how much it took out of you keeping Maelstrom at bay while Ember and Cyra sucked up the lava. Powers come with a cost. You can't afford to be exhausted when the Denizens return."

"So what, I'm just supposed to walk around making pretty ice sculptures without learning my limits?"

Una raised an eyebrow, her one blue eye piercing my retort.

"I'm sorry," I sighed, rubbing my face. "I'm..."

"Exhausted," Una said.

I dipped my head. "If my energy depletes so easily, how will I know the right time to use it?"

Ember walked over to us, planted a hand on my shoulder. "You and me both, buddy. We'll practice a little every day. Hopefully our stamina will improve. And remember, we're in this together. It's not all on you."

I stared at my cousin. The power he contained was tremendous. For the first time, I didn't feel like saving Atlantis was all on me.

Feeling a burst of emotion, I wrapped my arms around Ember and pulled him into a hug.

"Wait for me." Una leaped into our huddle.

With a chuckle, Ember gasped for air. "Alright, alright! I'm flammable, you know. If I burst into flames, it's on you two."

I ducked under Ember's wing as his body temperature rose and pulled Una with me. The frost under Ember's feet melted, leaving a patch of grass twisting with shadows.

"I think you might need a rest too," I said.

"Before I explode, or something," Ember muttered.

"I hate this place." Una stepped over a particularly thick and twisting shadow.

I grabbed her hand and tugged her close to me, swishing the trident to make the shadows stay back. "It won't always be like this."

I didn't mention what we would have to do to reclaim Atlantis. No one needed to dwell on the darkness, metaphorically or figuratively.

"I'll grab Ash and head back to the palace," Ember said as he shifted his wing away. "Let's reconvene in the morning and see what we can do once we're rested."

I bumped his fist with mine to seal the agreement. Once Una positioned her spear on her back once more, she took my hand and led me toward the palace.

"Wait," I said, looking over my shoulder, deciding it was the right time for her surprise.

"What?" she asked.

I smiled. "I want to show you something."

Her gaze followed mine to the frosted tree line. With the colder temperatures that Dagonar had brought, my ice and frost would be sticking around. "It's beautiful, but I'm not sure I'm in the mood for a midnight walk...not in these shadows."

"Trust me." Using the trident to light our way, I guided her toward the woods, veering around the thicker shadows, my feet crunching over frost. When we passed the path that led to Una's house, she hesitated, giving a quick glance over her shoulder as we moved through the dark forest.

"Are we safe in here?"

"Shadows are just shadows."

"Until Dagonar returns. Then they become something else."

"But not tonight."

Una laughed. "You don't know that."

I nudged her ribs. "I'm the Prince of Atlantis, and I know everything."

Her laugh turned into a deep, throaty chuckle, and if it weren't for the presence of the dancing shadows, I might have lifted her into my arms and laid her on a grassy patch, made love to her right here in the woods. The thought sent a rush of heat through me. We hadn't had enough time alone lately. The wounds Nautalun had caused were still fresh. But I didn't relish the idea of a shadowy tendril sneaking up my ass while I was butt naked, so I smothered my growing desire.

I led her deeper into the forest, where the trees stood like silent sentinels, their trunks cloaked in inky darkness. The only sound was the crunch of our feet across a layer of dead leaves, their crispness breaking the enveloping silence. The rustle of animals and the hoots of owls were eerily absent, giving the suggestion that Una and I were the only two souls in existence.

As we walked, the shadows twisted and curled around us, snaking around our ankles. I moved the trident in wide arcs, stirring the shadows, using its glow to fight a path against the darkness.

"Where are we going, Gal?" Una clung to my arm, her gaze darting into the shadows.

My excitement built with each step. "You'll love it, I promise."

We finally reached the clearing, and I paused, savoring the moment. The house stood before us, crafted from the surrounding materials—a blend of stone and wood, adorned with intricate carvings that told stories of Atlantis' history.

Vines twisted around the beams, their leaves shimmering with frost when I swept a hand in the air and evoked my new power. I had designed the house myself, every detail meticulously chosen, hoping to create a place for us away from royal duties and intrusive prophecies. The palace was all well and good, but my entire extended family lived there, and I wanted a place for Una and me to call our own.

"I had planned to wait until you turned eighteen," I said, my knees oddly weak. "You spend so many nights in my suite, I never understood why we had to wait to move in together, but I wanted to respect your parents' wishes."

"Move in together?" Una's fingers dug into my arm.

I turned to face her, leaned the trident against a tree. "We haven't really spoken about it."

"About what?"

"Our future. But I know it's what we both want. I think. Being together. Forever. At least, I hope that's what you want...and now I'm weirdly nervous..." I imagined all the moments we could share within those walls.

"Don't be nervous," she whispered. "Go on."

"I mean, I'm still the prince, and you're still an oracle, and we have duties and I'm not asking you to run away with me into the sunset or anything like that, but I thought we could use a bit of space, and have a place of our own without anyone intruding on us...Am I saying the wrong thing?"

A tear rolled out of Una's eye. I leaned over her and pressed my lips to it, kissing it away. "I don't want you to cry."

"I'm happy," she said. "Despite everything that's going on, I never knew you were planning this...I didn't think you were planning that far ahead...I didn't realize how much you loved me..." She shook her head, swiping at her glistening eye.

I lifted her chin, capturing her gaze as I kissed her. "You are my everything." I dropped my forehead so it was resting against hers. "You made me what I am."

Una wrapped her arms around me, drew my bottom lip into her mouth, gave it a gentle nip.

"I hate you sneaking off in the middle of the night to go back home. Everyone knows what we're up to—not that we have anything to hide—and it's time we had a home of our own. If you like it. I'm mean...if you'd rather live in the palace..." I rubbed the back of my neck, a cold flush chilling my skin. I had never been in a relationship before Una. I'd been woefully inexperienced in matters of love, and sex. She'd taught me everything I knew. Taught me about the kind of man I wanted to be. But I was suddenly terrified I'd misjudged the situation.

"No!" Una cried. "I love it. It's perfect. But..."

"But?"

"It's in the middle of nowhere."

I chuckled. "It's only a five-minute walk from your parents, and the palace. It took us longer because of the darkness. The path will be lit at night when it's finished."

"I don't know what to say."

"That's a first."

She slapped my arm, then looked over the house once more.

"It's...beautiful," she whispered, stepping closer to examine the details, running her hand across the window ledge. The walls seemed to glow, almost as if they were alive, reflecting the warmth I felt inside. A swell of pride hit me, but even more, I felt hope. This was our haven, a place where we could escape the chaos of our lives and begin to heal together. "I just hope we have the time to appreciate it."

Her words sucked the hope right out of my heart.

CHAPTER TWENTY-ONE

The morning brought no relief to the darkness, not that I had expected it to. But there was always that grain of hope I held inside that someone, namely one of the High Council members, would figure out a way to reclaim the sun. To harness some kind of fake light so we didn't lose our crops, or our minds. We were ocean shifters built to remain in the depths for days or months, but we still needed the sun.

I dropped a kiss on Una's cheek, careful not to disturb her sleep, and left my suite. Shadows twisted through the palace halls, thickening in corners, skittering across surfaces, crawling down drains. They clung to my clothing, iced across the back of my neck, and burrowed beneath furniture. Almost taking on physical form. And yet, if I swept my hand through them, I made no contact. When touched, they would drift or scurry away, only to regain their initial positions a few minutes later.

It wasn't any better when I headed outside. At least

within the palace walls we could keep candles burning and lights turned on. But in the garden where I'd come to train, the cold, nebulous tendrils slithered around my ankles and blanketed the landscape in darkness. Ford stood near the edge of the garden, silhouetted against the lingering gloom.

With the trident in my hand, I trudged across the lawns until I reached Ford, then dropped it on the grass where it could offer a small cone of light for me to train by.

Ford patted my shoulder. "I've already seen Ember this morning. He's exhausted himself already, so it will just be you and me."

I nodded. I had slept well, Una curled into my side, her head on my chest, her leg wrapped around my waist. How I wanted it to be every night. How it soon would be. Today, she planned to study *The Mermaid Chronicles* in the great hall with the rest of the High Council and senate, ahead of a meeting I'd called.

Feeling refreshed, I was eager to test my new ability, to see how far I could push it before I exhausted myself. Power pulsed within me as steady as a heartbeat. Despite the suffocating nature of the shadows, I had grown somewhat used to them and refused to let them distract me now.

"Let's see what you've got," Ford said.

I turned to face one of the jellyfish-infested water channels. The water pulsed, a rhythmic flow beneath the surface. I reached deeper, searching for a connection, allowing the cold to wash over me, wrapping me in its embrace. This was part of me now, my lineage entwined with the depths of the ocean and the bite of frost.

Something shifted inside me. I lifted my arm. The water

quivered at my command, responding to my call. Slowly, it began to swirl, drawing upward into a spiraling column of ice and liquid, capturing the essence of both.

But then, the darkness shifted, curling like smoke around my ankles, hungry and insatiable. Dagonar's presence lingered, as if he were watching from the shadows, waiting for me to falter. A chill gripped my spine. I had to push harder.

I directed the swirling column toward the tree line, where the shadows writhed with a life of their own. With a sharp flick of my wrist, the column shot forward, slamming into the darkness with a thunderous crack, sending shards of ice cascading through the air.

"Nice," Ford said. "What else?"

"Wasn't that enough?" I asked, already drained.

"To impress me? Yes. But Dagonar and Karkenloth need more."

I didn't comment, but extended my hand, turning my palm to face the water, willing it to respond. The surface rippled, a shiver racing across the liquid as ice spread like veins. Power hummed beneath my skin, urging me to embrace it. I extended my other hand. Slowly, and with a great shifting of ice, a large section of the frozen channel rose into the air, bringing the pulsing jellyfish with it. I counted five or more of the venomous creatures. I spun my hand and the block of ice transformed into a spear, the jellyfish falling to the ground, desiccated and drained of water. One last pulse, and they were all dead.

Leaping back as a rogue tentacle rolled over my foot, my control crashed, slipping away like grains of sand through my fingers, the spear crashing to the ground and shattering into a million pieces.

I blew out a breath, stood with my hands on my hips, staring at the ice and jellyfish and snaking shadows.

"Try again," Ford said, gesturing to an area away from the jellyfish.

I turned my attention to the water vapor in the air. That was what I'd had the most success with yesterday. I focused on the droplets, narrowing my vision until they blurred into a shimmering haze. A rush of adrenaline surged through me, a mixture of fear and excitement. I sensed the potential buried inside me.

I inhaled deeply, grounding myself against the clamor of shadows that licked at my skin. I extended my hand, cold seeping into my palm, frost curling around my fingers. With a flick of my wrist, I directed the droplets toward me.

The droplets whirled, swirling into a crystalline shape of solid ice that hovered above my palm. Triumph surged through me as the shape grew into something heavier than I could ever dare to lift. A towering ice structure. But the shadows responded, curling and twisting, drawn to the power I controlled. They pressed closer, dark tendrils stretching to snuff out my triumph.

"Keep it together, Gal. Don't let them distract you." Ford's voice cut through the thick shadows.

With a determined shout, I thrust my hands forward, shooting shards of ice from my structure. They sliced through the darkness, scattering the shadows like leaves caught in a gale, until there was nothing left.

"Now, let's see you freeze that channel," Ford called, pointing to the water.

The command ignited a fire in my chest. I turned to the river flowing nearby. Power flowed through me, a freezing wave that beckoned the water to obey. A sudden gust of wind howled through the trees, rattling the branches overhead. With a shout, I pushed my hand forward, envisioning the water rising in a graceful arch, thinking of how beautiful Una would look surrounded by a dress of water and ice...but instead, it erupted violently. The icy tendrils shot upward, forming jagged spikes that pierced the air, each one reflecting the golden glow of the trident.

I doubled over, resting my hands on my thighs.

"You okay?" Ford asked.

"Give me a minute." I drew in a couple of breaths. "It's unpredictable. I'm never quite sure how the power is going to manifest."

"It's new," Ford said by way of explanation.

"I think it goes haywire when I'm tired...or distracted."

Ford nodded. "It was the same with your mother."

"Didn't she almost destroy the island with her fireballs?"

Ford chuckled. "Once or twice."

"Great."

Ford smiled, the kind that carried more weight than words alone. "Listen, Gal. Power like yours—like your mother's—it's not about being perfect from the start. It's about learning to control the storm inside you, not letting it control you. Yeah, you'll slip up. Probably break a few things along the way." He glanced at the frozen river and the shattered jellyfish. "But each time you push yourself, you get closer to mastering it."

He rested a hand on my shoulder. "Your power is unpredictable because *you're* still figuring it out. But trust me, every misstep is just a step forward. Don't fear the moments you lose control—use them. That's where real strength is born. You've got this. You're more than your mistakes."

Ford gave my shoulder a firm squeeze. "Remember, it's not about how you fall, it's about how you get back up and keep fighting."

"Okay," I replied. "I'm ready to give this another go."

"That's what I'm talking about."

Straightening, I held my palms outward, the temperature dropping immediately as if the water were waiting for me to command it. Ice crept along the surface of the water channel, spreading like winter's breath, inching toward the depths.

I poured everything I had into it, pushing against the encroaching shadows and my own fatigue. The water froze, forming thick, glimmering layers that crackled as they expanded. A sharp pull of tension ripped through my arms, the muscles in my back coiled tight, my legs sang with tension. I gritted my teeth, but I refused to give in.

The river responded, solidifying under my command. A loud crack echoed through the air as the last of the liquid froze, transforming the water into a glacial expanse. I stood before it, chest heaving, heart racing, as I examined what I had done.

Ford clapped a hand on my shoulder. "You did it. You've taken a step toward mastery, Gal. But this is only the beginning. We've got to keep training; there's more to learn. I was reading the book last night. You can make weapons from ice, freeze entire bodies of water, freeze the moisture within someone's body, even create floods to wash an enemy away."

Catching my breath, I raised both brows. "I don't know what to say. I'm a long way from freezing an ocean. And I'm exhausted."

Ford smiled. "A little bit every day will increase your stamina. It's just going to take a bit of time."

"I don't have time." I glanced at the shadows creeping along the ground. "The darkness gets thicker every day. I have a feeling Dagonar is waiting for just the right moment to return, when everyone is despairing that they'll never see the sun again. When the crops die. When people lose hope." I paused, my voice dropping lower. "And when he does, no amount of ice will be enough to stop him. Ember and I need to be ready...or we're all dead."

Ford opened his mouth to respond, and I knew he was going to give me a hard time about optimism or pessimism or facing the darkness even when I was scared, but before any words could come out, a frisbee of fire sailed past my face and skidded across the frozen river.

I leaped away from the blur of heat and sizzling shadows, clocking Ember walking along the path, a huge grin on his face.

"How cool was that?" he asked with a wink.

"Definitely *not* cool," I said. "Considering you almost singed my eyebrows off."

"Haha. You can barely see them anyway they're so pale." Ember fell into a low bow. "Just wanted to keep you on your toes."

"Your powers are back?" Ford said.

"Not entirely. But an hour's cat nap recharged the furnace," Ember replied. "That's as big as I can make the shield at the moment. But it's cool I can throw it."

"Good to know." I circled my hand in the direction of Ember's sizzling frisbee, covering it with ice and dimming its fiery glow.

"Looks like you've been doing cool shit too."

"I guess I have." I looked at Ford for approval, but then realized I didn't need it. My manipulation of water had a long way to go, but the latent power humming in my veins gave me a new sense of confidence.

When I'd left to find Zale, I'd only had the power of anger spurring me on. No plan. No skills. No support. I hadn't cared for anyone's approval then, and yet I'd desperately needed guidance. Since then, I had grown up, more so in the last few weeks. The stakes were real. As serious as they could get, and yet...I felt strangely calm. Maybe it was the calm before the storm. Maybe I was appreciating everything I had in my life. Maybe I had finally let my mother go.

"Come on." Ember slung an arm around my shoulders. "Let's go to the meeting and see if the big guns have discovered any new information."

I picked up the trident and the three of us walked to the palace, Ember letting off little puffs of fire that smoked the smaller shadows into non-existence.

When we arrived in the great hall, my entire extended family was in attendance, along with the senate and High Council. The lights were turned on and candles flickered on every surface, doing their best to vanquish the gloom. Una was nestled in an armchair with *The Mermaid Chronicles* on her lap. Its pages were disappointingly dim, meaning it had no new information to offer, and judging by the frown on her forehead, she hadn't discovered anything new that could help us.

As I moved to place the trident in its brackets, I walked by my father, who touched my arm and gave it a squeeze. We shared a look. In his eyes, I saw a man who'd fought many battles. And won. But at great costs. No one could predict what kind of condition we'd be in after the battle with the remaining Denizens. We could only hope and pray. And I knew as well as my father that some losses were too much to bear. But I couldn't think about that now. By letting my mother go, I'd had to create room for something new. Neither optimism nor pessimism, or fear or hope, but a mixture of them all, an understanding of reality, and that whatever I faced, I would, somehow, survive.

The pressure on my arm tightened as my father communicated all the things he wanted to say without words. Did he too sense we were on the eve of battle? Words were inadequate. They couldn't change our stars. All we could do was try to grasp them and hope they didn't burn us in the process.

Raina stood by his side, her hand curled around his waist, her gaze as equally serious. "Is there anything in particular either of you want me to say in the next press release?" She looked between my father and me.

"I trust you to know what the right thing is to say," I replied. "But we can go over it after the meeting if you like."

"I don't want to cause a panic," she said. "No more than there already is."

Aunt Riana had been a journalist on the mainland before the nuclear war, and since she'd moved to Atlantis, had developed her own press office with a handful of junior staff. And she was damn good at it too. Not just weaseling out a story, but presenting both sides of an argument. When I'd returned to Atlantis after hunting Zale, she had smoothed the way with the people for me.

"I appreciate you more than you'll ever know," I told her. The truth of it hit me at that moment. And it wasn't because I was saying goodbye, but because I wanted to give everyone something to cling to. Maybe I was becoming a prince after all. A true leader, understanding how to motivate people and encourage morale. If I could do that half as well as my dad, I'd be happy.

It was Raina alone who had made my father smile again. And she had nudged me toward releasing the emotional shackles my mother's death had left behind. For that, I would always be grateful.

"Thank you for saying that, Gal." She touched my arm as I moved away.

I stood behind Una, my hand cupping her face, my thumb brushing over the healing wound on her cheek. She grasped my wrist, holding onto me. We would weather this together.

I cleared my throat. "I've called you all here to discuss the remaining two Denizens. With darkness choking our island, we can't wait for the next attack to happen. We must prepare."

I moved my gaze over each person in the room, holding their eyes, letting the weight of my words sink in. The tension was palpable, the air thick with the unspoken fears that clung to us like the shadows outside. Ford stood with his arms crossed, his expression grim but resolute. Beside him, Jordan, my father's cousin, flexed his toned forearms. Blaze shifted his weight, eyes narrowed, his gaze drifting to the orb of Fire and Heat, which he had become guardian of after my mother's death. Even Rob, the head of the army and usually unflappable, pressed his lips into a thin, anxious line.

"We can't afford any mistakes," I continued, leaning into a new, growing confidence. Anticipation was always worse. But now that we were in the middle of it, now that I had developed a new power, it was time to embrace the darkness and reclaim our right to Atlantis. "The Denizens will strike again, and when they do, we need to be ready to face them head-on —before they tear this island apart."

"How are we supposed to fight shadows?" Uncle Dylan asked. He stood by the window, looking into the darkness, a muscle ticking in his jaw.

All eyes turned to Maya, Una's mother. She was our oracle, she was the one who knew *The Mermaid Chronicles* inside and out.

She rose from where she sat beside Trent. "Una and I have been studying the book. There is no information about how to defeat Dagonar, but as Gal experienced at the bay, we know his appendages can be severed from his body."

"That's all we have to go on?" Jordan grimaced, shoving a hand through his hair.

"My son and Ember have developed some impressive new abilities," Dad said, a quick glance at both of us. "Granted by the Power of the Sea when they were healed. I think that is Atlantis' way of telling us how to defeat the remaining two Denizens."

"My pyro shield can sizzle shadows," Ember said, brushing his hand over his shoulder in an exaggerated display of confidence. "I reckon I can burn Dagonar to a crisp." He clicked his fingers.

Blaze rolled his eyes at his son. "Don't get too cocky. Your power has not grown to its full strength yet."

My ability to freeze water with a wave of my hand didn't sound quite so impressive, but if I could control the moisture that surrounded Karkenloth when he arrived, we might have a chance.

"And you, Gal?" Uncle Dylan asked, stepping away from the window. "What can you do?"

I tilted my head. "I'm still learning the limits of it..."

"It's impressive," Ford said, surprising me. "And puts the odds in our favor."

I broke out in a sweat, the burden of responsibility rearing its head for a few seconds. I shook it away, drawing on the strength from the trident and my new ability. There was no one more powerful than me on the island. I wasn't sure why Atlantis had chosen me to wield these gifts, and why the fountain stubbornly refused to heal me—as if I had something more to learn—but I was learning to embrace them. Hell, I was even learning to enjoy them. The idea of freezing an entire lake and sending it flying through the sky...or arcing the trident and teleporting all over the island...when this was all over, there was a lot of fun to be had. I grinned at the thought of scaring the crap out of Ember by appearing in front of him on a dark and lonely night. As long as he didn't retaliate with his pyro shield. On second thought, maybe pranks on Ember should be off limits from now on.

"Ember may be able to handle Dagonar," Grams said, her face a mask of concern. "But how will we get rid of the jellyfish? They came right back on the tide when you last tried, Gal."

"People need to swim. To shift," Aunt Marina added.

My ears burned, still smarting from the failure. "I don't have all the answers, and there are so many unknowns, as is typical when it comes to the prophecies, but my hope is that when Dagonar is destroyed, the jellyfish will either disappear, or I will be able to vanquish them permanently."

"Let's worry about Dagonar first," Dad said. "Jellyfish second."

The lights in the room flickered. Even the candles guttered on their wicks, and everyone glanced at the windows. Una gripped my hand.

"Are they here?" Pops asked, rising to his feet.

Everyone stared at the windows. It would be impossible to tell if Dagonar had arrived. But my gut told me we had a bit longer. After a few minutes of uneasy silence, scattered conversations resumed.

"The army are on standby," Rob volunteered. "Sleeping in shifts so that no matter when the Denizens arrive, we will have a strong force. Most of the spears have now been retrofitted with explosives too."

A few impressed eyebrows rose. Una gave me a small grin.

"Thank you," Dad replied.

"There's something else I want to try." My gaze fell over

the guardians. Una, who was responsible for the orb of Spirit and Soul. Dylan, who guarded Air and Flight. Blaze, who tended to Fire and Heat. Ford, who had always been suited to Earth and Rock. And of course, I was the guardian of the orb of Snow and Ice. Babette used to protect the Power of the Sea, our largest and most powerful orb, but since her death, it hadn't chosen a replacement. I wasn't sure whether to be comforted by that or not. Perhaps the orb no longer needed a guardian, or perhaps it didn't trust anyone enough with the responsibility.

"I'd like to ask the orbs for a blessing," I said, watching the orbs from the corner of my eye. They hovered on stone plinths in the middle of the vast room, their magic emitting occasional pulses of light, as if clinging to my words. "When I made the ice flute, Una and I carried our orbs with us and they blessed the flute. I believe they enchanted it, made it more powerful. I'd like to ask the guardians here if they'd allow me to do the same for the trident, with all the orbs."

Ford stepped forward. "Of course. It's a good idea."

Dylan smiled, shaking his head. "You didn't even need to ask. You know that orb and I have a love-hate relationship. If you want to adopt it, it's all yours."

I chuckled at his response. When he'd been attacked by Zale as a young teen, it had traumatized him. He'd been stolen from his family. He'd never gotten over the trauma, and although he always stepped up to battle when he was needed, he preferred to live in the shadows, nursing his scars.

Blaze clapped my back. "Absolutely." His red orb glowed a little brighter.

Una squeezed my hand, kissed the back of it. "A great idea, prince."

"We have no one to agree for the Power of the Sea," Maya said, sweeping a hand toward the pulsing blue orb. It was the size of a basketball, somehow nebulous and solid at the same time. It hovered above the central stone plinth, swirling with all the hues of blue, situated in the center of the other five smaller orbs. "But I have a feeling it will approve."

Gratified to have received approval, I stepped toward the trident and lowered it from its brackets. It pushed its golden light into the room, sending both hope and warmth to envelop us. As I approached the orbs, each of the guardians came to stand by the one they were connected to. First, I arced the trident through my own white orb, much smaller than the others because of its heavy use during the hunt for Zale. Its power hadn't replenished yet, and it would take several years, but it was capable of a blessing.

White and gold light mixed, a meeting of magic that sent sparks dancing over our heads. Next, I approached Una and her purple orb. She gave me an encouraging smile as I brushed the trident through the magical sphere. Coils of purple light spilled into the room and wound around the trident, disappearing into its hilt.

The third orb I approached was Air and Flight. Uncle D gave me a chagrined smile, opened his hand to offer it to me. Air and Flight had always been the most temperamental of orbs, not allowing Dylan to have full mastery of the abilities it came with, and so with caution, I poked the three prongs into its mass of yellow. The yellow brightened, sent a shockwave of bright light into the room, making us all stumble. A few laughed.

Dylan frowned, glowering at the orb. "As I said, happy to put it up for adoption any time."

Taking a breath, I approached Ford and the orb of Earth and Rock. He gave me an encouraging nod. The green and brown orb seemed more solid than the others. Fittingly, I supposed. I brought the trident close and a shower of green light sprinkled over the prongs and skittered down the hilt. I felt flecks of something land on my hand, but when I glanced down, couldn't see anything to cause the sensation.

Blaze put a hand on my shoulder as I drew near to the orb of Fire and Heat. I'd always been most fearful of this one. Mostly because I was more suited to Snow and Ice. But partly because it had belonged to my mother. I let out a breath when warm, red light flooded my face and made the trident glow.

Lastly, I faced the Power of the Sea. Maya stood beside it to represent Babette. I whispered a silent prayer as I stared into its nebulous depths, asking it for protection. This one didn't make me nervous. Babette had been my friend. She'd died helping me. I knew she'd want this for me. She would want me to succeed.

Hands caressed my face, or at least, that's what it felt like as probes of blue light swept over my head and shoulders and skimmed over the trident.

Before I turned to face the others, I shared a solemn look with the guardians, then raised the trident above my head. The weapon itself remained golden, but the glow it emitted pulsed in all the colors of the rainbow.

Power hummed through my veins. Ice covered my hands. Sparks of color danced over my head and shoulders.

I glanced at Una. Her mouth hung open as her one beautiful blue eye widened at the sight of me.

The power built, whispering promises, urging me to release it. I barely felt human anymore. I was on my way to becoming something else. Something that could save Atlantis. Something that could protect the woman I loved. Something that could defeat two of the most evil gods in our world.

And I was ready.

CHAPTER TWENTY-TWO

I stood at the window of my bedroom, peering into the darkness, attempting to burn it away with only the anger of my glare. But defeating Dagonar wouldn't be that easy.

Una stood behind me, her presence a quiet, steady warmth. Without a word, she slipped her arms around my waist, holding me in a way that made my heart beat a little faster. A soft sigh escaped her as her lips pressed a lingering kiss between my shoulder blades.

"We should sleep," she said. "You've been training all day with that new power of yours. You must be exhausted."

"In a minute," I replied, placing my hand over hers. My gaze fell to the statue of my mother in the courtyard below. She was captured in action, throwing her orb of Fire and Heat. Instead of letting the grief overwhelm me, I drew on the strength she represented.

Una rested her head against my back, her warm breath

MARISA NOELLE

fanning across my skin. I didn't know when the Denizens would attack, but I planned to spend every minute I could either training or soaking in Una's presence. I wouldn't be separated from her again. From now on, she would sleep in my bed.

Her hands drifted lower, fingertips tracing the contours of my stomach. Her fingers paused, teasing lightly as they skimmed the trail of hair that disappeared beneath my waistband. My breath hitched, tension building as her movements became more purposeful. Her touch sent heat rushing through my veins. A quiet hunger stirred in the space between us, the unspoken desire tightening like a thread drawn taut, ready to snap.

I leaned back into her, my pulse quickening as her hands continued their slow exploration, her body pressed close enough that I could feel her heartbeat syncing with mine. Her touch claimed each part of me with deliberate tenderness, yet left enough space for the tension to build, for the unspoken need to simmer between us.

I turned in her arms, cradling her face between my hands, my thumbs brushing over her soft skin as I drew her closer. Our gazes locked for a brief second before I leaned in, pressing a kiss to her lips, slow and savoring. I luxuriated in the feel of her, the taste of her. The ocean and salt and jasmine. I never wanted to smell or taste anything else.

"Gal..." She traced the dark circles under my eyes with her thumbs. "You're exhausted."

I shook my head, unwilling to let my weariness pull me away from her. "I'm never too exhausted for you."

A tender smile curved her lips, softening her expression

as her fingers drifted lower, wrapping around my back. Her hands worked their way into my muscles, kneading away the knots of tight muscle. I groaned, my eyes slitting, my head falling forward.

But then her lips found mine again, and this time, I kissed her deeper. I parted her mouth with the tip of my tongue, tasting her fully. Sliding my hands into her hair, I tangled them in the wild blonde strands as I tilted her head back, eager to explore every inch of her mouth. The kiss deepened, a soft moan escaping her as she pressed closer, her body molding perfectly against mine.

The curve of her body against me sparked a slow burn that began in my chest and spread like molten heat, every part of me awakening to her touch. The softness of her skin beneath my fingers, the way she moved against me, every subtle shift sending shockwaves of desire rippling through me. My pulse quickened, the tension ratcheting up, the space shrinking until nothing remained but the two of us.

With every kiss, every press of her body, the fire inside me grew stronger, more demanding. It coiled low in my stomach, twisting tighter, stirring a hunger that surged through my veins. All I could think about was her—how she felt, how she tasted, the way her body fit so perfectly against mine. She deserved to be worshipped, especially after what had happened with Nautalun.

Time slowed, everything narrowing to the feel of her skin, the sound of her breath, the rhythm of our hearts.

"I want you," I murmured between kisses.

"You can have me," Una whispered into the shell of my ear. Her teeth grazed the edge of my earlobe, a gentle nip that sent a jolt of pleasure down my spine. Every nerve in my body hummed in response, the heat between us growing more insistent.

With a low growl, I plucked her off her feet, cradling her against my chest as I carried her to the bed. Laying her gently on the sheets, I smoothed her hair away from her face and swept my thumb gently across the fading wound on her cheek. The sight of it stirred something protective deep inside me. "You are the bravest person I know."

She laughed and swatted my arm. "Says the guy who teleports into volcanoes."

I gave her a sheepish grin. "I didn't intend to land *in* the volcano," I muttered, marveling at how she could make even the most dangerous moments feel like memories we could laugh about.

Una ran a fingernail down my arm, eliciting a shiver from me. "Well, the volcano isn't there anymore, so you have at it."

My thoughts flickered briefly to the battles we'd fought, and the ones still ahead of us. "I can't believe how Ember and Cyra sucked up all that lava."

Una tugged me onto the bed with her, rolling me until I hovered over her, my weight resting on my elbows. Her fingers curled around the back of my neck, pulling me closer. "Less battle talk," she murmured, her lips brushing mine, "more kissing."

Smiling, I lowered my head. Our lips met in a slow, deep kiss that sent heat spiraling through me. I slid my thigh between her legs, pressing gently, and she let out a soft groan, her head falling back into the pillows. Her eye fluttered closed, her body arching into mine as she whispered my name, her voice a breathy plea that made my stomach tighten. "Gal..."

I trailed kisses along her jaw, my lips lingering on her silken skin, savoring the way she responded to every touch. I moved down the curve of her neck, pressing feather-light kisses along the column of her throat. She shivered beneath me, her fingers digging into my waist as she pulled me closer.

Heat skated beneath my skin, growing more intense with every second. I slid my hand down, splaying it across her taut stomach. Her muscles quivered under my touch as my fingers drifted over her skin, exploring, teasing. Una raised her arms, wrapped them around my waist, and tugged me closer until my chest lay flush with hers. I cradled her head in my hands as I devoured her lips, licking and nipping and somehow not getting enough of her.

Her fingernails raked over my back, leaving tiny trails of fiery pleasure in their wake. My body ached with the need for her, every nerve on edge, every muscle tight with anticipation. I'd been ready to be inside her long before now, but something held me back, a desire to make this moment last, to stretch the tension between us until it was unbearable.

She groaned again, her hips shifting beneath mine. We were both teetering on the edge of something we could no longer hold back.

Lifting myself onto an elbow, I wound my arm beneath Una and undid the clasp of her bra. She shrugged out of the fabric, her skin revealed in the dim light, her nipples already hardening in anticipation. She lay back on the bed, her eye half-lidded as my gaze roamed over her curves, desperate to touch every single one.

I cupped her breast in my hand, molding the soft mound with gentle pressure. As her nipple stiffened beneath my touch, Una gasped, her back arching off the bed, pressing herself harder against my thigh. The sound of her soft, breathless reaction shot through, tightening the coil of desire low in my stomach.

Unable to resist, I replaced my hand with my mouth, drawing her nipple between my lips. I swirled my tongue over the sensitive peak, tasting her, the essence of her oceanic scent mixed with her warmth. I trailed my tongue across the swell of her breast, tracing a line into the valley between, before moving to her other nipple. I devoured it with the same slow, deliberate hunger, each flick of my tongue earning me another delicious moan from her.

"Gal..." She exhaled my name like it was the only thing keeping her tethered to the moment.

"I love you," I said.

Her eye blinked open. She looked up at me with a mixture of heat and adoration. I didn't know whether to make love to her or fuck her. The way she looked at me, like I was both her sanctuary and her wildest desire, sent a fresh wave of heat rushing through me.

With a devilish smile, Una undid the button of my pants, slid them over my hips, tugging them down just enough to free me. With my erection released, the ache in my length intensified, and I clenched my jaw to prevent things from happening too soon.

Shifting beside her, I let my fingers drift across her stomach, tracing the soft, delicate skin as I slid them lower, past the thin elastic of her panties. My hand moved over the small patch of soft hair, then to her slick center, where her body welcomed me with warm, wet readiness. The sensation of her against my fingers nearly unraveled me, but I held on, wanting to draw this out, to take my time savoring every gasp, every shudder of pleasure from her.

Una bucked beneath my hand, her hips rising off the bed as she gripped my wrist, her head pressing back into the pillow. Her expression was all heat and need. I pressed my thumb to her sensitive bud, moving in slow, deliberate circles that had her hips chasing the rhythm.

Keeping my thumb steady, I slipped two fingers inside her, feeling the wet, satisfying heat of her. She was so ready, so warm, and the sensation nearly undid me. As I moved my fingers in and out of her center, I dropped kisses onto her cheek, the taste of her filling my senses again.

Una bit down on her bottom lip, her hands wrapping around my arm, holding tight as she bucked against me. Her breath came in short, quick bursts, my name tumbling out of her lips on repeat.

I leaned down, capturing her nipple between my teeth, nipping gently before soothing the skin with my tongue. Her body shuddered beneath me, and I felt the tension in her muscles coil tighter, the wave of her release building. I increased the pace of my thumb and fingers, matching the rhythm of her hips as she moved against me, chasing the edge of her pleasure.

Her body tensed all at once, her back arching as she clenched around my fingers, her muscles tightening in rhythmic spasms. She moaned my name, her voice breaking as the ecstasy rolled through her, her grip on my arm tightening as she rode out the wave of her release, her body trembling with each aftershock.

I left my fingers inside her, waiting until her eye blinked open, still clouded with the heat of desire. Her breath came in shallow, rapid bursts, but there was no mistaking the hunger in her gaze.

"That wasn't enough," she said.

I raised a brow. "It sounded like enough."

But her smile, slow and seductive, told me otherwise. She wanted more, and I was more than willing to give it. Reluctantly, I withdrew my fingers from her, and rolled onto my back. Bringing them to my lips, I tasted her—her sweet, intoxicating flavor. I nearly lost myself in the bliss of it, my senses overwhelmed by her flavor.

Then I felt her hand, warm and confident, wrap around my length. *Shit, that felt good.* The sharp surge of pleasure that followed had me groaning, hips jerking involuntarily into her grasp. Her touch was slow— agonizingly slow—as she ran her hand up and down the length of my erection, each stroke stoking a restless burn.

With a growl, I flipped her onto her back, positioning myself between her legs. I paused to admire the swell of her breasts, the dip of her waist, the curve of her hips, and the delicate flutter of her pulse in her neck...*breathtaking*. And mine.

Our gazes locked, the unspoken connection between us buzzing with electricity as I sank into her. Her body welcomed me, tight and slick, enveloping me in a heat so intense it stole my breath. Her gaze never left mine as her expression shifted, her banked heat sizzling over with every inch I pushed inside.

I began to move, slow at first, savoring the feel of her beneath me, the way her body arched to meet mine, her nails clawing my back as she urged me on. She gripped my hips as I moved, rising and falling in a timeless rhythm as old as the tides, urging me on with breathless pleas.

Soaking in the feel of her, I reveled in the sensation of a sharp tightening deep inside. She released a breathy moan as I filled the deepest part of her. Her hips rose to meet each of my movements, circling in perfect rhythm with mine. A sheen of sweat misted her skin as her muscles gripped me tighter with every thrust. The deeper I went, the more she gasped, her breath coming in ragged bursts.

My skin ached. Hot blood thundered through my veins. My stomach fluttered.

Una's muscles clamped around me, causing a flash of ecstasy to shoot through me in a blinding rush. The heat in my stomach unraveled. Turned into an aching spike of pleasure. Tension mounted. Coiling tight as I thrust into Una again and again. Unbearable. Biting shudders took my limbs hostage. My skin hummed with heat.

Una dug her fingers into my rear, yanking me deeper inside her, encouraging my hips to move faster. Harder. Deeper. Faster. *More.*

She drove me to the edge, pushed me past the point of control.

"Una..."

Her name slipped from my lips in a ragged groan, my body shuddering as the tension inside me exploded, a primal rush of release burning through my limbs. Every inch of me spasmed, the sensation obliterating all thought, leaving only the feel of her, the scent of her, the sight of her.

"Una..." I groaned again, burying myself deeper inside her as she unraveled around me. Her core tightened, spasming with her own release, pulling me deeper into her. We clung to each other as wave after wave of aftershocks claimed us, our hips jerking in unison, bodies pressed together, lips crashing in desperate, heated kisses.

We stayed like that for a long time, our bodies tangled, our breaths mingling as the last of the aftershocks rippled through us. Gradually, the world came back into focus.

I rested my forehead against hers, both of us catching our breath. Her skin was slick with sweat, her chest rising and falling against mine in a steady rhythm that calmed me.

I kissed her forehead, the need in my body giving way to a softer feeling. I traced the line of her jaw, brushing over the delicate skin of her throat before settling at the curve of her waist.

"You're incredible," I murmured, my voice still hoarse from the rawness of it all.

Una smiled, her lips brushing against mine in a featherlight kiss before pulling back to meet my gaze. Her eye sparkled with warmth and affection, but there was still that mischievous glint that made my heart stutter.

"So are you," she whispered, her fingers sliding lazily across my back. "But if you keep doing that thing with your thumb...I might never let you leave this bed."

I chuckled. "I think I could live with that."

I shifted, sliding to the side, but kept her close, her body molding against mine as we lay together, skin to skin. The bed felt like a world of our own, where nothing else mattered but the softness of her body pressed against me, and the steady beat of her heart beneath my hand.

She nestled into me, resting her head on my chest, her breath a soft sigh against my skin. For a while, neither of us said anything. We didn't need to. The silence was full, comfortable, like we were soaking in the afterglow of something sacred. I ran my fingers through her hair, untangling the wild blonde strands, and she hummed in contentment, the sound vibrating through me, soothing.

"Una?" I finally said.

"Yeah?" Her voice was sleepy.

I cupped her cheek, brushing my thumb over her skin. "You're staying here tonight."

"I know." She raised her head to look at me. "As long as you promise not to lock me in here when everything starts."

I laced my fingers through hers and held them against my chest. "I need you by my side."

Her smile was small but full of trust. She settled back into my arms, locking our fingers tighter together. "Good."

I held her closer, staring at the window, at the darkness pressing against our small haven. Shadows coiled beneath the glass, snaking their way into the room, drifting to the floor where they skated beneath the bed. Others weaved up the curtains and pooled on the ceiling. Several drifted to the lights and snuffed out their illumination.

I frowned, watching their sinister movements as they thickened and coiled into menacing shapes.

I sat up.

"What's wrong?" Una asked, her gaze falling to the window where dense shadows knocked against the frame.

A scream tore through the courtyard. Then another. The lights went out. The only illumination in the room came from the trident where it rested against the wall.

"Dagonar's here," I said, leaping out of bed.

CHAPTER TWENTY-THREE

I yanked on a pair of shorts, my fingers trembling as I fumbled with the waistband. The sound of battle outside seeped through the walls—screams, so many agonizes screams—but I forced myself to focus.

"Gal, wait!" I turned to see Una threading her arms through her shirt, her body visibly shaking.

"What is it?" I asked as I plucked the trident from its resting place.

More screams came from outside. Followed by the roar of flames. No doubt one of the dragon kings.

She cupped her hands over her mouth, her gaze bouncing between me and the window, panic flaring in her eye. It was still pitch-black outside, but the occasional fireball streaked through the inky darkness. "I'm scared."

My heart softened. I walked back over to her and folded an arm around her waist. "You don't have to come," I whispered, resting my forehead against hers. "You can stay here."

She shook her head and laid her palm on my chest, right over my heart. "Never."

"It's going to be okay." Her throat flexed as she swallowed. "I have the trident, blessed by the orbs, and my new ability. I can do this, Una."

She nodded, her fingers curling into a fist against my chest. "I know you can."

I kissed her forehead, then her cheek, then pressed my lips to hers. "We have to go."

I took Una's hand, and we moved together. We sprinted toward the grand staircase, the sound of soldiers' boots echoing against the marble beneath us, the steady thrum of battle growing louder as we drew closer. Smoke and tension clouded the air, bringing a metallic bite of impending violence. Violence I would wield.

We dashed down the grand staircase. Below us guards and soldiers ran out the front door grabbing explosively charged spears as Rob handed them out at the entrance. He looked up at me as I hurried down the steps, his gaze heavy with gravity.

"Good luck," Rob said to Una as he handed her a spear. "I've seen what you can do with this. You're a true asset."

Una blushed. She nodded once, lips tight, and then we sprinted out the front doors together.

I skidded to a halt at the top of the stone steps. The battle wasn't merely underway—it was total anarchy. I couldn't take it all in.

Blaze roared overhead, his massive wings spread wide against the ink-black sky. He banked sharply, exhaling torrents of searing flames onto a dark, towering figure below. Dagonar.

The sight of him hit me like a punch to the chest. He was monstrous, his vaguely humanoid, amorphous form shifting like a storm cloud, darker than the night surrounding him. The black mass of his body swirled and pulsed, thick tendrils of shadow lashing out in every direction, snatching soldiers from the ground like they were nothing more than insects. Screams echoed through the air, merging with the roar of fire and the crack of explosive spears.

I glanced at Una beside me, her face illuminated by the bursts of fire and explosions, her earlier panic twisted into an expression of shock.

Blaze dove again, spewing fire at Dagonar's core. The flames licked across the swirling shadows, and for a few seconds, parts of Dagonar disintegrated, scattering into ash-like particles. But the reprieve was short-lived. The shadows reformed, creeping back toward the central mass, their tendrils whipping across the courtyard. There must have been over two hundred soldiers scurrying across the cobbles, thrusting their spears into the blackness, explosions momentarily severing the shadowy limbs. But each time a tendril was cut, it writhed on the cobblestones, then snaked its way back toward Dagonar, rejoining his body.

There had to be a way to stop him. Permanently. I couldn't tear my eyes from the sight—the futility of it all—and the sickening realization hit me that we were running out of time. We didn't have enough spears, and the soldiers couldn't fight forever. There was no time to stop by the fountain.

Fatigue would catch them eventually, and Dagonar wasn't slowing down.

Movement to my left caught my eye—my father. He stood in the thick of the battle, his muscular form wrestling with a thick coil of shadow wrapped around his waist, his muscles straining as he fought against it. A chill gripped my chest. I clenched my teeth. I prepared to teleport to him, to help. But before I could act, he let out a growl, ripping the shadow in half with his brute strength. Tossing the writhing tendrils to the ground, he went to grab another.

I swallowed hard, watching him for a second longer.

I'd never seen his strength in action. Not since the battle with the ghost pirates, and I'd only caught glimpses then. His power was incredible. He tore another shadow from around Cyra's neck, then scooped the young teen into his arms and carried her to safety. She barely flinched as she got back to her feet, inhaling streams of her father's fire from the air, her small frame radiating with determination. Without hesitation, she sprinted forward, darting between the thrashing shadows, and unleashed a burst of flames into a thick mass of darkness. She had guts, I'd give her that.

The trident buzzed in my hand, its energy coursing through me, urging me forward.

As I was about to dash down the steps, my hand still connected to Una's, a blur in the sky snagged my attention. Ford, caught in a shadowy vine, dangled helplessly above.

I turned to Una. "I have to go."

She pressed a quick kiss to my cheek. "I love you. Be safe."

I hung on to her gaze for a heartbeat longer, then I arced

the trident and surged into action. I hadn't practiced the series of quick maneuvers I had in mind to rescue Ford, could only hope the trident would bend to my will.

I sailed through the air, time almost standing still, and appeared in the sky next to Ford. Slashing the trident in the air as the power of teleportation gave way to gravity, I cut through one of the vines clinging to Ford. I flicked the trident once more and teleported behind Ford's back, sliced through a second vine trapping his legs. Before we both plummeted to earth, I grabbed his wrist with my free hand and arced the trident again. A second later we stood in the courtyard together, soldiers raging around us.

Ford gave me a sharp nod, his gratitude silent but clear. He grabbed a spear from the ground and dashed back into the thick of the fight.

Dagonar's roar shook the sky as shadows twisted around him like a living storm, slithering across the ground and lashing out at anyone who dared approach. He raised his arms, tendrils of darkness snapping from his arms like whips. Two soldiers nearby screamed as the shadowed tendrils coiled around their bodies, lifting them into the air. The grotesque sounds of bones snapping and flesh tearing hit my ears as they were torn in half, their blood splattering the stone courtyard.

Blaze roared above, his massive wings beating against the sky as he swooped down and unleashed a torrent of fire. The flames seared the air, engulfing Dagonar in a blistering inferno. For a moment, the shadows recoiled, hissing and thrashing as they retreated from the fire. But the moment was brief—Dagonar stepped through the flames unscathed, his eyes gleaming with dark power as his shadows reformed, stronger and more vicious than before.

Cyra unleashed a blast of fire from her mouth, aiming at the shadowy whips. One of the tendrils sizzled and burned away under the heat, but more replaced it, snaking through the flames and lashing toward her.

"Cyra! Watch out!" Blaze's voice thundered from above as he dove again to protect his daughter.

Dagonar's attention shifted, his gaze snapping toward the soldiers armed with explosive spears. One of them hurled a spear at the swirling shadows surrounding Dagonar's feet. The explosion shattered the tendrils, sending pieces of shadow flying in every direction—but almost immediately, the darkness slithered back together, reforming into a lethal wave. The soldiers had little time to react before more shadow whips lashed out, grabbing two of them by the throats, squeezing until they went limp.

I caught a flash of movement from the corner of my eye— Una. She faced the Denizen, spear in hand, her face burning with resolve. She pulled her arm back and launched the spear. It sailed through the air, aimed directly at Dagonar. But before it struck, a whip of shadow shot out, catching Una around the waist and yanking her off the ground.

"Una!" I shouted, panic surging through me. Memories of the bay threatened to distract me.

Her scream cut through my heart as the shadow constricted around her, tightening. She struggled, her hands clawing at the darkness as it coiled tighter, threatening to crush her.

I arced the trident, focusing on the crackling tension in

the air where the shadows gripped her. A flash of light blinded me for an instant as I disappeared from the ground and reappeared in mid-air, right next to Una.

I didn't hesitate. With a fierce slash, I swung the trident, the blade cutting through the shadow like it was smoke. The tendril recoiled, hissing, as it disintegrated under the power of the trident. I grabbed Una's arm, pulling her free of the suffocating grasp, and teleported us to safety, landing in a crouch behind a pile of rubble.

Una gasped for air, her hand clutching her side where the shadow had squeezed her. "I'm fine," she panted, seeing the fear in my eyes. "Just...a little bruised."

Before I could respond, a deafening crash echoed across the courtyard. I turned to see Uncle Dylan charging toward Dagonar, a spear in each hand. With a feral yell, he hurled both spears at the shadow-wielding tyrant. The explosive heads detonated on impact, blowing apart the shadows once again. But as before, the dark tendrils reformed, snapping back into place like they were made of water.

Dagonar had hold of at least ten people in his shadowy ropes of death, including my father. He raised them high. So very high. If he let them go, they would fall and die on impact. I focused my attention on my father and teleported into the air.

"You need to focus on taking him down, not rescuing everyone," Dad said as I hovered in the air beside him. "I've got this." His eyes gleamed as he ripped the shadow apart.

Before I fell, I teleported once more, the sharp prongs of the trident held prone, and arrived in front of Dagonar's head.

Our eyes locked—his an endless, swirling abyss of hatred and shadow, mine blazing with fury. The cold emptiness in his gaze swept through me, as relentless and freezing as an arctic tide, but I didn't flinch.

"Give me the trident." His voice in my head.

I didn't bother with a reply. I slashed the trident in a wide arc, aiming for his throat.

Dagonar roared, his voice like grinding stone, and twisted at the last second. The trident grazed his cheek, leaving a trail of dark mist instead of blood. Did he even bleed? I wasn't sure.

Before he retaliated, I teleported again, this time to his left, swiping at his ribs. The strike landed, cutting through more shadow, but it reformed in an instant, swirling back into place.

I teleported again and again—slashing at his head, his back, his legs—each strike landing before I vanished and appeared elsewhere. Dagonar snarled in frustration, trying to follow my movements, but I was persistent, never staying in one place long enough for him to counter, the power of the blessed trident thrumming through me, lighting me up in an otherworldly glow.

But despite my rapid attacks, he wasn't weakening. The more I struck, the faster his shadows reformed, swallowing every wound I dealt. I needed something more—something that would break him from the inside.

Heart pounding, I made a decision. In a flash, I teleported directly into Dagonar's chest. His amorphous body, swirling with darkness, enveloped me. I was inside him now—surrounded by pure blackness, the cold shadows pressing in on all sides. My senses were overloaded. It felt like drowning in ink, my breath coming in ragged gasps as I fought against the clinging void.

I swung the trident wildly in the blackness, feeling the resistance of shadow but never landing a solid hit. The darkness was alive, shifting and swirling too fast for me to keep up. It was like trying to fight a storm. The shadows slipped through my fingers, slashing at me from all directions, their cold tendrils sapped my strength with every passing second.

"Give me the trident, Gal."

"Never!"

Dagonar's laughter thundered through my head, deep and mocking, as if it came from every corner of my mind. The oppressive weight of the shadows bore down on me, dragging me deeper. My arms grew heavy, the trident more difficult to swing. My legs faltered beneath me as the blackness swirled faster, suffocating me.

I couldn't breathe. Every time I tried to strike, the shadows reformed quicker than I could react. It was as if Dagonar was toying with me, letting me struggle in vain.

I had to get out, but my thoughts were sluggish, my mind clouded by the all-consuming dark. The shadows squeezed tighter around my chest, crushing my lungs, my pulse slowing as exhaustion crept in. Desperation gnawed at the edges of my fading strength.

I need to find a way out.

Una.

I gripped the trident tighter, forcing my body to move. Shadows curled around my limbs, twisting and tightening, every movement slowed by the oppressive darkness. Dagonar's laughter echoed in my ears, a hollow sound that reverberated through my soul. My vision flickered as exhaustion crept deeper into my bones.

Suddenly, a blinding flash of light erupted from the courtyard below. The weight around me loosened, the shadows retreating enough for me to catch my breath. Ember's fiery shield pulsed beneath me, creating a dome of crackling flames that deflected the shadowy tendrils and sent waves of heat into the air. The heat was intense, scorching even from a distance, but it was the only thing keeping Dagonar's relentless attack at bay.

Ember stood at the center of the courtyard, his hands raised high and his one wing pounding the air as flames danced around his body, sheltering him and several others behind a protective barrier. The shield grew, protecting more people by the second, pushing against Dagonar's invading shadows.

His eyes locked on Dagonar as he advanced, the flames licking at the edges of the Denizen's shadowy form. Every step Ember took scorched the ground, leaving molten rock in his wake, the heat from his pyro shield burning away the shadows before they could rejoin the Denizen's body. Dagonar recoiled, his shapeless body writhing and shifting to avoid the flames, but Ember pressed forward, unyielding.

This was my chance.

With a surge of adrenaline, I teleported out of the blackness and reappeared in the courtyard, gasping for air. Dagonar's shadows swirled around me, desperate to latch on again, but Ember's flames drove them back. I found Una, a little bloody and bruised, but mercifully alive. She yanked the tiny shadows still clinging to my body away, throwing them into Ember's shield.

"Thank you," I whispered, landing a kiss on her head.

"Please don't jump into the body of another Denizen again. Please, Gal, you scared the crap out of me—"

I shushed her with a kiss. I wasn't scared of Dagonar, even though he was strong. I knew I could kill him. And now Ember was here, this was my chance.

Ember's face bunched with tension. The effort it took to maintain the shield and protect the people still fighting below tested every ounce of strength he bore. The shield was larger than I'd seen him produce it before, large enough to protect two hundred people. A dome of flames and fire. A force field of sizzling heat. But I caught the odd patch of darkness, the flames struggling to stay alight. He was tiring already.

Cyra stood beside him, her small hands glowing with the heat of her own fire, exhaling blasts of flame toward any shadow that dared approach.

I tightened my grip on the trident. Dagonar's form shimmered, his shadows wispier, lighter, the once-solid darkness now fraying at the edges. A glimmer of light appeared in the sky; the sun trying to break through.

Taking a breath, I teleported again, landing behind Dagonar's head, and swiped at his dimming form with the trident. The sharp prongs sliced through the darkness, severing pieces of it that dissolved in the air. But Dagonar wasn't done yet. He lashed out with shadowy tendrils, but this time, they crumbled under the heat of Ember's flames before they could rejoin the evil god's body.

With Dagonar's strength waning, I seized my moment. I

raised the trident high, its prongs crackling with energy, light pulsing along its shaft, and drove it into the heart of Dagonar.

The Denizen's form convulsed, a guttural roar escaping as the trident pierced him.

With a final pulse of power, the trident exploded with light, sending shockwaves through the courtyard. Dagonar's form shattered, the shadows dissipating into nothingness.

When I teleported back to the ground, Ember released his shield and a cool breeze swept through the courtyard, easing the heat on flushed faces. Faces I could now see under the bright light of the sun.

Exhausted, I sank to my knees, flopped onto my side, and then rolled onto my back. I splayed my arms and legs, looked up at the sun, trying not to blink as I digested its brightness. I had no idea how long we'd been enduring the darkness. It was hard to tell time when the sun never rose, but now that it was back, warming my cheeks, caressing my tired muscles, I realized its absence had festered inside of me worse than I'd thought.

Ember flopped down next to me, wrapped his fingers around my wrist and pumped our fists in the air.

"How you doing?" he asked.

"I'm alive."

Ember chuckled. "I'm freaking exhausted."

"I hear that."

He shifted beside me. "Think I may have singed off my pubes."

I laughed, which turned into a coughing fit, which turned into a muscle spasm of pain. "Please don't make me laugh. Everything hurts."

Pushing myself into a sitting position, I scanned the area for Una. My gaze skimmed over heaps of rubble, smoldering fires, and deep craters. The courtyard was a mess of ruined stone and chucks of marbles and bright, hopeful sunshine. But even as I took in the damage of the battle, the island began to repair itself. Cobblestones flew back into place, cement fixing them in place. Marble columns grew from the ashes, and withered vines turned ripe and plump once more. Within minutes, everything was as it had been before Dagonar arrived. Even the water sparkled with new clarity, although the jellyfish remained.

Dad came by and pulled me to my feet. "I'm proud of you."

"I couldn't have done it without you," I replied as he gave me a tight hug. He stank of ash and fire and burned things.

"I'm going to check on the others. Then address our people."

As he wandered off, I caught sight of Una near the fountain. Most people huddled around the healing water. Una stood in the middle of the fountain, even though it didn't heal her, handing out shells filled with water, making sure everyone was cared for.

She was dirty and bloody, burned and disheveled, her eyepatch lost in battle, but she had never looked more powerful. More beautiful. My heart leaped inside my chest. I charged across the repaired courtyard, elbowed my way through the people, ignoring the aches in my limbs, and swept her into my arms.

Una wrapped her arms around my neck. "You were amazing."

I shook my head. "Just doing my job."

She threw her head back and laughed. "Not so long ago I remember a time when you would have done anything to get out of your responsibilities."

I smiled at her. She was right. But life had changed me. I'd grown up. I hoped. I'd become worthy of the trident and the Power of the Sea's blessing. I couldn't turn my back on that. My mother had been terrified of losing people too, and yet she'd fought viciously during every war.

I glanced at her statue, standing tall and proud, and no longer felt the pull of grief. Just love. And pride. And power.

There was so much power beneath my fingertips. I could feel it buzzing, urging me to use it, already replenishing my depleted energy reserves.

As Una turned to help more people drink from the fountain, I glanced down at my body, surprised by the flow of energy rolling through my limbs. The aches and pains vanished. There were no cuts or bruises or burns. I felt...*alive*. More than alive. As if the fountain had healed me. But I hadn't taken a single drop.

CHAPTER TWENTY-FOUR

Sunlight streamed down, casting long shadows, almost too bright after the choking darkness that had smothered the island only hours before.

I threaded through the crowd with the trident in hand, the weight of its power pulsing through my arm with every step. People pressed close, their hands brushing my arms, their eyes wide with awe—a scrutiny I'd never experienced before. I felt a little uncomfortable, but when I realized I wouldn't get away without engaging in conversation and reenacting blow-by-blow accounts, I embraced their attention. Maybe allowing myself to feel a little pride wasn't a bad thing.

I shook hands, hugged little kids, kissed the cheeks of grateful mothers.

"You saved us!" they murmured. "You're a hero."

The words sunk into me, their admiration sparking something deeper than the rush of victory. It was a soft, intoxicating warmth, more tender than the raw power of the trident —but it fed me all the same.

"You were so brave, Your Highness!" a man shouted, his voice thick with gratitude.

I squared my shoulders, straightened my spine, and lifted my chin. The crowd parted as I moved, eager faces turned toward me. I couldn't remember the last time I'd felt so seen. So *needed*. Not even when I'd defeated Zale. Of course, I had also destroyed *The Mermaid Chronicles*, and most people weren't too happy about that.

I stood in the middle of the courtyard with the sun on my back, recounting action scenes, acting them out with the trident. Laughter rippled through the crowd, followed by cheers. A couple of kids tugged at my legs, their eyes shining. I scooped them up, tossing them into the air, their squeals filling the courtyard.

"Can you teleport me?" a woman asked.

Smiling, I obliged. With a flick of the trident, we blinked to the north shore and back, the brief journey leaving the crowd awestruck. The northern beaches, once shrouded in shadow, gleamed under the sun's rays. The sight made something tighten in my chest—pride? Power? Maybe both. The way they looked at me, the gasps of admiration—it fueled a hunger I didn't know I had.

I caught Uncle Dylan's eye across the courtyard. He was leaning against a pillar in the shade, arms crossed, his gaze unreadable. He gave me a nod, but something about his expression made my pulse skip. What was his problem? The battle was over. Dagonar was dead. I'd saved them all. Yet there he was, lurking in the shadows like a storm cloud on the horizon. Maybe it was the aftermath of another battle. They always re-traumatized him. Hopefully, no one he cared about had been hurt. Which reminded me I hadn't checked on all my friends and family members.

Shaking off the unease, I scanned the crowd, ticking off names and faces. Ember sat at a table with a bunch of our friends, downing cups of wine. His dad hovered nearby with his wings still in the open. Cyra and Ash were there too, retelling their own versions of events.

I found Maya and Trent. Aunt Marina. My grandparents. Rob and Jordan. Una's three younger siblings. Then there was my father and Aunt Raina walking the path to the beach with their arms wrapped around each other. I still couldn't get used to the idea of them together, but I was happy for them. I caught sight of the back of Ford's head as he trudged up the steps toward the palace. Everyone was accounted for. Alive.

I heaved a sigh of relief, but the peace around me felt too fragile, too fleeting, as if one wrong step would shatter it. I turned back to the crowd, and the moment I made eye contact, the questions came.

"The jellyfish?" a man's voice rose from somewhere in the back. "Is there anything you can do?"

I nodded, wiping the sweat from my brow. "Let me try."

Jumping from the chair I'd been standing on, I pushed through the throng. The crowd parted in a wave of hushed anticipation, eyes glued to me as I approached a water channel. The jellyfish were there, their blood-red bodies undulating through the water, their tentacles swaying like lethal ribbons. They pulsed with an eerie light, casting long, crimson shadows on the stones beneath them.

The sight made my skin prickle. We'd reclaimed the sun, but the water was still poisoned by their presence, and without it, ocean shifters would suffer. We may have saved our crops, but without the water, morale would sink deeper than Dagonar's darkness. And I was sick of the sight of them.

The crowd parted as I raised the trident, its brilliant glow of rainbow light pulsing into the sky. Arcing the golden weapon in the air, I envisioned the toxic creatures flowing out, far beyond the island, banished to the endless ocean.

As I swished the trident in gentle arcs, the venomous animals began to move, their bodies pulsing with bright red light, their tentacles reaching for currents. One by one, they joined the invisible tide I'd conjured, swept away toward the open ocean. The crowd murmured, a ripple of hushed conversations moving through it.

For the next few hours, I teleported across the island, clearing every channel, stream, lake, and pond of the toxic creatures. With each flash of light and each successful sweep of the trident, I felt a surge of pride—but it came with a dangerous edge. I had power, more than I'd ever dreamed of. And it wasn't confined to the trident. It was inside me.

When the last of the jellyfish disappeared into the deep, I made my way back to the courtyard, my limbs heavy with fatigue but my chest buzzing with fierce satisfaction. The crowd was still thick, voices loud with celebration. They cheered when they saw me return, but I waved them off, collapsing into a chair by the fountain. There were only so many questions and back slaps I could take before I craved anonymity.

Una brought me a cup of wine and fell onto my lap. I wound my fingers into her hair, then gripped the back of her neck, turning her head for a kiss. The world shrunk to the two of us, her warmth grounding me against the building sense of unease inside my head. The sky above was cloudless, impossibly blue, but there was a thickness in the air, a tension beneath the laughter that lingered like an aftertaste. No one else seemed to notice it, though. It was probably just me. I might be powerful, but that hadn't cured me of overthinking.

Across the courtyard, the bar heaved with people and spilled onto the walkways. Servers pushed through the crowd, trolleys of wine and beer clinking as they went. People mingled by the fountain, drinks in hand, faces flushed with the glow of victory. It looked like a festival, but it didn't feel like one—not to me. There was still one Denizen out there. One more lurking in the shadows, waiting for the perfect moment to strike. And while they celebrated, I couldn't shake the creeping sensation that the real battle was yet to come. Karkenloth was the biggest of the lot.

As the hours stretched on, the courtyard transformed into a raucous scene. Laughter bubbled from every corner, faces glowing not only from the candles flickering on tables, but from the heady mix of relief and wine. The bar ran out of beer and I was sent to one of the western villages to beg for a spare keg. Of course, teleportation made that task much easier. I changed the pipes over for Uncle Dylan, took the empty kegs into the back alley, dancing around stray hands still wanting to touch me.

It felt like the island was exhaling all its tension in one long, wild breath. People danced near the fountain, swirling to the rhythm of an invisible song that had started with victory and was fueled by alcohol.

Ember held court by a large crowd of our friends, cracking jokes with anyone who would listen. His words were slurred, his grin wide, and his energy infectious.

"If this is what happens after a battle," he said, raising his drink, "sign me up for the next one. I could get used to this hero business!" He winked at a group of women nearby, who giggled and clinked their glasses in response.

Una sat beside me, her fingers tracing lazy patterns on my arm as she laughed at something Cyra had said. I watched her, the way her shoulders relaxed, the way her head tilted back with laughter, and for a moment, I allowed myself to imagine our future free of Denizens and prophecies.

"It's going to his head," Una said with a smile.

"He did save us."

"*You* saved us." She kissed me, right in the middle of the crowd, probing her tongue into my mouth and taking it hostage until I softened against her.

I still carried the trident. I wouldn't let it out of my sight until the last battle was over. Its energy continued to pulse through me, reminding me an attack could happen at any moment. I seemed to be the only one who remembered that. The only one sober.

"You alright, buddy?" Ember's voice broke through my thoughts. He stood behind me, swaying, an empty cup dangling from one hand. His eyes were bloodshot. "You look like you're carrying the weight of the whole damn ocean on your shoulders."

I forced a smile. "Just thinking. You know me, always thinking."

"Well, stop thinking," he said, slinging an arm around my shoulder. "We saved the day. Enjoy it! For all we know, Karkenloth's out there somewhere crying into its fishy pillow because it knows how powerful we are." He sniggered, and I couldn't help but chuckle too, but the knot in my stomach didn't loosen.

The night dragged on, the celebrations getting louder, sloppier. People staggered between tables, their movements slow and clumsy, fueled by too much drink and too little sleep. Some sang off-key songs, others sprawled on the grass, laughing at nothing. How could they be so cavalier when the worst Denizen was yet to appear?

I guess I couldn't blame them. They'd been cooped up in darkness for weeks, crops dying, food sources low, depression running rampant...and all they could do was wait.

I spent the evening forcing smiles, laughing too late at jokes, mishearing comments, jumping at sudden sounds. But every shadow stretched too long, every gust of wind carried the scent of something wrong. I scanned the horizon, where the sea met the sky, half-expecting to see Karkenloth rising from the depths.

Una dozed off against my shoulder sometime after midnight, her soft breaths a rhythm I tried to match, but my heart continued to race. Ember had cracked one-liners for hours, but when his voice grew hoarse, the jokes thinned. One by one, the crowd dwindled.

The sky shifted from pitch black to a bruised blue, the first hints of dawn creeping over the horizon. I leaned back in my chair, exhaustion weighing down my limbs, but my mind wouldn't shut off. The trident rested across my lap, its glow still strong, its power pulsing in the back of my mind. Eventually, my eyes drifted shut.

I must have dozed off because when I opened my eyes again, the sky was brighter, the sun edging over the ocean. Everything was still, the world caught in the quiet lull before day truly begins. The sun danced across the water, making it glisten and shimmer. It was a sight I'd sorely missed. A genuine smile warmed my lips. But then I saw it—something on the horizon. A shape. Massive and dark, it broke the smooth line of the sea, too big to be a ship, too solid to be anything natural.

The shape on the horizon grew clearer with every passing second. My heart stuttered as I rose from my chair. The light from the rising sun stretched across the waves, but the shape didn't disappear. Its dark outline solidified into something far more sinister.

Karkenloth.

Its body breached the surface like an ancient leviathan pulled from the depths, a dark orange behemoth covered in gleaming wet scales, thick as armor, stretching from head to tail. Tentacles emerged, one by one, unfurling like nightmarish serpents from beneath the water. They were enormous, each one lined with row after row of suckers, their edges rimmed with spines that glinted in the early morning light. There had to be dozens of them, writhing in the air, thick and strong enough to crush a ship in their grip. I could hear the suction even from where I sat, a sickening, wet sound as they slithered and pulsed, tasting the air, tasting the island.

The breath stalled in my lungs, my pulse a frantic rhythm. This was the moment I'd been waiting for. The ultimate showdown. Dagonar was nothing compared to this. Karkenloth was the last Denizen, the deadliest, the one who would wipe us out if I didn't stop it. But I would. I had to.

I flexed my fingers around the trident, and its golden light pulsed, feeding me a sense of strength, a sense of certainty. This was history in the making. I would become a legend. I possessed Vorago's trident after all.

Power swam through my arm, electrifying every nerve, filling me with something more than adrenaline—something close to invincibility. I'd taken down Dagonar, hadn't I? I'd saved the island, cleared the waters, restored the sun. What was one more Denizen? Why had I been so worried?

A part of me knew it was reckless, that overconfidence was dangerous, but another part of me—the part that had reveled in the cheers and praise last night—was already imagining the celebration after this was done. The *real* celebration. One where I'd be the undisputed hero, the one who saved the entire island, who rid the world of the Denizens for good. Una and I could start our future. We could live in our cocoon in the woods away from all the attention. She would be mine, always and forever, night after night after night.

But first, Karkenloth.

I'd cut through its tentacles, slice open its belly, and watch its dark blood stain the sea. Then we'd party properly —drinks flowing, the sun bright, the people chanting my name like they had last night, but louder. *I'll kill it,* I thought, *and we'll finally be free.*

But as Karkenloth's massive body surged closer, the water frothing and boiling beneath it, a flicker of doubt trickled through me. The sheer size of it was overwhelming, its tentacles coiling and twisting, each movement deliberate and menacing. It wasn't just a beast, it was a force of nature, ancient and relentless.

I shoved the doubt down, hard. This was what I'd trained for, what I was made for. My destiny was written in *The Mermaid Chronicles*. This was a fate I would control.

I would not let fear creep in now, not when the entire island was depending on me. I squared my shoulders, lifting the trident high, its glow intensifying until it was almost blinding in the early light. The time had come, and I was ready. Ready to strike, ready to kill, ready to end this nightmare once and for all.

The time had come to face Karkenloth—and win.

CHAPTER TWENTY-FIVE

*K*arkenloth.

I tracked the dark, hulking mass on the horizon, still far off, but moving fast. Tentacles coiled and thrashed beneath the water's surface, the beast's dark orange body a blot against the rising sun.

"We need to move," I called.

I glanced around the courtyard. Soldiers and civilians alike lay slumped over tables, chairs, or each other. Some were even sprawled out on the cobble ground, mouths open, completely knocked out. The stench of wine and stale beer filled the air.

I clapped my hands, shaking the nearest person awake—a guard with a spear still clutched in his hand. "Up! Karkenloth's coming!"

Ember, sprawled on the ground with his back propped against a fountain, groaned and dragged a hand over his face. "Can't a guy catch a few hours of peace after saving the world?" His voice was raspy with sleep, and as he sat up, his wild hair stuck out in every direction.

"We haven't saved it yet," I shot back, shaking another soldier awake. "Get up, everyone! Karkenloth's on the horizon!"

Ember grumbled as he finally stood, rolling his shoulders. His gaze snagged on the horizon before he retched into a bush. "If I pass out mid-swing, tell everyone I went down heroically."

"You'll be okay, buddy," I muttered, scanning the courtyard for Una. I found her curled up against a pillar, her blonde hair a tangled mess over her shoulders. My chest tightened at the sight of her. She looked so peaceful, unaware of the impending doom.

I rushed over, gently shaking her awake. "Una, we need to go."

She blinked, then rubbed her eye. "What's happening?"

"Karkenloth's coming," I said, trying to keep my voice steady. "Stay close to me. I don't want you getting hurt."

She nodded, a quiver running across her lips as she pushed her eyepatch into place. I hated seeing Una scared. And that only fed the fire burning in my chest. I would create a safe island. A haven where she no longer had to live in fear. I would embrace every power surging through me, and more, if it meant Una could sleep easy once again.

Across the courtyard, Ember stretched, staring at the horizon. "I swear, that thing's bigger than half the island. You sure this trident of yours can handle it, Gal? Or should we start praying to the gods for backup?"

"I do *not* need the gods. They abandoned us centuries ago. So fuck them," I said, gripping the trident tight in my hand.

"Yeah, fuck 'em." Ember gave me a high-five. "But also, have you seen the size of it?"

Power thrummed through me, stronger than the pounding of my heart against my ribs, feeding me strength. "I've handled everything else. This is no different. We'll kill it, and then—then we'll have a real celebration."

Ember snorted. "Overconfident much?"

"I'm serious." I turned to him. "We've got this. *I've* got this. I'm not just a prince sitting on a throne. Karkenloth won't know what hit him."

But even as the words left my mouth, a small voice inside whispered doubts. This was Karkenloth, the biggest and most dangerous Denizen. One wrong move could cost us everything. Could cost *Una* everything. But no—this was my moment. My chance to prove to everyone, and to myself, that I was ready for this. There was no room for doubt. I'd come this far, and I wasn't about to stop now.

As the courtyard came alive with movement—soldiers staggering to their feet, civilians rushing for cover—I planted my feet on the ground and stared at the massive shape inching across the water. This was it. The final test. And I was ready.

I was more than ready.

I didn't wait for the others. The second I locked eyes with that monstrous shape on the horizon, something flicked on inside me—something fierce and impatient. The trident hummed, begging for action. The buzz was addictive. I could almost hear it whisper: *Go.*

I arced the trident through the air, felt the pull of space bending around me as I teleported, leaving the noise of the courtyard behind. Wind lashed against my face, cold and salty, as I reappeared high above the ocean. Below me, Karkenloth loomed larger than I'd imagined, its massive body churning the sea like a living storm. Tentacles, thick as tree trunks and covered in grotesque suckers, thrashed in and out of the water, sending waves crashing against the shore. The dark orange of its body glistened in the early light, a sickly hue that only seemed to intensify the creature's otherworldly presence.

Before I could orient myself, one of those tentacles shot toward me. The trident jerked in my hand, hard, as the tentacle coiled around it, yanking me off balance. I cursed, feeling the pull, and in an instant, the trident slipped from my grip. I grasped at air.

For a breathless few seconds, panic swelled—free-falling from this height into the thrashing sea would be a death sentence. But no. I wasn't helpless. I wasn't the same kid who'd stumbled through his first battles, unsure of his powers. Not anymore.

Focus, Gal.

I stretched out my arms and summoned the chill inside me, the ice that flowed in my veins. The air around me dropped in temperature and the power rippled through me. The surface of the water below began to crack and freeze, ice spreading in thin sheets, then rising into jagged steppingstones. With a sharp exhale, I threw my body forward, planting one foot on the nearest block of ice. It wobbled beneath me, but I kept my balance, steadying myself as I created more. A path of ice stretching across the churning ocean, supporting me like a bridge over hell.

The wind bit at my skin, but it didn't stop the rush of exhilaration from flowing through me. I couldn't comprehend the amount of power I commanded. Didn't want to quantify it. The scope of it was terrifying. But I wouldn't shy away from it anymore. I would put it to use. And save my island. Destroy the Denizens, and any other threat that came my way. With this amount of power at my fingertips, I had nothing to be afraid of anymore. *The Mermaid Chronicles* was merely a bunch of words. The Power of the Sea a nebulous blue orb. Objects. Relics. Nothing more.

I glared at Karkenloth, whose monstrous tentacles writhed beneath the water. My trident—*my* trident—was still trapped in its grasp, sinking deeper into the beast's coils. It pulsed with faint light, trying to resist, but Karkenloth's grip was too strong.

"Not today," I growled.

I stretched out my hand, fingers splayed, and called the trident back to me. The pull between us vibrated through the air, a connection that seized the breath in my lungs. The tentacle jerked in resistance, tightening around the golden weapon, but it wasn't enough. The trident belonged to me. And only me.

With a sharp snap, it wrenched free, flying back into my outstretched hand with a force that made my arm tingle.

Karkenloth screeched, its voice a guttural roar that emptied both the air and sea of wildlife. But I didn't react. Instead, I spun the trident in a wide arc. Energy crackled at the tips of the three prongs.

I slammed the trident toward the nearest tentacle, and with a flash of light, the blade cut clean through the flesh. Dark blood spewed into the water, staining the ice. Karkenloth shrieked again, thrashing wildly as the severed limb danced a death throw. I could see its eyes now, massive and furious, glaring at me with a rage that seemed to shake the ocean itself.

Whatever.

It was merely an overgrown excuse for a seafood buffet.

Karkenloth, the last Denizen, was going down—and I was going to be the one to kill it. Maybe serve it on a platter during the celebration ceremony.

While I was preparing for a second strike, Ash and Blaze erupted from the clouds, their wings beating in synch. Blaze's fiery breath filled the sky, scorching one of Karkenloth's massive tentacles, the flesh crackling and curling in on itself. Ash flung an explosive spear with pinpoint precision, aiming straight for the beast's enormous head. But the winds whipped violently, tossing the blade off course as towering waves surged beneath it. The spear missed its mark, disappearing into the waves.

"No!" I roared at them both, ice and spray coating my skin. "I can handle him."

Ash beat his wings against the cold thermals, gaping at me.

Blaze swooped low, his fire unable to penetrate the biting cold around me as he shook his head.

"It's bigger than the Hound of the Sea," he called, his voice gruff, his eyes hard. "You *cannot* do this alone."

I balanced on my icy steps, reinforcing its solidity when I felt it begin to crack or melt. To prove my point, I directed my power at the water surrounding Karkenloth. It took more effort than I thought as ten-foot swells whipped across the ocean and Karkenloth's trashing tentacles whisked them higher, but after a minute or two, the water surrounding him turned to ice.

I grinned at Blaze, triumph swelling in my chest. One swift teleport and I'd have it—straight to one of its hearts. But that brief second of pride was all it took for Karkenloth to shatter my control. With a deafening roar, the Denizen's twisting tentacles smashed through the ice. Cracks splintered in every direction, icebergs crumbling into the sea. The ice cage I'd fought to create exploded into shards, swept away by the creature's violent thrashing.

"Dammit!" *If Blaze hadn't distracted me.*

A strangled shout pulled my attention to the other side of the beast. I saw Ash, coiled tight in one of the Denizen's monstrous tentacles, his body nearly swallowed by its thick, slimy flesh. Only his head remained visible, his eyes wide with terror.

"Shit!" Blaze and I muttered in unison.

Without waiting for him to act, I teleported, my body snapping through the cold air. One heartbeat I was on the ice, the next I was beside Ash, swinging the trident. I slashed through the thick appendage, the power of the weapon searing the tentacle's slick skin. It took three sharp strokes before the tentacle loosened its hold, finally falling away from Ash's limp body.

But instead of flying, Ash's eyes drooped closed, and he dropped out of the sky.

Blaze dove beneath him, catching him mid-fall, the impact pushing Blaze into the path of another searching tentacle, but I teleported to the insidious appendage and sliced through it before it could snare father and son. With a screech, the severed limb fell, splashing into the waves below, sending Karkenloth into another fit of enraged thrashing. Blaze, clutching his unconscious son, shot toward the safety of the shoreline.

I glanced over my shoulder to see soldiers lining the beach. During the few moments of battle, Karkenloth had crept closer to the coastline than I'd realized, its massive body casting a shadow over the sand. Its tentacles lashed out in every direction, slick with seawater and glistening dark orange. Its body rippled as if the very ocean had given birth to him. Each move sent waves crashing toward the shore, the waters swirling with its malevolent presence.

Thank God the jellyfish were gone.

Selachii dove into the shallows, turning full shark before they even hit the water, reappearing as they coasted up the crests of waves and chomped through tentacles with their jagged teeth. This. This is what selachii were made for, why they'd been the original protectors of Atlantis.

I kissed the trident. "You and me, baby."

Karkenloth could appear as any ocean creature it chose, and it could morph to another at any moment. There was little wonder it'd come as a giant squid; human history was filled with numerous legendary battles against such creatures. The sheer size of the Denizen was enough to instill desertion into the bravest soldiers. But Karkenloth had never battled the trident before. He'd never battled me.

A squid possessed three hearts. And it was the reason I was sure Karkenloth had chosen to appear as one. Each one must be punctured. Each heart lay beneath a solid wall of thick muscle and scaled skin, not to mention the lashing tentacles that prevented me from getting close. It would not be easy.

A shriek cut through the pandemonium as one of Karkenloth's tentacles crashed into the shore, sending soldiers scattering.

I planted my feet on the nearest chunk of ice I had formed and forced the surrounding water to freeze again. Cold blue energy poured from my body, spreading outward in jagged lines across the sea, forming ice platforms in rapid succession. If I could immobilize him—at least temporarily—I'd have a chance to get to his hearts.

"*Gal!*" a voice boomed from behind me.

I glanced back to see my father tearing through the mass of tentacles like a god risen from slumber. With his bare hands, he ripped into the flesh of one of Karkenloth's appendages. The tentacle burst, dark blood spraying into the air as Dad tore it in half. Its roar of defiance reverberated over the crashing waves.

Ember wasn't far behind, his wild grin only half-formed. His hands glowed with pyrokinetic energy, and with a sweeping motion, he unleashed a wall of fire between us and

Karkenloth, holding back the beast's advance. The heat from the pyro-shield was searing, evaporating the spray of salt-water before it touched us.

"That'll keep him busy," Ember called. "Now, what do you say we BBQ this oversized squid?"

I couldn't help but smirk. Even in the face of disaster, Ember never lost his humor.

"Focus on the tentacles! I'll go for the hearts," I shouted at anyone nearby.

Selachii continued to attack Karkenloth from beneath, their wide mouths gnashing and slicing and chewing. Blood filled the ocean. Black and red.

Before I rejoined the fray, I scanned the shore for Una. She and Uncle Dylan, stationed on the rocky cliffs above the shoreline, hurled spears with deadly precision. Each spear whistled through the air, embedding itself deep into Karkenloth's writhing limbs. Dylan's face was grim, his eyes dark with concentration, while Una's expression was fierce, her golden hair whipping in the wind. One of her spears sliced through the base of a tentacle, severing it, the explosion charge smattering black blood and tissue and tendons and suckers across the ice.

So gross.

I teleported to Karkenloth's rear, severing tentacles with fast swipes of the trident, freezing others and shattering them with a solid kick, trying to fight my way to its heart.

Ford fought in the shallows, slashing at the tentacles with his blade, every strike sending spurts of dark, inky blood into the water. He was fast, dodging and weaving between the waves as the water churned around him.

Karkenloth's tentacles lashed out at him, but Ford was a killing machine.

I spotted movement in the water below—two enormous shadows cutting through the waves. Trent and Pops had shifted into their full shark forms, their powerful jaws snapping at Karkenloth's submerged tentacles. The water churned black as they bit down, thrashing as they tore through the beast's flesh. Pops, the larger of the two, clamped onto one tentacle with a sickening crunch, while Trent darted between strikes, slicing at the twisting limbs with razor-sharp teeth.

I forced my attention back to the task at hand, channeling my ice powers once again. The air crackled as I pushed the cold further, creating a path of frozen steppingstones leading straight to the beast. I leaped from one to the next, closing in on Karkenloth's body. Its skin was thick, rough as stone. Piercing it would take every ounce of strength I had.

The trident pulsed in my hands, responding to my need. I lunged toward the center of Karkenloth's mass, aiming for the first heart. But just as I was about to strike, a tentacle whipped out of nowhere, wrapping around the trident and yanking it from my grasp. My balance wavered, and for a split second, I felt the icy abyss beneath me, ready to drag me down.

"Not today," I muttered through gritted teeth. I called on my cold power, freezing the water beneath me once more. An ice platform surged up just in time, and I leaped onto it, my feet skittering and sliding. Finally, I steadied myself, cold air rushing through my lungs, ice clinging to my limbs. I stretched out my hand, summoning the trident.

The golden weapon ripped free from the tentacle's grasp and flew back into my hand, humming with renewed power. With a fierce growl, I swung it in a wide arc, severing the tentacle that had dared to take it from me. The detached limb fell into the water with a satisfying splash, and Karkenloth bellowed.

"*Fuck you.*" I repositioned my grip on the trident as I stared into the beast's many dark, furious eyes.

Karkenloth's eyes locked onto mine, each of its pupils dilating with a mixture of hatred and primal fury. I could feel its hearts—three distinct pulses thrumming beneath its thick hide. The trident buzzed, guiding me toward those vital organs. But they were well-protected, buried beneath layers of slimy, armored skin and a mass of deadly, whipping appendages. The beast knew its weak points, and it wasn't about to let me near them without a fight.

"Gal, incoming!" Ember's voice tore through the storm of sounds, and suddenly a blazing shield of fire burst into existence around me, warding off the nearest tentacles. "I don't know how long I can hold it. You better move your ass!"

I darted forward, leaping from one melting ice step to the next.

"Fire and ice," I muttered.

The cold stung my legs as I raced toward Karkenloth's massive body. Dad crashed into one of the beast's nearby tentacles, tearing through it like it was made of paper. His roar was almost as loud as Karkenloth's, his muscles straining as he ripped tentacles apart. I caught sight of Pops as he swam beneath me, jaws wide open.

I took a deep breath, then thrust the trident forward. A

massive tentacle crashed toward me, but I froze the water beneath it, creating a slick surface that sent it sliding sideways. The tentacle slammed into the ice, cracking it, but not before I leaped into the air and teleported onto the monster's back. I was closer now—close enough to feel the pounding of its three hearts, each pulse vibrating through my bones. The stench of the beast's briny flesh filled my nostrils as I balanced on its slick skin.

My limbs shook with the effort to hold on, with the fatigue of using my ice ability. The trident's power was eternal, but the cyro-aquaism drained me quickly. I needed to get in and out. End this shit before I ran out of steam.

I plunged the trident into Karkenloth's thick hide, the weapon sinking deep. The beast shrieked, a deafening, gut-wrenching sound that sent waves rippling across the ocean.

Gritting my teeth, I twisted the trident, ice surging from its tip, freezing the surrounding tissue as I sought the first heart.

Karkenloth thrashed, trying to dislodge me, but I held on, planting my feet as I drove the weapon deeper. My body strained, muscles trembling, but the first heart gave way, the trident piercing through its tough shell. Dark, black blood spurted from the wound, showering me in a frozen, viscous substance that stank worse than death. Ancient. Evil and ancient. All the bad things I'd ever smelled rolled into one putrefying spout of gushing monster blood.

The creature screamed again, but its movements slowed, its strength faltering. I yanked the trident free and teleported to another spot on its body just as a tentacle whipped past where I'd been standing.

"Two more," I whispered, both sweat and ice coating my skin.

Behind me, Blaze tore through more tentacles with his fire, flames trailing from his open mouth. "You've got this, Gal! Finish the bastard off!"

I spun the trident, its golden surface slick with the beast's blood. With a war cry ripping out of me, I plunged the weapon toward the second heart. Karkenloth writhed beneath me, its tentacles flailing. The ice beneath my feet solidified, keeping me steady as I drove the weapon home. Another sickening pop, and the second heart burst.

Karkenloth's bellow of pain echoed across the sea, its massive form sagging under the weight of its wounds. One more heart. One more strike.

"Just one more!" I shouted, more to myself than anyone else.

Despite the building exhaustion, power danced across my limbs, flowed down my spine, curled in the pit of my stomach. A golden light covered me from head to toe, spurring me on, whispering sweet nothings to rival Una's.

I lunged for the final heart, thrusting the weapon with everything I had. Karkenloth's last tentacle came crashing down, but I froze the air around it, halting its momentum long enough for me to land the killing blow.

The third heart exploded beneath the trident's tip, and with it, the great beast released one final, shuddering cry.

The ocean stilled.

The tentacles fell limp.

Karkenloth was dead.

I stood atop its hulking body, chest heaving, the trident

glowing. The surrounding water was stained dark with the creature's blood, but the horizon was clear. Finally.

I sucked in breath after breath, marveling at the sheer size of the Denizen's corpse as it floated on the water, me still standing on top of it.

I had killed it, this thing. I had dealt with the prophecy that had been hanging over me for months. And now I would reclaim my island. And my woman.

CHAPTER TWENTY-SIX

I placed the trident in its brackets, stepping back to take in its gleaming surface. Even polished and cleaned, the weapon pulsed with a dull, hungry light, as though unsatisfied by my neglect. I frowned, resisting the urge to reach for it again. My hand twitched at my side, itching to grab it, to feel its weight, its power. But there was nothing left to fight. No Denizens rising from the deep. No monsters threatening the shores. No reason to sleep with it by the side of my bed or listen to its whisperings.

"You sure you don't want it with you in the new house?" Ember's voice broke through my thoughts. He stood beside me, arms crossed over his chest, hair still damp from a recent swim. "If you need it, it'll be closer."

With my hands on my hips, I stood in the middle of the great hall staring at the thing that had made me feel...immortal. To think I'd once been terrified of Zale, trembling at the idea of facing him. Now, after Karkenloth? A beast a thousand times larger and infinitely more dangerous? Zale seemed like a distant memory. One that barely scratched at my mind.

"It'll come if I call it." I tried to sound casual, dismissive, but the truth was far more complicated. I didn't want the trident *too* close. Not anymore.

When I realized my hands were shaking, I clasped them together, squeezing hard, attempting to ignore the building whispers and the way my hand wanted to reach for the weapon like it was a magnet. Like it was now part of me. Like it should always be by my side.

It had given me strength, confidence beyond what I'd ever imagined, but...it had also whispered things. Things that didn't always feel like my own thoughts. I could still hear the echoes from the battle—fleeting moments when it felt like the trident was leading, pushing me to act. Had I been fully in control? Was that even possible?

Anything was possible in Atlantis.

"True," Ember said with a grin, clapping me on the back. "That's some next-level magic shit you've got going on there."

"And you." I returned his grin, though it felt hollow.

The Power of the Sea had blessed us both with abilities far beyond what either of us could've imagined. But that was the problem, wasn't it? The power. The attention. The adoration. It was addictive. It was easy to let it go to your head. Too easy. I had seen it in others, and recently, I'd felt it in myself. In the last two battles, the high that came with victory—I'd relished it a little too much. I didn't want to become *that* person.

I shuddered as I stepped away from the weapon toward

the exit. I didn't want to become addicted to the trident's power. I didn't want to need it, crave it, or not be able to think of anything else. And so here it would stay, in the great hall, where its power would have less of a hold on me. That's what I was hoping, anyway.

"Preparations are in full swing for the party at the bar tonight," Ember reminded me. "You are coming, right?"

I'd rather stay home with Una. In the week since Karkenloth had been killed, any time I stepped into public view, I was battered with questions. Initially, I'd enjoyed giving accounts of my brave deeds. Then a little voice in the back of my head had chimed in, telling me I was exaggerating, embellishing, peacocking. The old Gal would have run for the hills and secluded himself in a remote location until the fuss blew over. The new Gal relished every moment of retelling every tiny event. And that's what worried me. It was better if I stayed away from the party and had a quiet night with Una.

"I'll think about it." I didn't want to disappoint Ember either. "No doubt Ash will be trying to steal drinks."

Ember chuckled. "That kid has no sense of modesty. Cyra on the other hand, has more grace than all the merfolk combined." He shook his head. "And she's calling him Jackass any chance she gets."

I laughed, amused the fleeting nickname had stuck. "That'll bring him down a peg or two." Which is exactly what it had done for me when Babette had called me it. "They're okay, though, after the battle? Any nightmares?"

Ember tilted his head. "They're going be just fine."

Nightmares always lingered. You can't escape past

trauma. But you can learn to move around it. To minimize it. To not let it have power over you. "If they need any help..." I was the resident trauma expert, after all.

Ember clapped my shoulder. "Noted. But right now, I think they're happy to enjoy the sunshine and a few quite days on the beach."

"Amen to that."

As we turned to leave, I noted the plinth that held *The Mermaid Chronicles* was empty. It would be with one of the High Council members, or Una. I was no longer afraid of the book, but I had zero interest in learning of any new prophecies. I needed a vacation. Una and I were in the middle of moving into the house, christening every room. Atlantis could take care of itself for the time being.

Outside the doors to the great hall, Ember nudged me. "You better show up tonight, or I'll drag your ass out myself. Even if it's naked."

"I'm sure the Atlanteans would love that." They'd probably cast my ass in bronze.

I smirked, but my thoughts lingered on how quickly the fame had twisted something inside me. Even Ember, with all his powers, didn't seem to feel the same gnawing pressure I did. Maybe he was better at handling it. Or maybe he wasn't so haunted by the weight of responsibility. But I had the creeping sense I was becoming someone I didn't want to be.

When we parted, Ember left to harvest some weed for the party. He'd had to relocate his marijuana farm, considering the fight with Maelstrom had decimated his crops, and he could no longer fly to the original location, anyway.

I shut the doors to the great hall behind me, nodded at the

guards, then made my way through the palace gardens to my new home. Breathing deep, I reveled in the scents of the plants and trees. Not that I knew what any of them were called, but they looked good, smelled nice, and I hoped the sun would never disappear on us again.

When I entered through the garden gate, the air was thick with the fragrance of blooming jasmine and the soft chirping of insects. I'd insisted the jasmine be planted throughout the garden so that even when Una was away from the house, I could smell her. It was the one plant I had acquainted myself with.

I found Una nestled on the swing chair, one leg tucked beneath her, a book resting on her lap, and a half-empty carafe of wine perched on the table next to her. Her fingers gripped the stem of her glass, and with each slow push of her toes against the ground, the swing moved in a gentle rhythm, a sway even softer than the breeze that rustled the leaves overhead.

I stepped behind her quietly, my lips finding the tender curve of her neck. She shrieked and threw her book across the patio. "Don't creep up on me like that! I've had enough scary moments for one lifetime."

I chuckled, circling around to face her. "Sorry," I murmured, sliding onto the swing beside her. Before she could protest, I pulled her onto my lap and nuzzled my nose into her neck. Her warmth pressed against me, the heat of her body intoxicating, and now we had all the time in the world to enjoy each other.

She reached behind her and grabbed her glass. "Would you mind? It's gone a bit warm."

"Clearly you don't drink fast enough. And pour one for me, will you?"

After she poured a second glass, I swept a hand over both. With a flick of my fingers, I chilled both glasses, watching as the frost crawled down the stems like delicate lace.

"I knew you were useful for a reason," Una said, raising her glass with a grin.

I arched a brow, feigning offense. "Killing evil gods and terrifying sea monsters isn't good enough for you?"

She cocked a shoulder. "Eh, I don't know. It's a once-every-few-years kind of thing. Meh. But chilled drinks when I'm too lazy to go to the freezer. Now that's a quality I can get behind."

Placing my glass on the ground, I grinned, and before she could say more, I seized her around the waist, fingers digging into her sides, tickling her until laughter burst from her lips. Her wine sloshed over the rim of the glass, spilling onto her chest. Without a second thought, I dipped my head and trailed my tongue across her skin, savoring the sweet, sharp taste of the wine mixed with the natural warmth of her body.

"There's more," I murmured, my lips brushing the delicate skin between her breasts. "It's trickling down right...here." I traced a slow, languid path with my tongue, following the line of the spilled wine.

"It managed to get all the way down my stomach too," Una said, her voice husky as she placed her glass on the table.

I chuckled, pulling her shirt up, baring the soft curve of her breasts. Slowly, deliberately, I swirled my tongue over one nipple, feeling it harden beneath my touch, then moved to the other, taking my time, drawing each peak into my mouth with a lazy, unhurried pace that had her shivering in my arms.

Her hands gripped my shoulders, her nails digging in as her body responded to each teasing movement of my mouth. Una shifted on the swing, her head falling back, her soft moans mingled with the sounds of the garden.

"Down here?" I trailed my tongue down the middle of her stomach, circled her belly button, and blew lightly over it.

"Even lower," Una murmured, her hips arching against me.

I slid my hand beneath the waistband of her shorts and underwear, dipping my fingers into her slick center. "You're pretty wet here too."

"That's where it all ended up," Una said. "It will take you a while to clean up down there."

I smiled, pressing my thumb to her clit, drawing slow, deliberate circles. Her moans deepened, her hips bucking against my hand as I added more pressure, pushing two fingers inside her, feeling her tighten around me with each thrust.

As I was about to lower my head for a kiss, something flickered in the corner of my eye—a strange, golden flash reflecting in the window behind us. I paused, my fingers stilling inside her as I turned my head to look. The light was golden, warm, too much like the glow of the trident.

"Don't stop," Una muttered.

Frowning, I disentangled myself from Una and watched as golden light bathed the entire window.

"Keep going..."

But I couldn't ignore it. Frowning, I untangled myself

from her, standing as the light brightened and spilled over the garden.

"I'm sure I left the trident in the great hall," I said. Besides, it didn't glow if I wasn't holding it.

Una stiffened beside me, hastily pulling her shirt back down and fixing her shorts. "It's...it's...not the trident."

I glanced at Una, surprised to see her face flushed with guilt. "What's going on?"

I didn't wait for an answer, but marched around the side of the house and through the front door, following the glow of light. My gaze settled on a small trunk in our living area where we kept a blanket for winter nights. Golden light poured out of its cracks. Una joined me.

I pointed. "What's in there?"

She gnawed on her bottom lip. "Something I was hoping you wouldn't see."

I turned to look at her. "Explain."

"I have the book." She sighed. "Often when a prophecy is completed, that's when newer prophecies appear. I wanted to see if there was anything new."

I raked a hand through my hair, trying to decide if I was more pissed that Una had tried to hide the book from me, or because there did indeed seem to be a new prophecy.

"I can read the book, you know."

"I know," she said. We both stood there, not venturing any closer to the glowing chest. "But I don't want you to read it."

My heart skipped a beat. "What can be worse than the Denizens?"

Una's gaze remained fixed on the ground, her lips pressed

together. When she finally looked up, her expression drained the warmth from the room. "It's going to change everything."

My pulse quickened, the pleasant warmth of the previous moment evaporating into a cold, unsettling dread. But there was no reason to be afraid. I had defeated the evilest of gods. I had immense power at my fingertips to call on whenever needed.

But when I met her eyes again, there was no reassurance there. Only fear. A deep, gnawing fear that twisted something inside me. She wasn't afraid of me, or what I could do. She was afraid *for* me.

And that's when I knew. Whatever this was, it wasn't just a new obstacle to overcome or another battle to win. It was something bigger, something that could unravel the fabric of life we had fought so hard to secure. My heart pounded harder, each beat a reminder that everything I thought was safe, everything I thought was *certain*, could be ripped away.

"What does it say, Una?" I asked carefully.

She shook her head. "I don't want to lose you."

I frowned, pulling her into my arms, holding her close against my chest, as though my embrace could shield her from whatever was coming. "Why would you ever lose me?"

Her body trembled against mine, a soft, strangled sob escaping her lips.

With my thoughts spinning and a very real fear clawing at my spine, I marched away from Una, threw open the lid of the chest, uncurled the blanket the book was wrapped in, and grabbed *The Mermaid Chronicles*.

Its edges were golden and glowing, stronger than I'd ever

seen them before. I didn't know what that meant, but the hairs on the back of my neck took notice.

I placed it on the table, my heart thudding in my chest as it flicked open on its own. The pages turned, moving faster than I could comprehend, until it landed on the prophecy section, the ink on the page still fresh and black. It hadn't been there the last time I'd looked.

I read it quickly. It wasn't long. The words made no sense. It was impossible.

"Una..." I barely recognized my own voice, a rasp of disbelief. She stood there, her arms wrapped around herself, her face pale, her lips trembling as a tear slipped down her cheek. She splayed her hands helplessly. "I don't understand."

"Neither do I."

I glanced back at the book, the words burning into my mind like a brand. What did they mean?

The man becomes the god.

THANK you so much for making it all the way to the end. I hope you have enjoyed *Denizens of Darkness* and are excited for the next and final book (This time I am telling the truth!!!). If you did, leaving a review is the best possible present for an author! You can do it here: https://geni.us/Denizens

I had thought Gal's story would end with taking down Zale, but as I wrote *Vendetta*, I realized there was so much

MARISA NOELLE

more of his character to explore. Losing a mother in the way
he did will leave anyone with scars, and I wanted to explore
his journey with you for a little longer...

Keep an eye out for *Vorago Returns*...

THE MERMAID
CHRONICLES
BOOK SEVEN

VORAGO
RETURNS

MARISA NOELLE

FACEBOOK READERS GROUP

If you want to experience more of my books, do join my Facebook readers group where you can chat to other readers and discuss my books, as well as anything else you are reading. I am very active in this group, and you can expect book jokes, puzzles, riddles, quizzes, giveaways, the opportunity to name characters, as well as secret information about what I'm working on, cover reveals and so much more!

Just click here: https://www.facebook.com/groups/840324970233576

FREEBIE

If you'd like access to eleven novellas set in *The Unadjusteds* universe, completely FREE, all you have to do is subscribe to my newsletter!

https://www.marisanoelle.com/subscribe/

ACKNOWLEDGMENTS

Writing a book takes a village, and I am endlessly grateful for mine. I want to give a big shout-out to three teams who have kept me going through thick and thin!

To *The Rebel Alliance*—my incredible writing group. You all have been my ride-or-die crew for years, cheering me on through every word and chapter. I couldn't have reached this finish line without you!

And then there's *Team Swag*—the ones who held my hand while I navigated the wild world of publishing. We've tackled every twist and turn together, sharing laughs, support, and wisdom. You're an amazing bunch of writers and even better friends.

Anna, Emma & Sally—you guys are some of the best people I know. Friends on line, friends in real life, and you keep me smiling through the blood, sweat and tears. Couldn't do it without you!

To Fay—the cover is nothing short of gorgeous! I couldn't have asked for anything better.

Thank you to Melissa Nash for such wonderful map work and bringing Atlantis to life!

Neil, my rock and my "Steady Eddie"—you stole my heart in one night and still keep it safe every day. Love you endlessly.

Riley, Lucas, and Quinn—my biggest supporters, as long as I don't embarrass you at school fairs with my book stacks! You're my go-to brainstormers whenever I'm stuck, and you always help me find my way.

To my parents, Larry and Rita—your unwavering support means everything to me. And Mom, you're my super-sharp proofreader... unless there's a typo—then it's totally on you!

To my early supporters—Sasha Newell, Michelle Oliver, Nikki, Adrian, Darcy & Hetty Kane—thank you for your invaluable advice and feedback. You've each been a vital part of this journey.

And the fabulous Twitter writing community—thank you for making the highs sweeter and the lows lighter. You all know who you are, and I'm grateful for each one of you.

BookTok! You've been an absolute blast! From making me buy crowns (yes, multiple) to supporting my books with enthusiasm, you've given me so much. I've found the best beta and ARC readers here, and I know I've found my people.

To Michael Fox, my A-level English teacher, thank you for teaching me to think for myself and defend my ideas. That lesson has carried me far.

And last but not least, to my readers—thank you from the bottom of my heart. You make every word worth it. I hope you stick around for more adventures to come!

Oh, and if you fancy learning more about my books and want to be in with the chance to win exclusive giveaways, sign up to my website below!

(**www.marisanoelle.com**)

ABOUT THE AUTHOR

Marisa Noelle is the author behind a treasure trove of young adult and adult novels across multiple genres, but they all have running themes of mental health or the ocean. She tends to gravitate toward the speculative arena and loves to write science-fiction, fantasy, horror, dystopian, romance, romantasy, or a combination of them all.

Marisa's books include:

The Shadow Keepers—a spine-tingling tale to keep you up all night and semi-finalist of the BBNYA book awards.

The Unraveling of Luna Forester—a novel impossible to talk about because of its huge twist, but it snagged several awards, including: First Place Incipere Award, WriteBlend Finalist, BBYNA Semi-Finalist, Bookshelf Finalist shelf.

The Unadjusteds Trilogy delves into one of her favourite genres—dystopian. *The Unadjusteds, the Rise of the Altereds, and The Reckoning* make up the trilogy, but there are eleven further companion novellas that follow the secondary characters. *The Unadjusteds* also placed as a semi-finalist in the BBNYA awards. There are also eleven origin story novellas set in *The Unadjusteds* universe that are completely FREE when you subscribe to my website.

The Mermaid Chronicles is a seven book romantasy series that includes: *Secrets of the Deep, Quest for Atlantis, Fight for Freedom, Ghost Pirates, Vendetta, Denizens of Darkness, Vorago Returns,* as well as its own companion guide. The entire series is coming to audio with Tantor Media soon!

Marisa also writes steamy romance under the pen name Savannah Warner.

When Marisa's not weaving literary spells, she's helping mold the future of MG and YA authors as a mentor for the Write Mentor program. She also likes to imagine herself as a mermaid, and can often be found in the local pool...or lake... or ocean. Despite her undeniable bookworm credentials since she was knee-high to a grasshopper, the author gig took Marisa by surprise. You see, she had a secret past as a bit of a science geek during her school days. But hey, science and storytelling make a surprisingly magical concoction! Currently, Marisa calls Woking, UK, her home sweet home, where she resides with her trusty squad, including her husband, three amazing kids, and a furry four-legged friend named Copper.

Marisa loves to hear from her readers. You can find and connect with her at the links below.

Twitter & Instagram: **@MarisaNoelle77**
Tiktok: **@MarisaNoelle12**
Website: **www.MarisaNoelle.com**